THE GOLD OF THE GODS

ARTHUR B. REEVE

1st WORLD
LIBRARY
Literary Society

The Gold of the Gods

Arthur B. Reeve

© 1st World Library, 2008
PO Box 2211
Fairfield, IA 52556
www.1stworldlibrary.com
First Edition

LCCN: 2007940179

Softcover ISBN: 978-1-4218-9310-5
Hardcover ISBN: 978-1-4218-9410-2
eBook ISBN: 978-1-4218-9210-8

Purchase *"The Gold of the Gods"*
as a traditional bound book at:
www.1stWorldLibrary.com/purchase.asp?ISBN=978-1-4218-9310-5

1st World Library is a literary, educational organization
dedicated to:

- Creating a free internet library of downloadable ebooks

- Hosting writing competitions and offering book publishing
scholarships.

Interested in more 1st World Library books? contact:
literacy@1stworldlibrary.com
Check us out at: www.1stworldlibrary.com

1st World Library Literary Society

Giving Back to the World

"If you want to work on the core problem, it's early school literacy."

- James Barksdale, former CEO of Netscape

"No skill is more crucial to the future of a child, or to a democratic and prosperous society, than literacy."

- Los Angeles Times

"Literacy... means far more than learning how to read and write... The aim is to transmit... knowledge and promote social participation."

- UNESCO

"Literacy is not a luxury, it is a right and a responsibility. If our world is to meet the challenges of the twenty-first century we must harness the energy and creativity of all our citizens."

- President Bill Clinton

"Parents should be encouraged to read to their children, and teachers should be equipped with all available techniques for teaching literacy, so the varying needs and capacities of individual kids can be taken into account."

- Hugh Mackay

CONTENTS

I. THE PERUVIAN DAGGER................................. 9

II. THE SOLDIER OF FORTUNE.......................... 22

III. THE ARCHAEOLOGICAL DETECTIVE.............. 33

IV. THE TREASURE HUNTERS 43

V. THE WALL STREET PROMOTER...................... 54

VI. THE CURSE OF MANSICHE.......................... 65

VII. THE ARROW POISON................................ 76

VIII. THE ANONYMOUS LETTER........................ 87

IX. THE PAPER FIBRES 98

X. THE X-RAY READER 109

XI. THE SHOE-PRINTS 120

XII. THE EVIL EYE 130

XIII. THE POISONED CIGARETTE...................... 141

XIV. THE INTERFEROMETER 150

XV. THE WEED OF MADNESS 161

XVI. THE EAR IN THE WALL 171

XVII. THE VOICE FROM THE AIR 183

XVIII. THE ANTIDOTE.................................. 193

XIX. THE BURGLAR POWDER........................... 203

XX. THE PULMOTOR................................... 214

XXI. THE TELESCRIBE.. 225

XXII. THE VANISHER.. 235

XXIII. THE ACETYLENE TORCH............................ 247

XXIV. THE POLICE DOG... 258

XXV. THE GOLD OF THE GODS 270

I

THE PERUVIAN DAGGER

"There's something weird and mysterious about the robbery, Kennedy. They took the very thing I treasure most of all, an ancient Peruvian dagger."

Professor Allan Norton was very much excited as he dropped into Craig's laboratory early that forenoon.

Norton, I may say, was one of the younger members of the faculty, like Kennedy. Already, however, he had made for himself a place as one of the foremost of South American explorers and archaeologists.

"How they got into the South American section of the Museum, though, I don't understand," he hurried on. "But, once in, that they should take the most valuable relic I brought back with me on this last expedition, I think certainly shows that it was a robbery with a deep-laid, premeditated purpose."

"Nothing else is gone?" queried Kennedy.

"Nothing," returned the professor. "That's the strangest part of it—to me. It was a peculiar dagger, too," he continued reminiscently. "I say that it was valuable, for on the blade were engraved some curious Inca characters. I wasn't able to take the time to decipher them, down there, for the age of the metal made them almost illegible. But now that I have all my stuff unpacked and arranged after my trip, I was just about to try—when along comes a thief and robs me. We can't have the University Museum broken into that way, you know, Kennedy."

"I should say not," readily assented Craig. "I'd like to look the place over."

"Just what I wanted," exclaimed Norton, heartily delighted, and leading the way.

We walked across the campus with him to the Museum, still chatting. Norton was a tall, spare man, wiry, precisely the type one would pick to make an explorer in a tropical climate. His features were sharp, suggesting a clear and penetrating mind and a disposition to make the most of everything, no matter how slight. Indeed that had been his history, I knew. He had come to college a couple of years before Kennedy and myself, almost penniless, and had worked his way through by doing everything from waiting on table to tutoring. To-day he stood forth as a shining example of self-made intellectual man, as cultured as if he had sprung from a race of scholars, as practical as if he had taken to mills rather than museums.

We entered a handsome white-marble building in the shape of a rectangle, facing the University Library, a building, by the way, which Norton had persuaded several wealthy trustees and other donors to erect. Kennedy at once began examining the section devoted to Latin America, going over everything very carefully.

Arthur B. Reeve

I looked about, too. There were treasures from Mexico and Peru, from every romantic bit of the wonderful countries south of us—blocks of porphyry with quaint grecques and hieroglyphic painting from Mitla, copper axes and pottery from Cuzco, sculptured stones and mosaics, jugs, cups, vases, little gods and great, sacrificial stones, a treasure house of Aztec and Inca lore—enough to keep one occupied for hours merely to look at.

Yet, I reflected, following Norton, in all this mass of material, the thief seemed to have selected one, apparently insignificant, dagger, the thing which Norton prized because, somehow, it bore on its blade something which he had not, as yet, been able to fathom.

Though Kennedy looked thoroughly and patiently, it seemed as though there was nothing there to tell any story of the robbery, and he turned his attention at last to other parts of the Museum. As he made his way about slowly, I noted that he was looking particularly into corners, behind cabinets, around angles. What he expected to find I could not even guess.

Further along and on the same side of the building we came to the section devoted to Egyptology. Kennedy paused. Standing there, upright against the wall, was a mummy case. To me, even now, the thing had a creepy look. Craig pushed aside the stone lid irreverently and gazed keenly into the uncanny depths of the stone sarcophagus. An instant later he was down on his hands and knees, carefully examining the interior by means of a pocket lens.

"I think I have made a start," he remarked, rising to his feet and facing us with an air of satisfaction.

We said nothing, and he pointed to some almost undiscernible marks in a thin layer of dust that had collected in the sarcophagus.

"If I'm not mistaken," he went on, "your thief got into the Museum during the daytime, and, when no one was looking, hid here. He must have stayed until the place was locked up at night. Then he could rob at his leisure, only taking care to confine his operations to the time between the rather infrequent rounds of the night watchman."

Kennedy bent down again. "Look," he indicated. "There are the marks of shoes in the dust, shoes with nails in the heels, of course. I shall have to compare the marks that I have found here with those I have collected, following out the method of the immortal Bertillon. Every make of shoes has its own peculiarities, both in the number and the arrangement of the nails. Offhand, however, I should say that these shoes were American-made—though that, of course, does not necessarily mean that an American wore them. I may even be able to determine which of a number of individual pairs of shoes made the marks. I cannot tell that yet, until I study them. Walter, I wish you'd go over to my laboratory. In the second right-hand drawer of my desk you'll find a package of paper. I'd like to have it."

"Don't you think you ought to preserve the marks?" I heard Norton hint, as I left. He had been watching Kennedy in open-eyed amazement and interest.

"Exactly what I am sending Walter to do," he returned. "I have some specially prepared paper that will take those dust marks up and give me a perfect replica."

I hurried back as fast as I could, and Kennedy bent to the task of preserving the marks.

Arthur B. Reeve

"Have you any idea who might have an object in stealing the dagger?" Kennedy asked, when he had finished.

Norton shrugged his shoulders. "I believe some weird superstitions were connected with it," he replied. "It had a three-sided blade, and, as I told you, both the blade and the hilt were covered with peculiar markings."

There seemed to be nothing more that could be discovered from a further examination of the Museum. It was plain enough that the thief must have let himself out of a side door which had a spring lock on it and closed itself. Not a mark or scratch was to be found on any of the window or door locks; nothing else seemed to have been disturbed.

Evidently the thief had been after that one, to him priceless, object. Having got it, he was content to get away, leaving untouched the other treasures, some of which were even intrinsically valuable for the metal and precious stones in them. The whole affair seemed so strange to me, however, that, somehow, I could not help wondering whether Norton had told us the whole or only half the story as he knew it about the dagger and its history.

Still talking with the archaeologist, Kennedy and I returned to his laboratory.

We had scarcely reached the door when we heard the telephone ringing insistently. I answered, and it happened to be a call for me. It was the editor of the Star endeavouring to catch me, before I started downtown to the office, in order to give me an assignment.

"That's strange," I exclaimed, hanging up the receiver and turning to Craig. "I've got to go out on a murder case—"

"An interesting case?" asked Craig, interrupting his own train of investigation with a flash of professional interest.

"Why, a man has been murdered in his apartment on Central Park, West, I believe. Luis de Mendoza is the name, and it seems—"

"Don Luis de Mendoza?" repeated Norton, with a startled exclamation. "Why, he was an influential Peruvian, a man of affairs in his country, and an accomplished scholar. I—I—if you don't mind, I'd like to go over with you. I know the Mendozas."

Kennedy was watching Norton's face keenly. "I think I'll go, too, Walter," he decided. "You won't lack assistants on this story, apparently."

"Perhaps you can be of some assistance to them, also," put in Norton to Kennedy, as we left.

It was only a short ride downtown, and our cab soon pulled up before a rather ornate entrance of a large apartment in one of the most exclusive sections of the city. We jumped out and entered, succeeding in making our way to the sixth floor, where Mendoza lived, without interference from the hallboy, who had been completely swamped by the rush that followed the excitement of finding one of the tenants murdered.

There was no missing the place. The hall had been taken over by the reporters, who had established themselves there, terrible as an army with concealed pads and pencils. From one of the morning men already there I learned that our old friend Dr. Leslie, the coroner, was already in charge.

Somehow, whether it was through Kennedy's acquaintance with Dr. Leslie or Norton's acquaintance with the Mendozas and the Spanish tongue, we found ourselves beyond the barrier of the door which shut out my rivals.

As we stood for a moment in a handsome and tastefully furnished living room a young lady passed through hurriedly. She paused in the middle of the room as she saw us and eyed us tremulously, as though to ask us why we had intruded. It was a rather awkward situation.

Quickly Norton came to the rescue. "I hope you will pardon me, Senorita," he bowed in perfect Spanish, "but—"

"Oh, Professor Norton, it is you!" she cried in English, recognizing him. "I'm so nervous that I didn't see you at first."

She glanced from him to us, inquiringly. I recollected that my editor had mentioned a daughter who might prove to be an interesting and important figure in the mystery. She spoke in an overwrought, agitated tone. I studied her furtively.

Inez de Mendoza was unmistakably beautiful, of the dark Spanish type, with soft brown eyes that appealed to one when she talked, and a figure which at any less tragic moment one might have been pardoned for admiring. Her soft olive skin, masses of dark hair, and lustrous, almost voluptuous, eyes contrasted wonderfully with the finely chiselled lines of her nose, the firm chin, and graceful throat and neck. Here one recognized a girl of character and family in the depths of whose soul smouldered all the passion of a fiery race.

"I hope you will pardon me for intruding," Norton repeated. "Believe me, it is not with mere idle curiosity. Let me introduce my friend, Professor Kennedy, the scientific detective, of whom you have heard, no doubt. This is his assistant, Mr. Jameson, of the Star. I thought perhaps they might stand between you and that crowd in the hall," he added, motioning toward the reporters on the other side of the door. "You can trust them absolutely. I'm sure that if there is anything any of us can do to aid you in—in your trouble, you may be sure that we are at your service."

She looked about a moment in the presence of three strangers who had invaded the quietness of what had been, at least temporarily, home. She seemed to be seeking some one on whom to lean, as though some support had suddenly been knocked from under her, leaving her dazed at the change.

"Oh, madre de Dios!" she cried. "What shall I do? Oh, my father—my poor father!"

Inez Mendoza was really a pathetic and appealing figure as she stood there in the room, alone.

Quickly she looked us over, as if, by same sort of occult intuition of woman, she were reading our souls. Then, instinctively almost, she turned to Kennedy. Kennedy seemed to recognize her need. Norton and I retired, some-what more than figuratively.

"You—you are a detective?" she queried. "You can read mystery—like a book?"

Kennedy smiled encouragingly. "Hardly as my friend Walter here often paints me," he returned. "Still, now and then, we are able to use the vast knowledge of wise men the world over to help those in trouble. Tell me—everything," he soothed, as though knowing that to talk would prove a safety-valve for her pent-up emotions. "Perhaps I can help you."

Arthur B. Reeve

For a moment she did not know what to do. Then, almost before she knew it, apparently, she began to talk to him, forgetting that we were in the room.

"Tell me how the thing happened, all that you know, how you found it out," prompted Craig.

"Oh, it was midnight, last night; yes, late," she returned wildly. "I was sleeping when my maid, Juanita, wakened me and told me that Mr. Lockwood was in the living room and wanted to see me, must see me. I dressed hurriedly, for it came to me that something must be the matter. I think I must have come out sooner than they expected, for before they knew it I had run across the living room and looked through the door into the den, you call it, over there."

She pointed at a heavy door, but did not, evidently could not, let her eyes rest on it.

"There was my father, huddled in a chair, and blood had run out from an ugly wound in his side. I screamed and fell on my knees beside him. But," she shuddered, "it was too late. He was cold. He did not answer."

Kennedy said nothing, but let her weep into her dainty lace handkerchief, though the impulse was strong to do anything to calm her grief.

"Mr. Lockwood had come in to visit him on business, had found the door into the hall open, and entered. No one seemed to be about; but the lights were burning. He went on into the den. There was my father—"

She stopped, and could not go on at all for several minutes.

"And Mr. Lockwood, who is he?" asked Craig gently.

"My father and I, we have been in this country only a short time," she replied, trying to speak in good English in spite of her emotion, "with his partner in a—a mining venture—Mr. Lockwood."

She paused again and hesitated, as though in this strange land of the north she had no idea of which way to turn for help. But once started, now, she did not stop again.

"Oh," she went on passionately, "I don't know what it was that came over my father. But lately he had been a changed man. Sometimes I thought he was—what you call—mad. I should have gone to see a doctor about him," she added wildly, her feelings getting the better of her. "But it is no longer a case for a doctor. It is a case for a detective—for some one who is more than a detective. You cannot bring him back, but—"

She could not go on. Yet her broken sentence spoke volumes, in her pleading, soft, musical voice, which was far more pleasing to the ear than that of the usual Latin-American.

I had heard that the women of Lima were famed for their beauty and melodious voices. Senorita Inez surely upheld their reputation.

There was an appealing look now in her soft deep-brown eyes, and her thin, delicate lips trembled as she hurried on with her strange story.

"I never saw my father in such a state before," she murmured. "For days all he had talked about was the 'big fish,' the peje grande, whatever that might mean—and the curse of Mansiche."

The recollection of the past few days seemed to be too much for her. Almost before we knew it, before Norton, who had started to ask her a question, could speak, she excused herself and fled from the room, leaving only the indelible impression of loveliness and the appeal for help that was irresistible.

Kennedy turned to Norton. But just then the door to the den opened and we saw our friend Dr. Leslie. He saw us, too, and took a few steps in our direction.

"What—you here, Kennedy?" he greeted in surprise as Craig shook hands and introduced Norton. "And Jameson, too? Well, I think you've found a case at last that will baffle you."

As we talked he led the way across the living room and into the den from which he had just come.

"It is very strange," he said, telling at once all that he had been able to discover. "Senor Mendoza was discovered here about midnight last night by his partner, Mr. Lockwood. There seem to be no clues to how or by whom he was murdered. No locks had been broken. I have examined the hall-boy who was here last night. He seems to be off his post a good deal when it is late. He saw Mr. Lockwood come in, and took him in the elevator up to the sixth floor. After that we can find nothing but the open door into the apartment. It is not at all impossible that some one might have come in when the boy was off his post, have walked up, even have walked down, the stairs again. In fact, it must have been that way. No windows, not even on the fire-escape, have been tampered with. In fact, the murder must have been done by some one admitted to the apartment late by Mendoza himself."

We walked over to the couch on which lay the body covered

by a sheet. Dr. Leslie drew down the sheet.

On the face was a most awful look, a terrible stare and contortion of the features, and a deep, almost purple, discoloration. The muscles were all tense and rigid. I shall never forget that face and its look, half of pain, half of fear, as if of something nameless.

Mendoza had been a heavy-set man, whose piercing black eyes beetled forth, in life, from under bushy brows. Even in death, barring that horrible look, he was rather distinguished-looking, and his close-cropped hair and moustache set him off as a man of affairs and consequence in his own country.

"Most peculiar, Kennedy," reiterated Dr. Leslie, pointing to the breast. "You see that wound? I can't quite determine whether that was the real cause of death or not. Of course, it's a bad wound, it's true. But there seems to be something else here, too. Look at the pupils of his eyes, how contracted they are. The lungs seem congested, too. He has all the marks of having been asphyxiated. Yet there are no indications on his throat of violence such as would be necessary if that were the case. There could have been no such thing as illuminating gas, nor have we found any trace of any receptacles which might have held poison. I can't seem to make it out."

Kennedy bent over the body and looked at it attentively for several minutes, while we stood back of him, scarcely uttering a word in the presence of this terrible thing.

Deftly Kennedy managed to extract a few drops of blood from about the wound and transfer them to a very small test-tube which he carried in a little emergency pocket-case in order to preserve material for future study.

Arthur B. Reeve

"You say the dagger was triangular, Norton?" he asked finally, without looking up from his minute examination.

"Yes, with another blade that shot out automatically when you knew the secret of pressing the hilt in a certain way. The outside triangular blade separated into three to allow an inner blade to shoot out."

Kennedy had risen and, as Norton described the Inca dagger, looked from one to the other of us keenly.

"That blade was poisoned," he concluded quietly. "We have a clue to your missing dagger. Mendoza was murdered by it!"

II

THE SOLDIER OF FORTUNE

"I should like to have another talk with Senorita Inez," remarked Kennedy, a few minutes later, as with Dr. Leslie and Professor Norton we turned into the living room and closed the door to the den.

While Norton volunteered to send one of the servants in to see whether the young lady was able to stand the strain of another interview, Dr. Leslie received a hurry call to another case.

"You'll let me know, Kennedy, if you discover anything?" he asked, shaking hands with us. "I shall keep you informed, also, from my end. That poison completely baffles me—so far. You know, we might as well work together."

"Assuredly," agreed Craig, as the coroner left. "That," he added to me, as the door closed, "was one word for me and two for himself. I can do the work; he wants to save his official face. He never will know what that poison was—until I tell him."

Inez had by this time so far recovered her composure that she was able to meet us again in the living room.

Arthur B. Reeve

"I'm very sorry to have to trouble you again," apologized Kennedy, "but if I am to get anywhere in this case I must have the facts."

She looked at him, half-puzzled, and, I fancied, half-frightened, too. "Anything I can tell you—of course, ask me," she said.

"Had your father any enemies who might desire his death?" shot out Kennedy, almost without warning.

"No," she answered slowly, still watching him carefully, then adding hastily: "Of course, you know, no one who tries to do anything is absolutely without enemies, though."

"I mean," repeated Craig, carefully noting a certain hesitation in her tone, "was there any one who, for reasons best known to himself, might have murdered him in a way peculiarly likely under the circumstances, say, with a dagger?"

Inez flashed a quick glance at Kennedy, as if to inquire just how much or how little he really knew. I got the impression from it, at least, that she was holding back some suspicion for a reason that perhaps she would not even have admitted to herself.

I saw that Norton was also following the line of Kennedy's questioning keenly, though he said nothing.

Before Kennedy could take up the lead again, her maid, Juanita, a very pretty girl of Spanish and Indian descent, entered softly.

"Mr. Lockwood," she whispered, but not so low that we could not hear.

"Won't you ask him to come in, Nita?" she replied.

A moment later a young man pushed open the door—a tall, clean-cut young fellow, whose face bore the tan of a sun much stronger than any about New York. As I took his appraisal, I found him unmistakably of the type of American soldier of fortune who has been carried by the wander-spirit down among the romantic republics to the south of our own.

"Professor Kennedy," began Senorita Mendoza, presenting us all in turn, "let me introduce Mr. Lockwood, my father's partner in several ventures which brought us to New York."

As we shook hands I could not help feeling that the young mining engineer, for such he proved to be by ostensible profession, was something more to her than a mere partner in her father's schemes.

"I believe I've met Professor Norton," he remarked, as they shook hands. "Perhaps he remembers when we were in Lima."

"Perfectly," replied Norton, returning the penetrating glance in kind. "Also in New York," he added.

Lockwood turned abruptly. "Are you quite sure you are able to stand the strain of this interview?" he asked Inez in a low tone.

Norton glanced at Kennedy and raised his eyebrows just the fraction of an inch, as if to call attention to the neat manner in which Lockwood had turned the subject.

Inez smiled sadly. "I must," she said, in a forced tone.

I fancied that Lockwood noted and did not relish an air of

restraint in her words.

"It was you, I believe, Mr. Lockwood, who found Senor Mendoza last night?" queried Kennedy, as if to read the answer into the record, although he already knew it.

"Yes," replied Lockwood, without hesitation, though with a glance at the averted head of Inez, and choosing his words very carefully, as if trying hard not to say more than she could bear. "Yes. I came up here to report on some financial matters which interested both of us, very late, perhaps after midnight. I was about to press the buzzer on the door when I saw that the door was slightly ajar. I opened it and found lights still burning. The rest I think you must already know."

Even that tactful reference to the tragedy was too much for Inez. She suppressed a little convulsive sob, but did not, this time, try to flee from the room.

"You saw nothing about the den that aroused any suspicions?" pursued Kennedy. "No bottle, no glass? There wasn't the odour of any gas or drug?"

Lockwood shook his head slowly, fixing his eyes on Kennedy's face, but not looking at him. "No," he answered; "I have told Dr. Leslie just what I found. If there had been anything else I'm sure I would have noticed it while I was waiting for Miss Inez to come in."

His answers seemed perfectly frank and straight-forward. Yet somehow I could not get over the feeling that he, as well as Inez, was not telling quite all he knew—perhaps not about the murder, but about matters that might be related to it.

Norton evidently felt the same way. "You saw no weapon—a dagger?" he interrupted suddenly.

The young man faced Norton squarely. To me it seemed as if he had been expecting the question. "Not a thing," he said deliberately. "I looked about carefully, too. Whatever weapon was used must have been taken away by the murderer," he added.

Juanita entered again, and Inez excused herself to answer the telephone, while we stood in the living room chatting for a few minutes.

"What is this 'curse of Mansiche' which the Senorita has mentioned?" asked Kennedy, seeing a chance to open a new line of inquiry with Lockwood.

"Oh, I don't know," he returned, impatiently flicking the ashes of a cigarette which he had lighted the moment Inez left the room, as though such stories had no interest for the practical mind of an engineer. "Some old superstition, I suppose."

Lockwood seemed to regard Norton with a sort of aversion, if not hostility, and I fancied that Norton, on his part, neglected no opportunity to let the other know that he was watching him.

"I don't know much about the story," resumed Lockwood a moment later as no one said anything. "But I do know that there is treasure in that great old Chimu mound near Truxillo. Don Luis has the government concession to bore into the mound, too, and we are raising the capital to carry the scheme through to success."

He had come to the end of a sentence. Yet the inflection of his voice showed plainly that it was not the end of the idea that had been in his mind.

"If you knew where to dig," suddenly supplied Norton, gazing keenly into the eyes of the soldier of fortune.

Lockwood did not answer, though it was evident that that had been the thought unexpressed in his remarks.

The return of the Senorita to the room seemed to break the tension.

"It was the house telephone," she said, in a quiet voice. "The hall-boy didn't know whether to admit a visitor who comes with his sympathy." Then she turned from us to Lockwood. "You must know him," she said, somewhat embarrassed. "Senor Alfonso de Moche."

Lockwood suppressed a frown, but said nothing, for, a moment later, a young man came in. Almost in silence he advanced to Inez and took her hand in a manner that plainly showed his sympathy in her bereavement.

"I have just heard," he said simply, "and I hastened around to tell you how much I feel your loss. If there is anything I can do - "

He stopped, and did not finish the sentence. It was unnecessary. His eyes finished it for him.

Alfonso de Moche was, I thought, a very handsome fellow, though not of the Spanish type at all. His forehead was high, with a shock of straight black hair, his skin rather copper-coloured, nose slightly aquiline, chin and mouth firm; in fact, the whole face was refined and intellectual, though tinged with melancholy.

"Thank you," she murmured, then turned to us. "I believe you are acquainted with Mr. de Moche, Professor Norton?"

she asked. "You know he is taking post-graduate work at the University."

"Slightly," returned Norton, gazing at the young man in a manner that plainly disconcerted him. "I believe I have met his mother in Peru."

Senorita Mendoza seemed to colour at the mention of Senora de Moche. It flashed over me that, in his greeting Alfonso had said nothing of his mother. I wondered if there might be a reason for it. Could it be that Senorita Mendoza had some antipathy which did not include the son? Though we did not seem to be making much progress in this way in solving the mystery, still I felt that before we could go ahead we must know the little group about which it centred. There seemed to be currents and cross-currents here which we did not understand, but which must be charted if we were to steer a straight course.

"And Professor Kennedy?" she added, turning to us.

"I think I have seen Mr. de Moche about the campus," said Craig, as I, too, shook hands with him, "although you are not in any of my classes."

"No, Professor," concurred the young man, who was, however, considerably older than the average student taking courses like his.

I found it quite enough to watch the faces of those about me just then. Between Lockwood and de Moche it seemed that there existed a latent hostility. The two eyed each other with decided disfavour. As for Norton, he seemed to be alternately watching each of them.

An awkward silence followed, and de Moche seemed to take

the cue, for after a few more remarks to Inez he withdrew as gracefully as he could, with a parting interchange of frigid formalities with Lockwood. It did not take much of a detective to deduce that both of the young men might have agreed on one thing, though that caused the most serious of differences between them—their estimation of Inez de Mendoza.

Inez, on her part, seemed also to be visibly relieved at his departure, though she had been cordial enough to him. I wondered what it all meant.

Lockwood, too, seemed to be ill at ease still. But it was a different uneasiness, rather directed at Norton than at us. Once before I had thought he was on the point of excusing himself, but the entrance of de Moche seemed to have decided him to stay at least as long as his rival.

"I beg your pardon, Senorita," he now apologized, "but I really must go. There are still some affairs which I must attend to in order to protect the interests we represent." He turned to us. "You will excuse me, I know," he added, "but I have a very important appointment. You know Don Luis and I were assisting in organizing the campaign of Stuart Whitney to interest American manufacturers, and particularly bankers, in the chances in South America which lie at hand, if we are only awake to take advantage of them. I shall be at your service, Senorita, as soon as the meeting is over. I presume I shall see you again?" he nodded to Kennedy.

"Quite likely," returned Kennedy drily.

"If there is any assistance I can render in clearing up this dreadful thing," went on Lockwood, in a lower tone to us, "you may count on me absolutely."

"Thank you," returned Craig, with a significant glance. "I may have to take up that offer."

"Do so, by all means," he reiterated, bowing to Norton and backing out of the door.

Alone again with Inez Mendoza, Kennedy turned suddenly. "Who is this Senor de Moche?" he asked. "I gather that you must have known him in Peru."

"Yes," she agreed. "I knew him in Lima"; then adding, as if by way of confession, "when he was a student at the University."

There was something in both her tone and manner that would lead one to believe that she had only the kindliest feelings toward de Moche, whatever might be the case, as it seemed, with his mother.

For a moment Kennedy now advanced and took Senorita Inez by the hand. "I must go now," he said simply. "If there is anything which you have not told me, I should like to know."

"No—nothing," she answered.

He did not take his eyes from hers. "If you should recall anything else," he persisted, "don't hesitate to tell me. I will come here, or you may come to the laboratory, whichever is more convenient."

"I shall do so," she replied. "And thank you a thousand times for the trouble you are going to in my behalf. You may be sure that I appreciate it."

Norton also bade her farewell, and she thanked him for

Arthur B. Reeve

having brought us over. I noticed also that Norton, though considerably older than any of us, had apparently succumbed to the spell of her wonderful eyes and face.

"I also would be glad to help you," he promised. "You can usually find me at the Museum."

"Thank you all," she murmured. "You are all so kind to me. An hour ago I felt that I had not a friend in all this big city— except Mr. Lockwood. Now I feel that I am not quite all alone."

She said it to Norton, but it was really meant for Kennedy. I know Craig shared my own feelings. It was a rare pleasure to work for her. She seemed most appreciative of anything that was done for her in her defenceless position.

As we passed out of the apartment house and sought our cab again, Kennedy was the first to speak, and to Norton.

"Do you know anything more about these men, Lockwood and de Moche?" he queried, as we sped uptown.

"I don't know a thing," he replied cautiously. "I—I'd much prefer not to talk of suspicions."

"But the dagger," insisted Kennedy. "Have you no suspicions of what became of it and who took it?"

"I'd prefer not to talk of mere suspicions," he repeated.

Little was said as we turned in at the campus and at last drew up before Norton's wing of the Museum.

"You will let me know of any development, no matter how trivial?" asked Kennedy, as we parted. "Your dagger seems to have stirred up more trouble than there was any reason to suppose when you came to me first."

"I should say so," he agreed. "I don't know how to repay the interest you have shown in its recovery. If anything else materializes, I shall surely get word to you immediately."

As we turned to leave, I could not help thinking of the manner of Lockwood and Norton toward each other. The name Stuart Whitney ran through my head. Stuart Whitney was a trustee of the University who had contributed heavily, among other things, to Norton's various expeditions to South America. Was it that Norton felt a peculiar loyalty to Whitney, or was he jealous that any one else should succeed in interesting his patron in things South American?

The actions of the two young men, Lockwood and de Moche, recurred to me. "Well," I remarked, as we walked along, "what do you think it is—a romance or a simple crime-hunt?" "Both, I suspect," replied Craig abstractedly. "Only not simple."

III

THE ARCHAEOLOGICAL DETECTIVE

"I think I'll go into the University Library," Craig remarked, as we left Norton before his building. "I want to refresh my mind on some of those old Peruvian antiquities and traditions. What the Senorita hinted at may prove to be very important. I suppose you will have to turn in a story to the Star soon?"

"Yes," I agreed, "I'll have to turn in something, although I'd prefer to wait."

"Try to get an assignment to follow the case to the end," suggested Craig. "I think you'll find it worth while. Anyhow, this will give you a chance for a breathing space, and, if I have this thing doped out right, you won't get another for some time. I'll meet you over in the laboratory in a couple of hours."

Craig hurried up the long flight of white-marble steps to the library and disappeared, while I jumped on the subway and ran downtown to the office.

It took me, as I knew it would, considerably over a couple of hours to clear things up at the Star, so that I could take advantage of a special arrangement which I had made, so that I could, when a case warranted it, co-operate with Kennedy. My story was necessarily brief, but that was what I wanted just now. I did not propose to have the whole field of special-feature writers camping on my preserve.

Uptown I hurried again, afraid that Kennedy had finished and might have been called away. But when I reached the laboratory he was not there, and I found that he had not been. Up and down I paced restlessly. There was nothing else to do but wait. If he was unable to keep his appointment here with me, I knew that he would soon telephone. What was it, I wondered, that kept him delving into the archaeological lore of the library?

I had about given him up, when he hurried into the laboratory in a high state of excitement.

"What did you find?" I queried. "Has anything happened?"

"Let me tell you first what I found in the library," he replied, tilting his hat back on his head and alternately thrusting and withdrawing his fingers in his waistcoat pockets, as if in some way that might help him to piece together some scattered fragments of a story which he had just picked up.

"I've been looking up that hint that the Senorita dropped when she used those words peje grande, which mean, literally, 'big fish,'" he resumed. "Walter, it fires the imagi-nation. You have read of the wealth that Pizarro found in Peru, of course." Visions of Prescott flashed through my mind as he spoke.

"Well, where are the gold and silver of the conquistadores? Gone to the melting-pot, centuries ago. But is there none left? The Indians in Peru believe so, at any rate. And, Walter, there are persons who would stop at nothing to get at the secret.

"It is a matter of history that soon after the conquest a vast fortune was unearthed of which the King of Spain's fifth amounted to five million dollars. That treasure was known as the peje chica—the little fish. One version of the story tells that an Inca ruler, the great Cacique Mansiche, had observed with particular attention the kindness of a young Spaniard toward the people of the conquered race. Also, he had observed that the man was comparatively poor. At any rate, he revealed the secret of the hiding-place of the peje chica, on condition that a part of the wealth should be used to advance the interests of the Indians.

"The most valuable article discovered was in the form of a fish of solid gold and so large that the Spaniards considered it a rare prize. But the Cacique assured his young friend that it was only the little fish, that a much greater treasure existed, worth many times the value of this one.

"The sequel of the story is that the Spaniard forgot his promise, went off to Spain, and spent all his gold. He was returning for the peje grande, of which he had made great boasts, but before he could get it he was killed. Prescott, I believe, gives another version, in which he says that the Spaniard devoted a large part of his wealth to the relief of the Indians and gave large sums to the Peruvian churches. Other stories deny that it was Mansiche who told the first secret, but that it was another Indian. One may, I suppose, pay his money and take his choice. But the point, as far as we are concerned in this case, is that there is still believed to be the great fish, which no one has found. Who knows? Perhaps, somehow, Mendoza had the secret of the peje grande?"

Kennedy paused, and I could feel the tense interest with

which his delving into the crumbling past had now endowed this already fascinating case.

"And the curse?" I put in.

"About that we do not know," he replied. "Except that we do know that Mansiche was the great Cacique or ruler of northern Peru. The natives are believed to have buried a far greater treasure than even that which the Spaniards carried off. Mansiche is said to have left a curse on any native who ever divulged the whereabouts of the treasure, and the curse was also to fall on any Spaniard who might discover it. That is all we know—yet. Gold was used lavishly in the temples. That great hoard is really the Gold of the Gods. Surely, as we have seen it so far in this case, it must be cursed."

There was a knock on the laboratory door, and I sprang to open it, expecting to find that it was something for Kennedy. Instead there stood one of the office boys of the Star.

"Why, hello, Tommy," I greeted him. "What seems to be the matter now?"

"A letter for you, Mr. Jameson," he replied, handing over a plain envelope. "It came just after you left. The Boss thought it might be important—something about that story, I guess. Anyhow, he told me to take it up to you on my way home, sir."

I looked at it again. It bore simply my name and the address of the Star, not written, but, strange to say, printed in ungainly, rough characters, as though some one were either not familiar with writing English or desired to conceal his handwriting.

"Where did it come from—and how?" I asked, as I tore the

envelope open.

"I don't know where, sir," replied Tommy. "A boy brought it. Said a man uptown gave him a quarter to deliver it to you."

I looked at the contents in blank amazement. There was nothing in the letter except a quarter sheet of ordinary size note paper such as that used in typewritten correspondence.

Printed on it, in characters exactly like those on the outside of the envelope, were the startling words:

"BEWARE THE CURSE OF MANSICHE ON THE GOLD OF THE GODS."

Underneath this inscription appeared the rude drawing of a dagger in which some effort had evidently been made to make it appear three-sided.

"Well, of all things, what do you think of that?" I cried, tossing the thing over to Kennedy.

He took it and read it; his face puckered deeply. "I'm not surprised," he said, a moment later, looking up. "Do you know, I was just about to tell you what happened at the library. I had a feeling all the time I was there of being watched. I don't know why or how, but, somehow, I felt that some one was interested in the books I was reading. It made me uncomfortable. I was late, anyhow, and I decided not to give them the satisfaction of seeing me any more—at least in the library. So I have had a number of the books on Peru which I wanted reserved, and they'll be sent over later, here. No, I'm not surprised that you received this. Would you remember the boy?" he asked of Tommy.

"I think so," replied Tommy. "He didn't have on a uniform,

though. It wasn't a messenger."

There was no use to question him further. He had evidently told all that he knew, and finally we had to let him go, with a parting injunction to keep his eyes open and his mouth shut.

Kennedy continued to study the note on the quarter sheet of paper long after the boy had gone.

"You know," he remarked thoughtfully, after a while, "as nearly as I can make the thing out with the slender information that we have so far, the weirdest superstitions seem to cluster about that dagger which Norton lost. I wouldn't be surprised if it took us far back into the dim past of the barbaric splendour of the lost Inca civilization of Peru."

He waved the sheet of paper for emphasis. "You see, some one has used it here as a sign of terror. Perhaps somehow it bore the secret of the big fish—who knows? None of the writers and explorers have ever found it. The most they can say is that it may be handed down from father to son through a long line. At any rate, the secret of the hiding-place seems to have been safely kept. No one has ever found the treasure. It would be strange, wouldn't it, if it remained for some twentieth-century civilized man to unearth the thing and start again the curse that historians say was uttered and seems always to have followed the thing?"

"Kennedy, this affair is getting on my nerves already."

While Craig was speaking the door of the laboratory had opened without our hearing it, and there stood Norton again. He had waited until Craig had finished before he had spoken.

We looked at him, startled, ourselves.

　　　　　Arthur B. Reeve

"I had some work to do after I left you," went on Norton, without stopping. "In my letter-box were several letters, but I forgot to look at them until just now, when I was leaving. Then I picked them up—and—look at this thing that was among them."

Norton laid down on the laboratory table a plain envelope and a quarter sheet of paper on which were printed, except for his own name instead of mine, an almost exact replica of the note which I had received.

"BEWARE THE CURSE OF MANSICHE ON THE GOLD OF THE GODS."

Kennedy and I looked at him. Already, evidently, he had seen that Kennedy held in his hand the note that had come to me.

"I can't make anything out of it," went on Norton, evidently much worried. "First I lose the dagger. Next you say it was used to murder Mendoza. Then I get this. Now, if any one can get into the Museum to steal the dagger, they could get in to carry out any threat of revenge, real or fancied."

Looked at in that respect, I felt that it was indeed a real cause of worry for Norton. But, then, it flashed over me, was not my own case worse? I was to be responsible for telling the story. Might not some unseen hand strike at me, perhaps sooner than at him?

Kennedy had taken the two notes and was scanning them eagerly.

Just then an automobile drew up outside, and a moment later we heard a tap at the door which Kennedy had closed after the entrance of Norton. I opened it.

"Is Professor Kennedy here?" I heard a voice inquire. "I'm one of the orderlies at the City Hospital, next to the Morgue, where Dr. Leslie has his laboratory. I've a message for Profesor Kennedy, if he's in."

Kennedy took the envelope, which bore the stamp of Dr. Leslie's department, and tore it open.

"My dear Kennedy," he read, in an undertone. "I've been engaged in investigating that poison which probably surrounds the wound in the Mendoza case, but as yet have nothing to report. It is certainly none of the things which we ordinarily run up against. Enclosed you will find a slip of paper and the envelope which it came in—something, I take it, that has been sent me by a crank. Would you treat it seriously or disregard it? Leslie."

As Kennedy had unfolded Leslie's own letter a piece of paper had fluttered to the floor. I picked it up mechanically, and only now looked at it, as Craig finished reading.

On it was another copy of the threat that had been sent to both Norton and myself!

The hospital orderly had scarcely gone when another tap came at the door.

"Your books from the library, Professor," announced a student who was employed in the library as part payment of his tuition. "I've signed the slip for them, sir."

He deposited the books on a desk, a huge pile of them, which reached from his outstretched arms to his chin. As he did so the pressure of his arms released the pile of books and the column collapsed.

From a book entitled "New and Old Peru," which fell with the pile, slipped a plain white envelope. Kennedy saw it before either of us, and seized it.

"Here's one for me," he said, tearing it open.

Sure enough, in the same rude printing on a quarter sheet were the words:

"BEWARE THE CURSE OF MANSICHE ON THE GOLD OF THE GODS."

We could only stare at each other and at that tell-tale sign of the Inca dagger underneath.

What did it mean? Who had sent the warnings?

Kennedy alone seemed to regard the affair as if with purely scientific interest. He took the four pieces of paper and laid them down before him on the table. Then he looked up suddenly.

"They match perfectly," he said quietly, gathering them up and placing them in a wallet which he carried. "All the indentures of the tearing correspond. Four warnings seem to have been sent to those who are likely to find out something of the secret."

Norton seemed to have gained somewhat of his composure now that he had been able to talk to some one.

"What are you going to do—give it up?" he asked tensely.

"Nothing could have insured my sticking to it harder," answered Craig grimly.

"Then we'll all have to stick together," said Norton slowly. "We all seem to be in the same boat."

As he rose to go he extended a hand to each of us.

"I'll stick," repeated Kennedy, with that peculiar bulldog look of intensity on his face which I had come to know so well.

IV

THE TREASURE HUNTERS

Norton had scarcely gone, and Kennedy was still studying the four pieces of paper on which the warning had been given, when our laboratory door was softly pushed open again.

It was Senorita Mendoza, looking more beautiful than ever in her plain black mourning dress, the unnatural pallor of her face heightening the wonderful lustrous eyes that looked about as though half frightened at what she was doing.

"I hope nothing has happened," greeted Kennedy, placing an easy-chair for her. "But I'm glad to see that you have confidence enough to trust me."

She looked about doubtfully at the vast amount of para-phernalia which Craig had collected in his scientific warfare on crime. Though she did not understand it, it seemed to impress her.

"No," she murmured, "nothing new has happened. You told me to call on you if I should think of anything else."

She said it with an air as if confessing something. It was

apparent that, whatever it was, she had known it all the time and only after a struggle had brought herself to telling it.

"Then you have thought of something?" prompted Craig.

"Yes," she replied in a low tone. Then with an effort she went on: "I don't know whether you know it or not, but my family is an old one, one of the oldest in Peru."

Kennedy nodded encouragingly.

"Back in the old days, after Pizarro," she hurried on, no longer able to choose her words, but blurting the thing out directly, "an ancestor of mine was murdered by an Inca dagger."

She stopped again and looked about, actually frightened at her own temerity, evidently. Kennedy and his twentieth-century surroundings seemed again to reassure her.

"I can't tell you the story," she resumed. "I don't know it. My father knew it. But it was some kind of family secret, for he never told me. Once when I asked him he put me off; told me to wait until I was a little older."

"And you think that may have something to do with the case?" asked Kennedy, trying to draw out anything more that she knew.

"I don't know," she answered frankly. "But don't you think that it is strange—an ancestor of mine murdered and now, hundreds of years afterward, my father, the last of his line in direct descent, murdered in the same way, by an Inca dagger that has disappeared?"

"Then you were listening while I was talking to Professor

Norton?" shot out Kennedy, not unkindly, but rather as a surprise test to see what she would say.

"You cannot blame me for that," she returned simply.

"Hardly," smiled Kennedy. "And I appreciate your reticence —as well as your coming here finally to tell me. Indeed, it is strange. Surely you must have some other suspicions," he persisted, "something that you feel, even though you do not know?"

Kennedy was leaning forward, looking deeply into her eyes, as if he would read what was passing in her mind. She met his gaze for a moment, then looked away.

"You heard Mr. Lockwood say that he had become associated with a Mr. Whitney, Mr. Stuart Whitney, down in Wall Street?" she ventured.

Kennedy did not take his eyes from her face as he sought to extract the reluctant words from her.

"Mr. Whitney has been largely interested in Peru, in business and in mining," she went on slowly. "He has given large sums to scholars down there, to Professor Norton's expeditions from New York. I—I'm afraid of that Mr. Whitney!"

Her quiet tone had risen to a pitch of tremulous excitement. Her face, which had been pale from the strain of the tragedy, was now full of colour, and her breast rose and fell with suppressed emotion.

"Afraid of him—why?" asked Kennedy.

There was no more reticence. Once having said so much, she

seemed to feel that she must go on and tell her fears.

"Because," she went on, "he—he knows a woman—whom my father knew." A sudden flash of fire seemed to light up her dark eyes. "A woman of Truxillo," she continued, "Senora de Moche."

"De Moche," repeated Kennedy, recalling the name and a still unexplained incident of our first interview. "Who is this Senora de Moche?" he asked, studying her as if she had been under a lens.

"A Peruvian of an old Indian family," she replied, in a low tone, as if the words were forced from her. "She has come to New York with her son, Alfonso. You remember—you met him. He is studying here at the University."

Again I noted the different manner in which she spoke the two names of mother and son. Evidently there was some feud, some barrier between her and the elder woman, which did not extend to Alfonso.

Kennedy reached for the University catalogue and found the name, "Alfonso de Moche." He was, as he had told us, a post-graduate student in the engineering school and, therefore, not in any of Kennedy's own classes.

"You say your father knew the Senora?" asked Kennedy.

"Yes," she replied, in a low voice, "he had had some dealings with her. I cannot say just what they were; I do not know. Socially, of course, it was different. They did not belong to the same circle as ours in Lima."

From her tone I gathered that there existed a race prejudice between those of old Spanish descent and the descendants of the Indians. That, however, could not account for her attitude. At least with her the prejudice did not extend to Alfonso.

"Senora de Moche is a friend of Mr. Whitney?" queried Kennedy.

"Yes, I believe she has placed some of her affairs in his hands. The de Moches live at the Prince Edward Albert Hotel, and Mr. Whitney lives there, too. I suppose they see more or less of each other."

"H-m," mused Kennedy. "You know Mr. Whitney, I suppose?"

"Not very well," she answered. "Of course, I have met him. He has been to visit my father, and my father has been down at his office, with Mr. Lockwood. But I do not know much about him, except that he is what you Americans call a promoter."

Apparently, Inez was endeavouring to be frank in telling her suspicions, much more so even than Norton had been. But I could not help feeling that she was trying to shield some one, though not to the extent of consciously putting us on a wrong scent.

"I shall try to see Mr. Whitney as soon as possible," said Kennedy, as she rose to go. "And Senora de Moche, too."

I fancied that Senorita Inez, although she had not told us much, felt relieved.

Again she murmured her thanks as she left and again Kennedy repeated his injunction to tell everything that happened that could possibly have any bearing on the case.

"That's a rather peculiar phase," he considered, when we were alone, "this de Moche affair."

"Yes," I agreed. "Do you suppose that woman could be using Whitney for some purpose?"

"Or Whitney using her," suggested Kennedy. "There's so much to be done at once that I hardly know where to begin. We must see both of them as soon as possible. Meanwhile, that message from Dr. Leslie about the poison interests me. I must at least start my tests of the blood samples that I extracted. Walter, may I ask you to leave me here in the laboratory undisturbed?"

I had some writing on my news story to do, and went into the room next to the laboratory, where I was soon busily engaged tapping my typewriter. Suddenly I became conscious of that feeling, which Kennedy had hinted at, of being watched. Perhaps I had heard a footstep outside and was not consciously aware of it. But, at any rate, I had the feeling.

I stopped tapping the keys and wheeled unexpectedly about in my chair. I am sure that I caught just a fleeting glimpse of a face dodging back from the window, which was on the first floor.

Whose face it was I am not prepared to assert exactly. But there was a face, and the fleeting glimpse of the eyes and forehead was just enough to give me the impression that they were familiar, without enabling me to identify them. At any rate, the occurrence made me feel decidedly uncomfortable, especially after the warning letters that we had all received.

I sprang to my feet and ran to the door. But it was too late. The intruder had disappeared. Still, the more I thought about

Arthur B. Reeve

it, the more determined I was to try to verify an indistinct suspicion, if possible. I put on my hat and walked hurriedly over to the office of the registrar.

Sure enough, I found that Alfonso de Moche had been at the University that day, must have attended a lecture an hour or so before. Having nothing else to do, I hunted up some of his professors and tried to quiz them about him.

As I had expected, they told me that he was an excellent student, though very quiet and reserved. His mind seemed to run along the line of engineering, and particularly mining. I could not help coming to the conclusion that undoubtedly he, too, was infected by the furore for treasure hunting, in spite of his Indian ancestry.

Yet there seemed to be surprisingly little known about him outside of the lecture room and laboratory. The profesors knew that he lived with his mother at a hotel downtown. He seemed to have little or nothing to do with the other students outside of class work. Altogether he was an enigma, as far as the social life of the University went. It looked very much as though he had come to New York quietly to prepare himself for the search for the buried treasure. Had the Gold of the Gods lured him into its net, too?

Reflecting on the tangle of events, the strange actions of Lockwood and the ambitions of Whitney, I retraced my steps in the direction of the laboratory, convinced that de Moche had employed at least a part of his time lately in spying on us. Perhaps he had seen Inez going in and out. Suddenly it flashed over me that the interchange of glances between de Moche and Lockwood indicated that she was more to him than a mere acquaintance. Perhaps it had been jealousy as well as treasure hunting that had prompted his eavesdropping.

Still reflecting, I decided to turn in at the Museum and have a chat with Norton. I found him nervously pacing up and down the little office that had been accorded him in his section of the building.

"I can't rid my mind of that warning," he remarked anxiously, pausing in his measured tread. "It seems inconceivable to me that any one would take the trouble to send four such warnings unless he meant it."

"Quite so," I agreed, relating to him what had just happened.

"I thought of something like that," he acquiesced, "and I have already taken some precautions."

Norton waved his hand at the windows, which I had not noticed before. Though they were some distance above the ground, I saw now that he had closed and barred them at the expense of ventilation. The warnings seemed to have made more of an impression on him than on any of the rest of us.

"One never can tell where or when a blow will fall with these people," he explained. "You see, I've lived among them. They are a hot-blooded race. Besides, as you perhaps have read, they have some queer poisons down in South America. I mean to run no unnecessary chances."

"I suppose you suspected all along that the dagger had something to do with the Gold of the Gods, did you not?" I hinted.

Norton paused before answering, as though to weigh his words. "Suspected—yes," he replied. "But, as I told you, I have had no chance to read the inscription on it. I can't say that I took it very seriously—until now."

"It's not possible that Stuart Whitney, who, I understand, is deeply interested in South America, may have had some inkling of the value of the dagger, is it?" I asked thoughtfully.

For a full minute Norton gazed at me. "I hadn't thought of that," he admitted at length. "That's a new idea to me."

Yet somehow I knew that Norton had thought of it, though he had not yet spoken about it. Was it through loyalty to the man who had contributed to financing his expeditions to South America?

"Do you know Senora de Moche well?" I ventured, a moment later.

"Fairly well," he replied. "Why?"

"What do you think of her?"

"Rather a clever woman," he replied noncommittally.

"I suppose all the people in New York who were interested in Peru knew her," I pursued, adding, "Mr. Whitney, Mendoza, Lockwood."

Norton hesitated, as though he was afraid of saying too much. While I could not help admiring his caution, I found that it was most exasperating. Still, I was determined to get at his point of view, if possible.

"Alfonso seems to be a worthy son, then," I remarked. "I can't quite make out, though, why the Senorita should have such an obvious prejudice against her. It doesn't seem to extend to him."

"I believe," replied Norton reluctantly, "that Mendoza had been on rather intimate terms with her. At least, I think you'll find the woman very ambitious for her son. I don't think she would have stopped at much to advance his interests. You must have noticed how much Alfonso thinks of the Senorita. But I don't think there was anything that could have overcome the old Castilian's prejudice. You know they pride themselves on never intermarrying. With Lockwood it would have been different."

I thought I began to get some glimmering of how things were.

"Whitney knows her pretty well now, doesn't he?" I shot out.

Norton shrugged his shoulders. But he could not have acquiesced better than by his very manner.

"Mr. Lockwood and Mr. Whitney know best what they are doing," he remarked, at length. "Why don't you and Kennedy try to see Senora de Moche? I'm a scientist, you know. I dislike talking about speculations. I'd prefer only to express opinions about things that are certainties."

Perhaps Norton wished to convey the impression that the subjects I had broached were worth looking into. At least it was the impression I derived.

"Still," he continued slowly, "I think I am justified in saying this much: I myself have been interested in watching both Alfonso de Moche and Lockwood when it comes to the case of the Senorita. All's fair, they say, in love and war. If I am any judge, there are both in this case, somewhere. I think you had better see the Senora and judge for yourself. She's a clever woman, I know. But I'm sure that Kennedy could make her out, even if the rest of us can't."

I thanked Norton for the hint that he had given, and after chatting a few moments more left him alone in his office.

In my room again, I went back to finish my writing. Nothing further occurred, however, to excite my suspicions, and at last I managed to finish it.

I was correcting what I had written when the door opened from the laboratory and Craig entered. He had thrown off his old, acid-stained laboratory smock and was now dressed to venture forth.

"Have you found out anything about the poison?" I asked.

"Nothing definite yet," he replied. "That will take some time now. It's a strange poison—an alkaloid, I'm sure, but not one that one ordinarily encounters. Still, I've made a good beginning. It won't take long to determine it now."

Craig listened with deep interest, though without comment, when I related what had happened, both Norton's conversation and about the strange visitor whom we had had peering into our windows.

"Some one seems to be very much interested in what we are doing, Walter," he concluded simply. "I think we'd better do a little more outside work now, while we have a chance. If you are ready, so am I. I want to see what sort of treasure hunter this Stuart Whitney is. I'd like to know whether he is in on this secret of the Gold of the Gods, too."

V

THE WALL STREET PROMOTER

Lockwood, as we now knew, had become allied in some way with a group of Wall Street capitalists, headed by Stuart Whitney.

Already I had heard something of Whitney. In the Street he was well known as an intensely practical man, though far above the average exploiter both in cleverness and education.

As a matter of fact, Whitney had been far-sighted enough to see that scholarship could be capitalized, not only as an advertisement, but in more direct manners. Just at present one of his pet schemes was promoting trade through the canal between the east coast of North America and the west coast of South America. He had spent a good deal of money promoting friendship between men of affairs and wealth in both New York and Lima. It was a good chance, he figured, for his investments down in Peru were large, and anything that popularized the country in New York could not but make them more valuable.

"Norton seemed rather averse to talking about Whitney," I ventured to Craig, as we rode downtown.

Arthur B. Reeve

"That may be part of Whitney's cleverness," he returned thoughtfully. "As a patron of art and letters, you know, a man can carry through a good many things that otherwise would be more critically examined."

Kennedy did not say it in a way that implied that he knew anything very bad about Whitney. Still, I reflected, it was astute in the man to insure the cooperation of such people as Norton. A few thousand dollars judiciously spent on archaeology might cover up a multitude of sins of high finance.

Nothing more was said by either of us, and at last we reached the financial district. We entered a tall skyscraper on Wall Street just around the corner from Broadway and shot up in the elevator to the floor where Whitney and his associates had a really palatial suite of offices.

As we opened the door we saw that Lockwood was still there. He greeted us with a rather stiff bow.

"Professor Kennedy and Mr. Jameson," he said simply, introducing us to Whitney, "friends of Professor Norton, I believe. I met them to-day up at Mendoza's."

"That is a most incomprehensible affair," returned Whitney, shaking hands with us. "What do you make out of it?"

Kennedy shrugged his shoulders and turned the remark aside without committing himself.

Stuart Whitney was a typical promoter, a large, full-blooded man, with a face red and inclined to be puffy from the congested veins. His voice alone commanded respect, whether he said anything worth while or not. In fact, he had but to say that it was a warm day and you felt that he had scored a telling point in the conversation.

"Professor Norton has asked me to look into the loss of an old Peruvian dagger which he brought back from his last expedition," explained Kennedy, endeavouring to lead the conversation in channels which might arrive somewhere.

"Yes, yes," remarked Whitney, with a nod of interest. "He has told me of it. Very strange, very strange. When he came back he told me that he had it, along with a lot of other important finds. But I had no idea he set such a value on it—or, rather, that any one else might do so. It would have been easy to have safeguarded it here, if we had known," he added, with a wave of his hand in the direction of a huge chrome steel safe of latest design in the outer office.

Lockwood, I noted, was listening intently, quite in contrast with his former cavalier manner of dismissing all consideration of ancient Inca lore as academic or unpractical. Did he know something of the dagger?

"I'm very much interested in old Peruvian antiquities myself," remarked Kennedy, a few minutes later, "though not, of course, a scholar like our friend Norton."

"Indeed?" returned Whitney; and I noticed for the first time that his eyes seemed fairly to glitter with excitement.

They were prominent eyes, a trifle staring, and I could not help studying them.

"Then," he exclaimed, rising, "you must know of the ruins of Chan-Chan, of Chima—those wonderful places?"

Kennedy nodded. "And of Truxillo and the legend of the great fish and the little fish," he put in.

Whitney seemed extraordinarily pleased that any one should be willing to discuss his hobby with him. His eyes by this time were apparently starting from their sockets, and I noticed that the pupils were dilated almost to the size of the iris.

"We must sit down and talk about Peru," he continued, reaching for a large box of cigarettes in the top drawer of his big desk.

Lockwood seemed to sense a long discussion of archaeology. He rose and mumbled an excuse about having something to do in the outer office.

"Oh, it is a wonderful country, Professor Kennedy," went on Whitney, throwing himself back in his chair. "I am deeply interested in it—its mines, its railroads, as well as its history. Let me show you a map of our interests down there."

He rose and passed into the next room to get the map. The moment his back was turned, Kennedy reached over to a typewriter desk that stood in a corner of the office, left open by the stenographer, who had gone. He took two thin second sheets of paper and a new carbon sheet. A hasty dab or two of the library paste completed his work.

Carefully Craig laid the prepared paper on the floor just a few inches from the door into the outer office and scattered a few other sheets about, as though the wind had blown them off the desk.

As Whitney returned, a big map unrolled in his hands, I saw his foot fall on the double sheet that Craig had laid by the door.

Kennedy bent down and began picking up the papers.

"Oh, that's all right," remarked Whitney brusquely. "Never mind that. Here's where some of our interests lie, in the north."

I don't think I paid much more attention to the map than did Kennedy as we three bent over it. His real attention was on the paper which he had placed on the floor, as though fixing in his mind the exact spot on which Whitney had stepped.

As Whitney talked rapidly about the country, we lighted the cigarettes. They seemed to be of a special brand. I puffed mine for a moment. There was a peculiar taste about it, however, which I did not exactly like. In fact, I think that the Latin-American cigarettes do not seem to appeal to most Americans very much, anyhow.

While we talked, I noticed that Kennedy evidently shared my own tastes, for he allowed his cigarette to go out, and, after a puff or two, I did the same. For the sake of my own comfort, I drew one of my own from my case as soon as I could do so politely, and laid the stub of the other in an ash-tray on Whitney's desk.

"Mr. Lockwood and Senor Mendoza had some joint interests in the country, too, didn't they?" queried Kennedy, his eye still on the pieces of paper near the door.

"Yes," returned Whitney. "Lockwood!"

"What is it?" came Lockwood's voice from outside.

"Show Professor Kennedy where you and Mendoza have those concessions."

The young engineer strode into the room, and I saw a smile of gratification cross Kennedy's face as his foot, also, fell on

Arthur B. Reeve

the paper by the door.

Unlike Whitney, however, Lockwood bent over to gather up the sheets. But before he could actually do so Kennedy reached down and swept them just out of his reach.

"Quite breezy," Kennedy covered up his action, turning to restore the paper to the desk.

Craig had his back to them, but not to me, and I saw him fumble for an instant with the papers. Quickly he pressed his thumb-nail on one side, as though making a rough "W," while on the other side he made what might be an "L." Then he shoved the two sheets and the carbon into his pocket.

I glanced up hastily. Fortunately, neither Whitney nor Lockwood had noted his action.

For the first time, now, I noticed as I watched him that Lockwood's eyes, too, were a trifle stary, though not so noticeable as Whitney's.

"Let me see," continued Whitney, "your concessions are all about here, in the north, aren't they?"

Lockwood drew a pencil from his pocket and made several cross-marks over the names of some towns on the large map.

"Those are the points that we had proposed to work," he said simply, "before this terrible tragedy to Mendoza."

"Mining, you understand," explained Whitney. Then, after a pause, he resumed quickly. "Of course, you know that much has been said about the chances for mining investments and about the opportunities for fortunes for persons in South America. Peru has been the Mecca for fortune hunters since the days of Pizarro. But where one person has been successful thousands have failed because they don't know the game. Why, I know of one investment of hundreds of thousands that hasn't yielded a cent of profit just because of that."

Lockwood said nothing, evidently not caring to waste time or breath on any one who was not a possible investor. But Whitney had the true promoter's instinct of booming his scheme on the chance that the interest inspired might be carried to some third party.

"American financiers, it is true," he went on excitedly, taking out a beautifully chased gold cigarette case, "have lost millions in mining in Peru. But that is not the scheme that our group, including Mr. Lockwood now, has. We are going to make more millions than they ever dreamed of—because we are simply going to mine for the products of centuries of labour already done—for the great treasure of Truxillo."

One could not help becoming infected by Whitney's enthusiasm.

Kennedy was following him closely, while a frown of disapproval spread over Lockwood's face.

"Then you know the secret of the hiding-place of the treasure?" queried Kennedy abruptly.

Whitney shook his head in the negative. "It is my idea that we don't have to know it," he answered. "With the hints that we have collected from the natives, I think we can locate it with the expenditure of comparatively little time and money. Senor Mendoza has obtained the concession from the government to hunt for it on a large scale in the big mounds about Truxillo. We know it is there. Is not that enough?"

If it had been any one less than Whitney, we should probably have said it was not. But it took more than that to deny anything he asserted. Lockwood's face was a study. I cannot say that it betrayed anything except disapproval of the mere discussion of the subject. In fact, it left me in doubt as to whether Whitney himself might not have been bluffing, in the certainty of finding the treasure—perhaps had already the secret he denied having and was preparing to cover it up by stumbling on it, apparently, in some other way. I recognized in Stuart Whitney as smooth an individual as ever we had encountered. His was all the sincerity of a crook. Yet he contrived to leave the whole matter in doubt. Perhaps in this case he actually knew what he was talking about.

The telephone rang and Lockwood answered it. Though he did not mention her name, I knew from his very tone and manner that it was Senorita de Mendoza who was calling up. Evidently his continued absence had worried her.

"There's absolutely nothing to worry about," we heard him say. "Nothing has changed. I shall be up to see you as soon as I can get away from the office."

There was an air of restraint about Lockwood's remarks, not as though he were keeping anything from the Senorita, but as though he were reluctant for us to overhear anything about his affairs.

Lockwood had been smoking, too, and he added the stubs of his cigarettes to the pile in the ash-tray on Whitney's desk. Once I saw Craig cast a quick glance at the tray, and I understood that in some way he was anxious to have a chance to investigate those cigarettes.

"You saw the dagger which Norton brought back, did you not?" asked Kennedy of Whitney.

"Only as I saw the rest of the stuff after it was unpacked," he replied easily. "He brought back a great many interesting objects on this last trip."

It was apparent that whether he actually knew anything about the secret of the Inca dagger or not, Whitney was not to be trapped into betraying it. I had an idea that Lockwood was interested in knowing that fact, too. At any rate, one could not be sure whether these two were perfectly frank with each other, or were playing a game for high stakes between themselves.

Lockwood seemed eager to get away and, with a hasty glance at his watch, rose.

"If you wish to find me, I shall be with Senorita de Mendoza," he said, taking his hat and stick, and bowing to us.

Whitney rose and accompanied him to the door in the outer office, his arm on his shoulder, conversing in a low tone that was inaudible to us.

No sooner, however, had the two passed through the door, with their backs toward us, than Kennedy reached over quickly and swept the contents of the ash-tray, cigarette stubs, ashes, and all, into an empty envelope which was lying with some papers. Then he sealed it and shoved it into his pocket, with a sidelong glance of satisfaction at me.

"Evidently Mr. Lockwood and the Senorita are on intimate terms," hazarded Kennedy, as Whitney rejoined us.

"Poor little girl," soliloquized the promoter. "Yes, indeed. And Lockwood is a lucky dog, too. Such eyes, such a figure—did you ever see a more beautiful woman?"

One could not help recognizing that whatever else Whitney might have said that did not ring true his admiration for the unfortunate girl was genuine. That was not so remarkable, however. It could hardly have been otherwise.

"You are acquainted, I suppose, with a Senora de Moche?" ventured Kennedy again, taking a chance shot.

Whitney looked at him keenly. "Yes," he agreed, "I have had some dealings with her. She was an acquaintance of old Mendoza's—a woman of the world, clever, shrewd. I think she has but one ambition—her son. You have met her?"

"Not the Senora," admitted Craig, "but her son is a student at the University."

"Oh, yes, to be sure," said Whitney. "A fine fellow—but not of the type of Lockwood."

Why he should have coupled the names was not clear for the moment. But he had risen, and was moving deliberately up and down the office, his thumbs in his waistcoat pockets, as though he were thinking of something very perplexing.

"If I were younger," he remarked finally, of a sudden, "I would give both of them a race for that girl. She is the greatest treasure that has ever come out of the country. Ah, well—as it is, I would not place my money on young de Moche!"

Kennedy had risen to go.

"I trust you will be able to unearth some clue regarding that dagger," said Whitney, as we moved toward the door. "It seems to have worried Norton considerably, especially since you told him that Mendoza was undoubtedly murdered with it."

Evidently Norton kept in close touch with his patron, but Kennedy did not appear to be surprised at it.

"I am doing my best," he returned. "I suppose I may count on your help as the case develops?"

"Absolutely," replied Whitney, accompanying us out into the hall to the elevator. "I shall back Norton in anything he wants to keep the Peruvian collection intact and protected."

Our questions were as yet unanswered. Not only had we no inkling as to the whereabouts of the dagger, but the source of the four warnings that had been sent us was still as much shrouded in mystery.

Kennedy beckoned to a passing taxicab.

"The Prince Edward Albert," he directed briefly.

VI

THE CURSE OF MANSICHE

We entered the Prince Edward Albert a few minutes later, one of the new and beautiful family hotels uptown.

Before making any inquiries, Craig gave a hasty look about the lobby. Suddenly I felt him take my arm and draw me over to a little alcove on one side. I followed the direction of his eyes. There I could see young Alfonso de Moche talking to a woman much older than himself.

"That must be his mother," whispered Craig. "You can see the resemblance. Let's sit here awhile behind these palms and watch."

They seemed to be engaged in an earnest conversation about something. Even as they talked, though we could not guess what it was about, it was evident that Alfonso was dearer than life to the woman and that the young man was a model son. Though I felt that I must admire them each for it, still, I reflected, that was no reason why we should not suspect them—perhaps rather a reason for suspecting.

Senora de Moche was a woman of well-preserved middle age, a large woman, with dark hair and contrasting full, red lips. Her face, in marked contradiction to her Parisian costume and refined manners, had a slight copper swarthiness about it which spoke eloquently of her ancestry.

But it was her eyes that arrested and held one's attention most. Whether it was in the eyes themselves or in the way that she used them, there could be no mistake about the almost hypnotic power that their owner possessed. I could not help wondering whether she might not have exercised it on Don Luis, perhaps was using it in some way to influence Whitney. Was that the reason why the Senorita so evidently feared her?

Fortunately, from our vantage point, we could see without being in any danger of being seen.

"There's Whitney," I heard Craig mutter under his breath.

I looked up and saw the promoter enter from his car. At almost the same instant the roving eyes of the Senora seemed to catch sight of him. He came over and spoke to the de Moches, standing with them several minutes. I fancied that not for an instant did she allow the gaze of any one else to distract her in the projection of whatever weird ocular power nature had endowed her with. If it were a battle of eyes, I recollected the strange look that I had noted about those of both Whitney and Lockwood. That, however, was different from the impression one got of the Senora's. I felt that she would have to be pretty clever to match the subtlety of Whitney.

Whatever it was they were talking about, one could see that Whitney and Senora de Moche were on very familiar terms. At the same time, young de Moche appeared to be ill at ease. Perhaps he did not approve of the intimacy with Whitney. At any rate, he seemed visibly relieved when the promoter excused himself and walked over to the desk to get his mail and then out into the cafe.

"I'd like to get a better view of her," remarked Kennedy, rising. "Let us take a turn or two along the corridor and pass them."

We sauntered forth from our alcove and strolled down among the various knots of people chatting and laughing. As we passed the woman and her son, I was conscious again of that strange feeling, which psychologists tell us, however, has no real foundation, of being stared at from behind.

At the lower end of the lobby Kennedy turned suddenly and we started to retrace our steps. Alfonso's back was toward us now. Again we passed them, just in time to catch the words, in a low tone, from the young man, "Yes, I have seen him at the University. Every one there knows that he is—"

The rest of the sentence was lost. But it was not difficult to reconstruct. It referred undoubtedly to the activities of Kennedy in unravelling mysteries.

"It's quite evident," I suggested, "that they know that we are interested in them now."

"Yes," he agreed. "There wasn't any use of watching them further from under cover. I wanted them to see me, just to find out what they would do."

Kennedy was right. Indeed, even before we turned again, we found that the Senora and Alfonso had risen and were making their way slowly to the elevators, still talking earnestly. The lifts were around an angle, and before we could place ourselves so that we could observe them again they were gone.

"I wish there was some way of adding Alfonso's shoe-prints to my collection," observed Craig. "The marks that I found in the dust of the sarcophagus in the Museum were those of a man's shoes. However, I suppose I must wait to get them."

He walked over to the desk and made inquiries about the de Moches and Whitney. Each had a suite on the eighth floor, though on opposite sides and at opposite ends of the hall.

"There's no use wasting time trying to conceal our identity now," remarked Kennedy finally, drawing a card from his case. "Besides, we came here to see them, anyhow." He handed the card to the clerk. "Senora de Moche, please," he said.

The clerk took the card and telephoned up to the de Moche suite. I must say that it was somewhat to my surprise that the Senora telephoned down to say that she would receive us in her own sitting room.

"That's very kind," commented Craig, as I followed him into the elevator. "It saves planning some roundabout way of meeting her and comes directly to the point."

The elevator whisked us up directly to the eighth floor and we stepped out into the heavily carpeted hallway, passing down to Room 810, which was the number of her suite. Further on, in 825, was Whitney's.

Alfonso was not there. Evidently he had not ridden up with his mother, after all, but had gone out through another entrance on the ground floor. The Senora was alone.

"I hope that you will pardon me for intruding," began Craig, with as plausible an explanation as he could muster, "but I have become interested in an opportunity to invest in a

Peruvian venture, and I have heard that you are a Peruvian. Your son, Alfonso, I have already met, once. I thought that perhaps you might be able to give me some advice." She looked at us keenly, but said nothing. I fancied that she detected the subterfuge. Yet she had not tried, and did not try now to avoid us. Either she had no connection with the case we were investigating or she was an adept actress.

On closer view, her eyes were really even more remarkable than I had imagined at a distance. They were those of a woman endowed with an abundance of health and energy, eyes that were full of what the old character readers used to call "amativeness," denoting a nature capable of intense passion, whether of love or hate. Yet I confess that I could not find anything especially abnormal about them, as I had about the eyes of Lockwood and Whitney.

It was some time before she replied, and I gave a hasty glance about the apartment. Of course, it had been rented furnished, but she had rearranged it, adding some touches of her own which gave it quite a Peruvian appearance, due perhaps more to the pictures and the ornaments which she had introduced rather than anything else.

"I suppose," she replied, at length, slowly, and looking at us as if she would bore right through into our minds, "I suppose you mean the schemes of Mr. Lockwood—and Mr. Whitney."

Kennedy was not to be taken by surprise. "I have heard of their schemes, too," he replied noncommittally. "Peru seems to be a veritable storehouse of tales of buried treasure."

"Let me tell you about it," she hastened, nodding at the very words "buried treasure." "I suppose you know that the old Chimu tribes in the north were the wealthiest at the time of the coming of the Spaniards?"

Craig nodded, and a moment later she resumed, as if trying to marshal her thoughts in a logical order. "They had a custom then of burying with their dead all their movable property. Graves were not dug separately. Therefore, you see, sometimes a common grave, or huaca, as it is called, would be given to many. That huaca would become a cache of treasure in time. It was sacred to the dead, and hence it was wicked to touch it."

The Senora's face betrayed the fact that, whatever modern civilization had done for her, it had not yet quite succeeded in eliminating the old ideas.

"Back in the early part of the seventeenth century," she continued, leaning forward in her chair eagerly as she talked, "a Spaniard opened a Chimu huaca and found gold that is said to have been worth more than a million dollars. An Indian told him about it. Who the Indian was does not matter. But the Spaniard was an ancestor of Don Luis de Mendoza, who was found murdered to-day."

She stopped short, seeming to enjoy the surprised look on our faces at finding that she was willing to discuss the matter so intimately.

"After the Indian had shown the Spaniard the treasure in the mound," she pursued, "the Indian told the Spaniard that he had given him only the little fish, the peje chica, but that some day he would give him the big fish, the peje grande. I see that you already know at least a part of the story, anyhow." "Yes," admitted Kennedy, "I do know something of it. But I should rather get it more accurately from your lips than from the hearsay of any one else."

She smiled quietly to herself. "I don't believe," she added, "that you know that the *peje grande* was not ordinary treasure. It was the temple gold. Why, some of the temples were literally plated over heavily with pure gold. That gold, as well as what had been buried in the huacas, was sacred. Mansiche, the supreme ruler, laid a curse on it, on any Indian who would tell of it, on any Spaniard who might learn of it. A curse lies on the finding—yes, even on the searching for the sacred Gold of the Gods. It is one of the most awful curses that have ever been uttered, that curse of Mansiche."

Even as she spoke of it she lowered her voice. I felt that no matter how much education she had, there lurked back in her brain some of the primitive impulses, as well as beliefs. Either the curse of Mansiche on the treasure was as real to her as if its mere touch were poisonous, or else she was going out of her way to create that impression with us.

"Somehow," she continued, in a low tone, "that Spaniard, the ancestor of Don Luis Mendoza, obtained some idea of the secret. He died," she said solemnly, flashing a glance at Craig from her wonderful eyes to stamp the idea indelibly. "He was stabbed by one of the members of the tribe. On the dagger, so I have heard, was marked the secret of the treasure."

I felt that in a bygone age she might have made a great priestess of the heathen gods. Now, was she more than a clever actress?

She paused, then added, "That is my tribe—my family."

Again she paused. "For centuries the big fish was a secret, is still a secret—or, at least, was until some one got it from my brother down in Peru. The tradition and the dagger had been intrusted to him. I don't know how it happened. Somehow he seemed to grow crazy—until he talked. The dagger was stolen from him. How it happened, how it came into Professor Norton's hands, I do not know.

"But, at any rate," she continued, in the same solemn tone, "the curse has followed it. After my brother had told the secret of the dagger and lost it, his mind left him. He threw himself one day into Lake Titicaca."

Her voice broke dramatically in her passionate outpouring of the tragedies that had followed the hidden treasure and the Inca dagger.

"Now, here in New York, comes this awful death of Senor Mendoza," she cried. "I don't know, no one knows, whether he had obtained the secret of the gold or not. At any rate, he must have thought he had it. He has been killed suddenly, in his own home. That is my answer to your inquiry about the treasure-hunting company you mentioned, whatever it may be. I need say no more of the curse of Mansiche. Is the Gold of the Gods worth it?"

There could be no denying that it was real to her, whatever we might think of the story. I recollected the roughly printed warnings that had been sent to Norton, Leslie, Kennedy, and myself. Had they, then, some significance? I had not been able to convince myself that they were the work of a crank, alone. There must be some one to whom the execution of vengeance of the gods was an imperative duty. Unsuperstitious as I was, I saw here a real danger. If some one, either to preserve the secret for himself or else called by divine mandate to revenge, should take a notion to carry out the threats in the four notes, what might not happen?

"I cannot tell you much more of fact than you probably already know," she remarked, watching our faces intently

Arthur B. Reeve

and noting the effect of every word. "You know, I suppose, that the treasure has always been believed to be in a large mound, a tumulus I think you call it, visible from our town of Truxillo. Many people have tried to open it, but the mass of sand pours down on them and they have been discouraged."

"No one has ever stumbled on the secret?" queried Kennedy.

She shook her head. "There have been those who have sought, there are even those who are seeking, the point just where to bore into the mounds. If they could find it, they plan to construct a well-timbered tunnel to keep back the sand and to drive it at the right point to obtain this fabulous wealth."

She vouchsafed the last information with a sort of quiet assurance that conveyed the idea, without her saying it directly, that any such venture was somehow doomed to failure, that desecrators were merely toying with fate.

All through her story one could see that she felt deeply the downfall and betrayal of her brother, followed by the tragedy to him after the age-old secret had slipped from his grasp. Was there still to be vengeance for his downfall? Surely, I thought to myself, Don Luis de Mendoza could not have been in possession of the secret, unless he had arrived at it, with Lockwood, in some other way than by deciphering the almost illegible marks of the dagger. I thought of Whitney. Had he perhaps had something to do with the nasty business?

I happened to glance at a huge pile of works on mining engineering on the table, the property of Alfonso. She saw me looking at them, and her eyes assumed a far-away, dreamy impression as she murmured something.

"You must know that we real Peruvians have been so educated that we never explore ruins for hidden treasure, not even if we have the knowledge of engineering to do so. It is a sort of sacrilege to us to do that. The gold was not our gold, you see. Some of it belongs to the spirits of the departed. But the big treasure belonged to the gods themselves. It was the gold which lay in sheets over the temple walls, sacred. No, we would not touch it."

I wondered cynically what would happen if some one at that moment had appeared with the authenticated secret. She continued to gaze at the books. "There are plenty of rare chances for a young mining engineer in Peru without that."

Apparently she was thinking of her son and his studies at the University as they affected his future career.

One could follow her thoughts, even, as they flitted from the treasure, to the books, to her son, and, finally, to the pretty girl for whom both he and Lockwood were struggling.

"We are a peculiar race," she ruminated. "We seldom inter-marry with other races. We are as proud as Senor Mendoza was of his Castilian descent, as proud of our unmixed lineage as any descendant of a 'belted earl.'"

Senora de Moche made the remarks with a quiet dignity which left no doubt in my mind that the race feeling cut deeply.

She had risen now, and in place of the awesome fear of the curse and tragedy of the treasure her face was burning and her eyes flashed.

"Old Don Luis thought I was good enough to amuse his idle hours," she cried. "But when he saw that Alfonso was in love with his daughter, that she might return that love, then I found out bitterly that he placed us in another class, another caste."

Kennedy had been following her closely, and I could see now that the cross-currents of superstition, avarice, and race hatred in the case presented a tangle that challenged him.

There was nothing more that we could extract from her just then. She had remained standing, as a gentle reminder that the interview had already been long.

Kennedy took the hint. "I wish to thank you for the trouble you have gone to," he bowed, after we, too, had risen. "You have told me quite enough to make me think seriously before I join in any such undertaking."

She smiled enigmatically. Whether it was that she had enjoyed penetrating our rather clumsy excuse for seeing her, or that she felt that the horror of the curse had impressed us, she seemed well content.

We bowed ourselves out, and, after waiting a few moments about the hotel without seeing Whitney anywhere, Craig called a car.

"They were right," was his only comment. "A most baffling woman, indeed."

VII

THE ARROW POISON

Back again in the laboratory, Kennedy threw off his coat and plunged again into his investigation of the blood sample he had taken from the wound in Mendoza's body.

We had scarcely been back half an hour before the door opened and Dr. Leslie's perplexed face looked in on us. He was carrying a large jar, in which he had taken away the materials which he wished to examine.

"Well," asked Kennedy, pausing with a test-tube poised over a Bunsen burner, "have you found anything yet? I haven't had time to get very far with my own tests yet."

"Not a blessed thing," returned the coroner. "I'm desperate. One of the chemists suggested cyanide, another carbon monoxide. But there is no trace of either. Then he suggested nux vomica. It wasn't nux vomica; but my tests show that it must have been something very much like it. I've looked for all the ordinary known poisons and some of the little-known alkaloids, but, Kennedy, I always get back to the same point. There must have been a poison there. He did not die primarily of the wound. It was asphyxia due to a poison that really killed him, though the wound might have done so, but not quite so quickly."

I could tell by the look that crossed Kennedy's face that at last a ray of light had pierced the darkness. He reached for a bottle on the shelf labelled spirits of turpentine.

Then he poured a little of the blood sample from the jar which the coroner had brought into a clean tube and added a few drops of the spirits of turpentine. A cloudy, dark precipitate formed. He smiled quietly, and said, half to himself, "I thought so."

"What is it?" asked the coroner eagerly, "nux vomica?"

Craig shook his head as he stared at the black precipitate. "You were perfectly right about the asphyxiation, Doctor," he remarked slowly, "but wrong as to the cause. It was a poison—one you would never dream of."

"What is it?" Leslie and I asked simultaneously.

"Let me take all these samples and make some further tests," he said. "I am quite sure of it, but it is new to me. By the way, may I trouble you and Leslie to go over to the Museum of Natural History with a letter?"

It was evident that he wanted to work uninterrupted, and we agreed readily, especially because by going we might also be of some use in solving the mystery of the poison.

He sat down and wrote a hasty note to the director of the Museum, and a few moments later we were speeding over in Leslie's car.

At the big building we had no trouble in finding the director and presenting the note. He was a close friend of Kennedy's and more than willing to aid him in any way.

"You will excuse me a moment?" he apologized. "I will get from the South American exhibit just what he wants."

We waited several minutes in the office until finally he returned carrying a gourd, incrusted on its hollow inside surface with a kind of blackish substance.

"That is what he wants, I think," the director remarked, wrapping it up carefully in a box. "I don't need to ask you to tell Professor Kennedy to watch out how he handles the thing. He understands all about it."

We thanked the director and hurried out into the car again, carrying the package, after his warning, as though it were so much dynamite.

Altogether, I don't suppose that we could have been gone more than an hour.

We burst into the laboratory, but, to my surprise, I did not see Kennedy at his table. I stopped short and looked around.

There he was over in the corner, sprawled out in a chair, a tank of oxygen beside him, from which he was inhaling laboriously copious draughts. He rose as he saw us and walked unsteadily toward the table.

"Why—what's the matter?" I cried, certain that m our absence an attempt had been made on his life, perhaps to carry out the threat of the curse.

"N-nothing," he gasped, with an attempt at a smile. "Only I—think I was right—about the poison."

Arthur B. Reeve

I did not like the way he looked. His hand was unsteady and his eyes looked badly. But he seemed quite put out when I suggested that he was working too hard over the case and had better take a turn outdoors with us and have a bite to eat.

"You—you got it?" he asked, seizing the package that contained the gourd and unwrapping it nervously.

He laid the gourd on the table, on which were also several jars of various liquids and a number of other chemicals. At the end of the table was a large, square package, from which sounds issued, as if it contained something alive.

"Tell me," I persisted, "what has happened. Has any one been here since we have been gone?"

"Not a soul," he answered, working his arms and shoulders as if to get rid of some heavy weight that oppressed his chest.

"Then what has happened that makes you use the oxygen?" I repeated, determined to get some kind of answer from him.

He turned to Leslie. "It was no ordinary asphyxiation, Doctor," he said quickly.

Leslie nodded. "I could see that," he admitted.

"We have to deal in this case," continued Kennedy, his will-power overcoming his weakness, "with a poison which is apparently among the most subtle known. A particle of matter so minute as to be hardly distinguishable by the naked eye, on the point of a lancet or needle, a prick of the skin not anything like that wound of Mendoza's, were necessary. But, fortunately, more of the poison was used, making it just that much easier to trace, though for the time the wound, which might itself easily have been fatal, threw us off the scent. But given these things, not all the power in the world—unless one was fully prepared—could save the life of the person in whose flesh the wound was made."

Craig paused a moment, and we listened breathlessly.

"This poison, I find, acts on the so-called endplates of the muscles and nerves. It produces complete paralysis, but not loss of consciousness, sensation, circulation, or respiration until the end approaches. It seems to be one of the most powerful agents of which I have ever heard. When introduced in even a minute quantity it produces death finally by asphyxiation—by paralyzing the muscles of respiration. This asphyxia is what puzzled you, Leslie."

He reached over and took a white mouse from the huge box on the corner of the table.

"Let me show you what I have found," he said. "I am now going to inject a little of the blood serum of the murdered man into this white mouse."

He took a needle and injected some of a liquid which he had isolated. The mouse did not even wince, so lightly did he touch it. But as we watched, its life seemed gently to ebb away, without pain, without struggle. Its breath simply seemed to stop.

Next he took the gourd which we had brought and with a knife scraped off just the minutest particle of the black, licorice-like stuff that incrusted it. He dissolved the particle in some alcohol, and with a sterilized needle repeated his experiment on a second mouse. The effect was precisely similar to that produced by the blood on the first.

I was intent on what Craig was doing when Dr. Leslie broke

Arthur B. Reeve

in with a question. "May I ask," he queried, "whether, admitting that the first mouse died at least apparently in the same manner as the second, you have proved that the poison is the same in both cases? And if it is the same, can you show that it affects human beings in the same way, that enough of it has been discovered in the blood of Mendoza to have caused his death? In other words, I want the last doubt set aside."

If ever Craig startled me, it was by his quiet reply:

"I've isolated it in his blood, extracted it, sterilized it, and I've tried it on myself."

In breathless amazement, with eyes riveted on him, we listened. "Then that was what was the matter?" I blurted out. "You had been trying the poison on YOURSELF?"

He nodded unconcernedly. "Altogether," he explained, as Leslie and I listened, speechless, "I was able to recover from both blood samples six centigrams of the poison. It is almost unknown. I could only be sure of what I discovered by testing the physiological effects. I was very careful. What else was there to do? I couldn't ask you fellows to try it, if I was afraid."

"Good heavens!" gasped Leslie, "and alone, too."

"You wouldn't have let me do it, if I hadn't got rid of you," he smiled quietly.

Leslie shook his head. "Tried it on the dog and made himself the dog!" exclaimed Leslie. "I need the credit of a successful case—but I'll not take this one."

Kennedy laughed.

"Starting with two centigrams of the stuff as a moderate dose," he pursued, while I listened, stunned at his daring, "I injected it into my right arm subcutaneously. Then I slowly worked my way up to three and then four centigrams. You see what I had recovered was far from the real thing. They did not seem at first to produce any very appreciable results other than to cause some dizziness, slight vertigo, a considerable degree of lassitude, and an extremely painful headache of rather unusual duration."

"Good night!" I exclaimed. "Didn't that satisfy you?"

"Five centigrams considerably improved on it," he continued, paying no attention to me. "It caused a degree of lassitude and vertigo that was most distressing, and six centigrams, the whole amount which I had recovered from the samples of blood, gave me the fright of my life right here in this laboratory a few minutes before you came in."

Leslie and I looked at each other and shook our heads.

"Perhaps I was not wise in giving myself so large an injection on a day when I was overheated and below par otherwise, because of the strain I have been under in handling this case, as well as other work. However that may be, the added centigram produced so much more on top of the five centigrams I had previously taken that for a time I had reason to fear that that additional centigram was just the amount needed to bring my experiments to a permanent close.

"Within three minutes of the time of injection the dizziness and vertigo had become so great as to make walking seem impossible. In another minute the lassitude rapidly crept over me, and the serious disturbance of my breathing made it apparent to me that walking, waving my arms, anything, was

Arthur B. Reeve

imperative. My lungs felt glued up, and the muscles of my chest refused to work. Everything swam before my eyes, and I was soon reduced to walking up and down the laboratory floor with halting steps, only preventing falling on the floor by holding fast to the edge of the table.

"I thought of the tank of oxygen, and managed to crawl over and turn it on. I gulped at it. It seemed to me that I spent hours gasping for breath. It reminded me of what I once experienced in the Cave of the Winds of Niagara, where water is more abundant in the atmosphere than air. Yet my watch afterward indicated only about twenty minutes of extreme distress. But that twenty minutes is one period I shall never forget. I advise you, Leslie, if you are ever so foolish as to try the experiment, to remain below the five-centigram limit."

"Believe me, I'd rather lose my job," returned Leslie.

"How much of the stuff was administered to Mendoza," went on Kennedy, "I cannot say. But it must have been a good deal more than I took. Six centigrams which I recovered from these small samples are only nine-tenths of a grain. You see what effect that much had. I trust that answers your question?"

Dr. Leslie was too overwhelmed to reply.

"What is this deadly poison that was used on Mendoza?" I managed to ask.

"You have been fortunate enough to obtain a sample of it from the Museum of Natural History," returned Craig. "It comes in a little gourd, or often a calabash. This is in a gourd. It is a blackish, brittle stuff, incrusting the sides of the gourd just as if it was poured in in the liquid state and left to dry. Indeed, that is just what has been done by those who manufacture it after a lengthy and somewhat secret process."

He placed the gourd on the edge of the table, where we could see it closely. I was almost afraid even to look at it.

"The famous traveller, Sir Robert Schomburgk, first brought it into Europe, and Darwin has described it. It is now an article of commerce, and is to be found in the United States Pharmacoepia as a medicine, though, of course, it is used in only very minute quantities, as a heart stimulant."

Craig opened a book to a place he had marked. "Here's an account of it," he said. "Two natives were one day hunting. They were armed with blow-pipes and quivers full of poisoned darts made of thin, charred pieces of bamboo, tipped with this stuff. One of them aimed a dart. It missed the object overhead, glanced off the tree, and fell down on the hunter himself. This is how the other native reported the result:

"'Quacca takes the dart out of his shoulder. Never a word. Puts it in his quiver and throws it in the stream. Gives me his blow-pipe for his little son. Says to me good-bye for his wife and the village. Then he lies down. His tongue talks no longer. No sight in his eyes. He folds his arms. He rolls over slowly. His mouth moves without sound. I feel his heart. It goes fast and then slow. It stops. Quacca has shot his last woorali dart.'"

Leslie and I looked at Kennedy, and the horror of the thing sank deep into our minds. Woorali. What was it?

"Woorali, or curare," explained Craig slowly, "is the well-known poison with which the South American Indians of the upper Orinoco tip their arrows. Its principal ingredient is derived from the Strychnos toxifera tree, which yields also the drug nux vomica, which you, Dr. Leslie, have mentioned. On the tip of that Inca dagger must have been a large dose of the dread curare, this fatal South American Indian arrow poison."

"Say," ejaculated Leslie, "this thing begins to look eerie to me. How about that piece of paper that I sent to you with the warning about the curse of Mansiche and the Gold of the Gods. What if there should be something in it? I'd rather not be a victim of this curare, if it's all the same to you, Kennedy."

Kennedy was thinking deeply. Who could have sent the messages to us all? Who was likely to have known of curare? I confess that I had not even an idea. All of them, any of them, might have known.

The deeper we got into it, the more dastardly the crime against Mendoza seemed. Involuntarily, I thought of the beautiful little Senorita, about whom these terrible events centred. Though I had no reason for it, I could not forget the fear that she had for Senora de Moche, and the woman as she had been revealed to us in our late interview.

"I suppose a Peruvian of average intelligence might know of the arrow poison of Indians of another country," I ventured to Craig.

"Quite possible," he returned, catching immediately the drift of my thoughts. "But the shoe-prints indicated that it was a man who stole the dagger from the Museum. It may be that it was already poisoned, too. In that case the thief would not have had to know anything of curare, would not have needed to stab so deeply if he had known."

I must confess that I was little further along in the solution of the mystery than I had been when I first saw Mendoza's body. Kennedy, however, did not seem to be worried. Leslie had long since given up trying to form an opinion and, now that the nature of the poison was finally established, was glad to leave the case in our hands.

As for me, I was inclined to agree with Dr. Leslie, and, long after he had left, there kept recurring to my mind those words:

BEWARE THE CURSE OF MANSICHE ON THE GOLD OF THE GODS.

VIII

THE ANONYMOUS LETTER

"I think I will drop in to see Senorita Mendoza," considered Kennedy, as he cleared up the materials which he had been using in his investigation of the arrow poison. "She is a study to me—in fact, the reticence of all these people is hard to combat."

As we entered the apartment where the Mendozas lived, it was difficult to realize that only a few hours had elapsed since we had first been introduced to this strange affair. In the hall, however, were still some reporters waiting in the vain hope that some fragment of a story might turn up.

"Let's have a talk with the boys," suggested Craig, before we entered the Mendoza suite. "After all, the newspaper men are the best detectives I know. If it wasn't for them, half our murder cases wouldn't ever be solved. As a matter of fact, 'yellow journals' are more useful to a city than half the detective force."

Most of the newspaper men knew Craig intimately, and liked him, possibly because he was one of the few people to-day who realized the very important part these young men played in modern life. They crowded about, eager to interview him.

But Craig was clever. In the rapid fire of conversation it was really he who interviewed them.

"Lockwood has been here a long time," volunteered one of the men. "He seems to have constituted himself the guardian of Inez. No one gets a look at her while he's around."

"Well, you can hardly blame him for that," smiled Craig. "Jealousy isn't a crime in that case."

"Say," put in another, "there'd be an interesting quarter of an hour if he were here now. That other fellow—de Mooch—whatever his name is, is here."

"De Moche—with her, now?" queried Kennedy, wheeling suddenly.

The reporter smiled. "He's a queer duck. I was coming up to relieve our other man, when I saw him down on the street, hanging about the corner, his eyes riveted on the entrance to the apartment. I suppose that was his way of making love. He's daffy over her, all right. I stopped to watch him. Of course, he didn't know me. Just then Lockwood left. The Spaniard dived into the drug store on the corner as though the devil was after him. You should have seen his eyes. If looks were bullets, I wouldn't give much for Lockwood's life. With two such fellows about, you wouldn't catch me making goo-goo eyes at that chicken—not on your life."

Kennedy passed over the flippant manner in view of the importance of the observation.

"What do you think of Lockwood?" he asked.

"Pretty slick," replied another of the men. "He's the goods, all right."

"Why, what has he done?" asked Kennedy.

"Nothing in particular. But he came out to see us once. You can't blame him for being a bit sore at us fellows hanging about. But he didn't show it. Instead he almost begged us to be careful of how we asked questions of the girl. Of course, all of us could see how completely broken up she is. We haven't bothered her. In fact, we'd do anything we could for her. But Lockwood talks straight from the shoulder. You can see he's used to handling all kinds of situations."

"But did he say anything, has he done anything?" persisted Kennedy.

"N-no," admitted the reporter. "I can't say he has."

Craig frowned a bit. "I thought not," he remarked. "These people aren't giving away any hints, if they can help it."

"It's my idea," ventured another of the men, "that when this case breaks, it will break all of a sudden. I shouldn't wonder if we are in for one of the sensations of the year, when it comes."

Kennedy looked at him inquiringly. "Why?" he asked simply.

"No particular reason," confessed the man. "Only the regular detectives act so chesty. They haven't got a thing, and they know it, only they won't admit it to us. O'Connor was here."

"What did he say?"

"Nothing. He went through all the motions—'Now, pens lifted, boys,' and all that—talked a lot—and after it was all over he might have been sure no one would publish a line of his confidences. There wasn't a stick of copy in the whole thing."

Kennedy laughed. "O'Connor's all right," he replied. "We may need him sorely before we get through. After all, nothing can take the place of the organization the police have built up. You say de Moche is in there yet?"

"Yes. He seemed very anxious to see her. We never get a word out of him. I've been thinking what would happen if we tried to get him mad. Maybe he'd talk."

"More likely he'd pull a gun," cautioned another. "Excuse ME."

Kennedy said nothing, evidently content to let the newspaper men go their own sweet way.

He nodded to them, and pressed the buzzer at the Mendoza door.

"Tell Senorita Mendoza that it is Professor Kennedy," he said to Juanita, who opened the door, keeping it on the chain, to be sure it was no unwelcome intruder.

Evidently she had had orders to admit us, for a second later we found ourselves again in the little reception room.

We sat down, and I saw that Craig's attention had at once been fixed on something. I listened intently, too. On the other side of the heavy portieres that cut us off from the living room I could distinguish low voices. It was de Moche and Inez.

Whatever the ethics of it, we could not help listening. Besides there was more at stake than ethics.

Arthur B. Reeve

Evidently the young man was urging her to do something that she did not agree with.

"No," we heard her say finally, in a quiet tone, "I cannot believe it, Alfonso. Mr. Whitney is Mr. Lockwood's associate now. My father and Mr. Lockwood approved of him. Why should I do otherwise?"

De Moche was talking earnestly but in a very muffled voice. We could not make out anything except a few scattered phrases which told us nothing. Once I fancied he mentioned his mother. Whatever it was that he was urging, Inez was firm.

"No, Alfonso," she repeated, her voice a little higher and excited. "It cannot be. You must be mistaken."

She had risen, and now moved toward the hall door, evidently forgetting that the folding doors behind the portieres were open. "Professor Kennedy and Mr. Jameson are here," she said. "Would you care to meet them?"

He replied in the negative. Yet as he passed the reception room he could not help seeing us.

As Inez greeted us, I saw that Alfonso was making a desperate effort to control his expression. He seemed to be concealing a bitter disappointment. Seeing us, he bowed stiffly, and, with just the murmur of a greeting, excused himself.

He had no sooner closed the door to run the gauntlet of the sharp eyes in the hall than the Senorita faced us fully. She was pale and nervous. Evidently something that he had said to her had greatly agitated her. Yet with all her woman's skill she managed to hide all outward traces of emotion that might indicate what it was that racked her mind.

"You have something to report?" she asked, a trifle anxiously.

"Nothing of any great importance," admitted Craig.

Was it actually a look of relief that crossed her face? Try as I could, it seemed to me to be an anomalous situation. She wanted the murderer of her father caught, naturally. Yet she did not seem to be offering us the natural assistance that was to be expected. Could it be that she suspected some one perhaps near and dear to her of having some knowledge, which, now that the deed was done, would do more harm than good if revealed? It was the only conclusion to which I could come. I was surprised at Kennedy's next question. Was the same idea in his mind, also?

"We have seen Mr. Whitney," he ventured. "Just what are Mr. Lockwood's relations with him—and yours?"

"Merely that Mr. Lockwood and my father were partners," she answered hastily. "They had decided that their interests would be more valuable by some arrangement with Mr. Whitney, who controls so much down in Peru."

"Do you think that Senora de Moche exercises a very great influence on Mr. Whitney?" asked Craig, purposely introducing the name of the Indian woman to see what effect it might have on her.

"Oh," she cried, with a little exclamation of alarm, "I hope not."

Yet it was evident that she feared so.

Arthur B. Reeve

"Why is it that you fear it?" insisted Kennedy. "What has she done to make you fear it?"

"I don't like her," returned Inez, with a frown. "My father knew her—too well. She is a schemer, an adventuress. Once she has a hold on a man, one cannot say—" She paused, then went on in a different tone. "But I would rather not talk about the woman. I am afraid of her. Never does she talk to me that she does not get something out of me that I do not wish to tell her. She is uncanny."

Personally, I could not blame Inez for her opinion. I could understand it. Those often baleful eyes had a penetrating power that one might easily fall a victim to.

"But you can trust Mr. Lockwood," he returned. "Surely he is proof against her, against any woman."

Inez flushed. It was evident that of all the men who were interested in the little beauty, Lockwood was first in her mind. Yet when Kennedy put the question thus she hesitated. "Yes," she replied, "of course, I trust him. It is not that woman whom I fear with him."

She said it with an air almost of defiance. There was some kind of struggle going on in her mind, and she was too proud to let us into the secret.

Kennedy rose and bowed. For the present he had come to the conclusion that if she would not let us help her openly the only thing to do was to help her blindly.

Half an hour later we were at Norton's apartment, not far from the University campus. He listened intently as Kennedy told such parts of what we had done as he chose. At the mention of the arrow poison, he seemed startled beyond measure.

"You are sure of it?" he asked anxiously.

"Positive, now," reiterated Kennedy.

Norton's face was drawn in deep lines. "If some one has the secret," he cried hastily, "who knows when and on whom next he may employ it?"

Coming from him so soon after the same idea had been hinted at by the coroner, I could not but be impressed by it.

"The very novelty of the thing is our best protection," asserted Kennedy confidently. "Once having discovered it, if Walter gives the thing its proper value in the Star, I think the criminal will be unlikely to try it again. If you had had as much experience in crime as I have had, you would see that it is not necessarily the unusual that is baffling. That may be the surest way to trace it. Often it is because a thing is so natural that it may be attributed to any person among several, equally well."

Norton eyed us keenly, and shook his head. "You may be right," he said doubtfully. "Only I had rather that this person, whoever he may be, had fewer weapons."

"Speaking of weapons," broke in Kennedy, "you have had no further idea of why the dagger might have been taken?"

"There seems to have been so much about it that I did not know," he returned, "that I am almost afraid to have an opinion. I knew that its three-sided sheath inclosed a sharp blade, yet who would have dreamed that that blade was poisoned?"

"You are lucky not to have scratched yourself with it by accident while you were studying it."

"Possibly I might have done it, if I had had it in my possession longer. It was only lately that I had leisure to study it."

"You knew that it might offer some clue to the hidden treasure of Truxillo?" suggested Kennedy. "Have you any recollection of what the inscriptions on it said?"

"Yes," returned Norton, "I had heard the rumours about it. But Peru is a land of tales of buried treasure. No, I can't say that I paid much more attention to it than you might have done if some one asserted that he had another story of the treasure of Captain Kidd. I must confess that only when the thing was stolen did I begin to wonder whether, after all, there might not be something in it. Now it is too late to find out. From the moment when I found that it was missing from my collection I have heard no more about it than you have found out. It is all like a dream to me. I cannot believe even yet that a mere bit of archaeological and ethnological specimen could have played so important a part in the practical events of real life."

"It does seem impossible," agreed Kennedy. "But it is even more remarkable than that. It has disappeared without leaving a trace, after having played its part."

"If it had been a mere robbery," considered Norton, "one might look for its reappearance, I suppose, in the curio shops. For to-day thieves have a keen appreciation of the value of such objects. But, now that you have unearthed its use against Mendoza—and in such a terrible way—it is not likely that that will be what will happen to it. No, we must look elsewhere."

"I thought I would tell you," concluded Kennedy, rising to go. "Perhaps after you have considered it over night some idea may occur to you."

"Perhaps," said Norton doubtfully. "But I haven't your brilliant faculty of scientific analysis, Kennedy. No, I shall have to lean on you, in that, not you on me."

We left Norton, apparently now more at sea than ever. At the laboratory Kennedy plunged into some microphotographic work that the case had suggested to him, while I dashed off, under his supervision, an account of the discovery of curare, and telephoned it down to the Star in time to catch the first morning edition, in the hope that it might have some effect in apprising the criminal that we were hard on his trail, which he had considered covered.

I scanned the other papers eagerly in the morning for Kennedy, hoping to glean at least some hints that others who were working on the case might have gathered. But there was nothing, and, after a hasty bite of breakfast, we hurried back to take up the thread of the investigation where we had laid it down.

To our surprise, on the steps of the Chemistry Building, as we approached, we saw Inez Mendoza already waiting for us in a high state of agitation. Her face was pale, and her voice trembled as she greeted us.

"Such a dreadful thing has come to me," she cried, even before Kennedy could ask her what the trouble was.

From her handbag she drew out a crumpled, dirty piece of paper in an envelope.

"It came in the first mail," she explained. "I could not wait to send it to you. I brought it myself. What can it mean?"

Arthur B. Reeve

Kennedy unfolded the paper. Printed in large characters, in every way similar to the four warnings that had been sent to us, was just one ominous line. We read:

"Beware the man who professes to be a friend of your father."

I glanced from the note to Kennedy, then to Inez. One name was in my mind, and before I knew it I had spoken it.

"Lockwood?" I queried inadvertently.

Her eyes met mine in sharp defiance. "Impossible," she exclaimed. "It is some one trying to injure him with me. Beware of Mr. Lockwood? How absurd!"

Yet it must have meant Lockwood. No one else could have been meant. It was he, most of all, who might be called a friend of her father. She seemed to see the implication without a word from us.

I could not help sympathizing with the brave girl in her struggle between the attack against Lockwood and her love and confidence in him. It did not need words to tell me that evidence must be overwhelming to convince her that her lover might be involved in any manner.

IX

THE PAPER FIBRES

Kennedy examined the anonymous letter carefully for several minutes, while we watched him in silence.

"Too clever to use a typewriter," he remarked, still regarding the note through the lens of a hand-glass. "Almost any one would have used a machine. That would have been due to the erroneous idea that typewriting cannot be detected. The fact is that the typewriter is perhaps a worse means of concealing identity than is disguised handwriting, especially printing like this. It doesn't afford the effective protection to the criminal that one supposes. On the contrary, the typewriting of such a note may be the direct means by which it can be traced to its source. We can determine what kind of machine it was done with, then what particular machine was used can be identified."

He paused and indicated a number of little instruments which he had taken from a drawer and laid on the table, as he tore off a bit of the corner of the sheet of paper and examined it.

"There is one thing I can do now, though," he continued. "I can study the quality of the paper in this sheet. If it were only torn like those warnings we have already received, it might

Arthur B. Reeve

perhaps be mated with another piece as accurately as if the act had been performed before our eyes."

He picked up a little instrument with a small curved arm and a finely threaded screw that brought the two flat surfaces of the arm and the end of the screw together.

"There is no such good fortune in this case, however," he resumed, placing the paper between the two small arms. "But by measurements made by this vernier micrometer caliper I can find the precise thickness of the paper as compared to the other samples."

He turned to a microscope and placed the corner of the paper under it. Then he drew from the drawer the four scraps of paper which had already been sent to us, as well as a pile of photographs.

"Under ordinary circumstances," he explained, "I should think that what I am doing would be utterly valueless as a clue to anything. But we are reduced to the minutiae in this affair. And to-day science is not ready to let anything pass as valueless."

He continued to look at the various pieces of paper under the microscope. "I find under microscopic examination," he went on, addressing Inez, but not looking up from the eye-piece as he shifted the papers, "that the note you have received, Senorita Mendoza, is written on a rather uncommon linen bond paper. Later I shall take a number of microphotographs of it. I have here, also, about a hundred microphotographs of the fibres in other kinds of paper, many of them bonds. These I have accumulated from time to time in my study of the subject. None of them, as you can see, shows fibres resembling this one in question, so that we may conclude that it is of uncommon quality.

"Here I have the fibres, also, of four pieces of paper that have already figured in the case. These four correspond, as well as the indentures of the torn edges. As for the fibres, lest you should question the accuracy of the method, I may say that I know of a case where a man in Germany was arrested, charged with stealing a government bond. He was not searched until later. There was no evidence, save that after the arrest a large number of spitballs were found around the courtyard under his cell window. This method of comparing the fibres of the regular government paper was used, and by it the man was convicted of stealing the bond. I think it is unnecessary to add that in the present case I can see definitely that not only the four pieces of paper that bore warnings to us were the same kind, but that this whole sheet, with its anonymous warning to you, is also the same."

Inez Mendoza looked at Kennedy as though he possessed some weird power. Her face, which had already been startled into an expression of fear at his mention of Lockwood, now was pale.

"Other warnings?" she repeated tremulously.

Quickly Kennedy explained what had already happened to us, watching the effect on her as he read of the curse of Mansiche and the Gold of the Gods.

"Oh," she cried, mastering her emotion with a heroic effort, "I wish my father had never become mixed up in the business. Ever since I was a little girl I have heard these vague stories of the big fish and the little fish, the treasure, and the curse. But I never thought they were anything but fairy tales. You remember, when I first saw you, I did not even tell them to you."

"Yes," returned Kennedy. "I remember. But had you no other

reason? Did you, down in your heart, think them really fairy tales?"

She shuddered. "Perhaps not," she murmured. "But I have heard enough of you detectives to know that you do not think a woman's fears exactly evidence."

"Still they might lead to evidence," suggested Kennedy.

She looked at him, more startled than ever, for already he had given her a slight exhibition of his powers.

"Mr. Kennedy," she exclaimed, "I am positively afraid of you, afraid that every little thing I do may lead to something I don't intend."

There was a frankness about the remark that would have been flattering from a man, but from her excited sympathy.

"No," she went on, "I have nothing tangible—only my feelings. I fear I must admit that my father had enemies, though who they are I cannot tell you. No, it is all in my heart—not in my head. There are those whom I dislike—and there are those whom I like and trust. You may call me foolish, but I cannot help trusting—Mr. Lockwood."

She had not meant to say his name, and Kennedy and I looked at her in surprise.

"You see?" she continued. "Every time I talk I say something, convey some impression that is the opposite of what I wish. Oh—what shall I do? Have I no one to trust?"

She was crying.

"You may trust me, Senorita," said Kennedy, in a low tone,

pausing before her. "At least I have no other interest than finding the truth and helping you. There—there. We have had enough to-day. I cannot ask you to try to forget what has happened. That would be impossible. But I can ask you, Senorita, to have faith—faith that it will all turn out better, if you will only trust me. When you feel stronger—then come to me. Tell me your fears—or not—whichever does you the most good. Only keep your mind from brooding. Face it all as you know your father would have you do."

Kennedy's words were soothing. He seemed to know that tears were the safety-valve she needed.

"Mr. Jameson will see that you get home safely in a taxicab," he continued. "You can trust him as you would myself."

I can imagine circumstances under which I would have enjoyed escorting Inez to her home, but today was not one of the times. Yet she seemed so helpless, so grateful for everything we did for her that I did not need even the pressure of her little hand as she hurried into the apartment from the car with a hasty word of thanks.

"You will tell Mr. Kennedy—you will both be—so careful?" she hesitated before leaving me.

I assured her that we would, wondering what she might fear for us, as I drove away again. There did not happen to be any of the newspaper men about at the time, and I did not stop.

Back in the laboratory, I found Kennedy arranging some-thing under the rug at the door as I came up the hall.

"Don't step there, Walter," he cautioned. "Step over the rug. I'm expecting visitors. How was she when she arrived home?"

I told him of her parting injunction.

"Not bad advice," he remarked. "I think there's a surprise back of those warnings. They weren't sent just for effect."

He had closed the door, and we were standing by the table, looking at the letters, when we heard a noise at the door.

It was Norton again.

"I've been thinking of what you told me last night," he explained, before Kennedy had a chance to tell him to step over the rug. "Has anything else happened?"

Kennedy tossed over the anonymous letter, and Norton read it eagerly.

"Whom does it mean?" he asked, quickly glancing up, then adding, "It might mean any of us who are trying to help her."

"Exactly," returned Kennedy. "Or it might be Lockwood, or even de Moche. By the way, you know the young man pretty well, don't you? I wonder if you could find him anywhere about the University this morning and persuade him to visit me?"

"I will try," agreed Norton. "But these people are so very suspicious just now that I can't promise."

Norton went out a few minutes later to see what he could do to locate Alfonso, and Kennedy replaced another blank sheet of paper for that under the rug on which Norton had stepped before we could warn him.

No sooner had he gone than Kennedy reached for the telephone and called Whitney's office. Lockwood was there, as he had hoped, and, after a short talk, promised to drop in on us later in the morning.

It was fully half an hour before Norton returned, having finally found Alfonso. De Moche entered the laboratory with a suspicious glance about, as though he thought something might have been planted there for him.

"I had a most interesting talk with your mother yesterday," began Kennedy, endeavouring by frankness to put the young man at ease. "And this morning, already, Senorita Mendoza has called on me."

De Moche was all attention at the words. But before he could say anything Kennedy handed him the anonymous letter. He read it, and his face clouded as he handed it back.

"You have no idea who could have sent such a note?" queried Craig, "or to whom it might refer?"

He glanced at Norton, then at us. It was clear that some sort of suspicion had flashed over him. "No," he said quickly, "I know no one who could have sent it."

"But whom does it mean?" asked Kennedy, holding him to the part that he avoided.

The young man shrugged his shoulders. "She has many friends," he answered simply.

"Yes," persisted Kennedy, "but few against whom she might be warned in this way. You do not think it is Professor Norton, for instance—or myself?"

"Oh, no, no—hardly," he replied, then stopped, realizing that he had eliminated all but Lockwood, Whitney, and himself.

"It could not be Mr. Lockwood?" demanded Craig.

"Who sent it?" he asked, looking up.

"No—whom it warns against."

De Moche had known what Kennedy meant, but had preferred to postpone the answer. It was native never to come to the point unless he was forced to do so. He met our eyes squarely. He had not the penetrating power that his mother possessed, yet his was a sharp faculty of observation.

"Mr. Lockwood is very friendly with her," he admitted, then seemed to think something else necessary to round out the idea. "Mr. Kennedy, I might have told her the same myself. Senorita Mendoza has been a very dear friend—for a long time."

I had been so used to having him evasive that now I did not exactly know what to make of such a burst of confidence. It was susceptible of at least two interpretations. Was he implying that it was sent to cast suspicion on him, because he felt that way himself or because he himself was her friend?

"There have been other warnings," pursued Kennedy, "both to myself and Mr. Jameson, as well as Professor Norton and Dr. Leslie. Surely you must have some idea of the source."

De Moche shook his head. "None that I can think of," he replied. "Have you asked my mother?"

"Not yet," admitted Kennedy.

De Moche glanced at his watch. "I have a lecture at this hour," he remarked, evidently glad of an excuse to terminate the interview.

As he left, Kennedy accompanied him to the door, careful himself to step over the mat.

"Hello, what's new?" we heard a voice in the hall.

It was Lockwood, who had come up from downtown. Catching sight of de Moche, however, he stopped short. The two young men met face to face. Between them passed a glance of unconcealed hostility, then each nodded stiffly.

De Moche turned to Kennedy as he passed down the hall. "Perhaps it may have been sent to divert suspicion—who can tell?" he whispered.

Kennedy nodded appreciatively, noting the change.

At the sound of Lockwood's voice both Norton and I had taken a step further after them out into the hall, Norton somewhat in advance. As de Moche disappeared for his lecture, Kennedy turned to me from Lockwood and caught my eye. I read in his glance that fell from me to the mat that he wished me quietly to abstract the piece of paper which he had placed under it. I bent down and did so without Lockwood seeing me.

"Why was he here?" demanded Lockwood, with just a trace of defiance in his voice, as though he fancied the meeting had been framed.

"I have been showing this to every one who might help me," returned Kennedy, going back into the laboratory after giving me an opportunity to dispose of the shoe-prints.

He handed the anonymous letter and the other warnings to

the young soldier of fortune, with a brief explanation.

"Why don't they come out into the open, whoever they are?" commented Lockwood, laying the papers down carelessly again on the table. "I'll meet them—if they mean me."

"Who?" asked Kennedy.

Lockwood faced Norton and ourselves.

"I'm not a mind reader," he said significantly. "But it doesn't take much to see that some one wants to throw a brick at me. When I have anything to say I say it openly. Inez Mendoza without friends just now would be a mark, wouldn't she?"

His strong face and powerful jaw were set in a menacing scowl. He would be a bold man who would have come between Lockwood and the lady under the circumstances.

"You are confident of Mr. Whitney?" inquired Kennedy.

"Ask Norton," replied Lockwood briefly. "He knew him long before I did."

Norton smiled quietly. "Mr. Kennedy should know what my opinion of Mr. Whitney is, I think," replied Norton confidently.

"I trust that you will succeed in running these blackmailers down," pursued Lockwood, still standing. "If I did not have more than I can attend to already since the murder of Mendoza I'd like to take a hand myself. It begins to look to me, after reading that letter, as though there was nothing too low for them to attempt. I shall keep this latest matter in mind. If either Mr. Whitney or myself get any hint, we'll turn it over to you."

Norton left shortly after Lockwood, and Kennedy again picked up the letter and scanned it. "I could learn something, I suppose, if I analyzed this printing," he considered, "but it is a tedious process. Let me see that envelope again. H-m, postmarked by the uptown sub-station, mailed late last night. Whoever sent it must have done so not very far from us here. Lockwood seemed to take it as though it applied to himself very readily, didn't he? Much more so than de Moche. Only for the fact that the fibres show it to be on paper similar to the first warnings, I might have been inclined to doubt whether this was bona fide. At least, the sender must realize now that it has produced no appreciable effect—if any was intended."

Kennedy's last remark set me thinking. Could some one have sent the letter not to produce the effect apparently intended, but with the ultimate object of diverting suspicion from himself? Lockwood, at least, had not seemed to take the letter very seriously.

X

THE X-RAY READER

"I think I'll pay another visit to Whitney, in spite of all that Norton and Lockwood say about him," remarked Kennedy, considering the next step he would take in his investigation.

Accordingly, half an hour later we entered his Wall Street office, where we were met by a clerk, who seemed to remember us.

"Mr. Whitney is out just at present," he said, "but if you will be seated I think I can reach him by telephone."

As we sat in the outer office while the clerk telephoned from Whitney's own room the door opened and the postman entered and laid some letters on a table near us. Kennedy could not help seeing the letter on top of the pile, and noticed that it bore a stamp from Peru. He picked it up and read the postmark, "Lima," and the date some weeks previous. In the lower corner, underscored, were the words "Personal— Urgent."

"I'd like to know what is in that," remarked Craig, turning it over and over.

He appeared to be considering something, for he rose suddenly, and with a nod of his head to himself, as though settling some qualm of conscience, shoved the letter into his pocket.

A moment later the clerk returned. "I've just had Mr. Whitney on the wire," he reported. "I don't think he'll be back at least for an hour."

"Is he at the Prince Edward Albert?" asked Craig.

"I don't know," returned the clerk, oblivious to the fact that we must have seen that in order to know the telephone number he must have known whether Mr. Whitney was there or elsewhere.

"I shall come in again," rejoined Kennedy, as we bowed ourselves out. Then to me he added, "If he is with Senora de Moche and they are at the Edward Albert, I think I can beat him back with this letter if we hurry."

A few minutes later, in his laboratory, Kennedy set to work quickly over an X-ray apparatus. As I watched him, I saw that he had placed the letter in it.

"These are what are known as 'low tubes,'" he explained. "They give out 'soft rays.'"

He continued to work for several minutes, then took the letter out and handed it to me.

"Now, Walter," he said brusquely, "if you will just hurry back down there to Whitney's office and replace that letter, I think I will have something that will astonish you—though whether it will have any bearing on the case remains to be seen. At least I can postpone seeing Whitney himself for a while."

I made the trip down again as rapidly as I could. Whitney was not back when I arrived, but the clerk was there, and I could not very well just leave the letter on the table again.

"Mr. Kennedy would like to know when he can see Mr. Whitney," I said, on the spur of the moment. "Can't you call him up again?"

The clerk, as I had anticipated, went into Whitney's office to telephone. Instead of laying the letter on the table, which might have excited suspicion, I stuck it in the letter slot of the door, thinking that perhaps they might imagine that it had caught there when the postman made his rounds.

A moment later the clerk returned. "Mr. Whitney is on his way down now," he reported.

I thanked him, and said that Kennedy would call him up when he arrived, congratulating myself on the good luck I had had in returning the letter.

"What is it?" I asked, a few minutes later, when I had rejoined Craig in the laboratory.

He was poring intently over what looked like a negative.

"The possibility of reading the contents of documents inclosed in a sealed envelope," he replied, still studying the shadowgraph closely, "has already been established by the well-known English scientist, Dr. Hall Edwards. He has been experimenting with the method of using X-rays recently discovered by a German scientist, by which radiographs of very thin substances, such as a sheet of paper, a leaf, an insect's body, may be obtained. These thin substances, through which the rays used formerly to pass without leaving an impression, can now be easily radiographed."

I looked carefully as he traced out something on the queer negative. On it, it was easily possible, following his guidance, to read the words inscribed on the sheet of paper inside. So admirably defined were all the details that even the gum on the envelope and the edges of the sheet of paper inside the envelope could be distinguished.

"It seems incredible," I exclaimed, scarcely believing what I actually saw. "It is almost like second sight."

Kennedy smiled. "Any letter written with ink having a mineral base can be radiographed," he added. "Even when the sheet is folded in the usual way, it is possible, by taking a radiograph, as I have done, stereoscopically. Then every detail can be seen standing out in relief. Besides, it can be greatly magnified, which aids in deciphering it if it is indistinct or jumbled up. Some of it looks like mirror-writing. Ah," he continued, "here's something interesting."

Together we managed to trace out the contents of several paragraphs laboriously, the gist of which I give here:

"LIMA, PERU.

"DEAR WHITNEY:

"Matters are progressing very favorably here, considering the stoppage of business due to the war. I am doing everything in my power to conserve our interests, and now and then, owing to the scarcity of money, am able to pick up a concession cheaply, which will be of immense value to us later."

"However, it is not so much of business that I wish to write you at the present time. You know that my friend Senora de Moche, with her son, Alfonso, is at present in New York.

Doubtless she has already called on you and tried to interest you in her own properties here. I need not advise you to be very careful in dealing with her."

"The other day I heard a rumour that may prove interesting to you, regarding Norton and his work here on his last trip. As we know, he has succeeded in finding and getting out of the country an Inca dagger which, I believe, bears a very important inscription. I do not know anything definite about it, as these people are very reticent. But no doubt he has told you all about it by this time. If it should prove of value, I depend on you to let me know, so that I may act at this end accordingly.

"What I am getting at is this: I understand that from rumours and remarks of the Senora she believes that Norton took an unfair advantage during her absence. What the inscription is I don't know, but from the way these people down here act one would think that they all had a proprietary interest in the relic. What it is all about I don't know. But you will find the Senora both a keen business woman and an accomplished antiquarian, if you have not already discovered it.

"In regard to Lockwood and Mendoza, if we can get them in on our side, it ought to prove a winning combination. There are stories here of how de Moche has been playing on Mendoza's passions—she's thoroughly unscrupulous and Don Luis is somewhat of a Don Juan. I write this to put you on guard. Her son, Alfonso, whom you perhaps have met also, is of another type, though I have heard it said that he laid siege to Inez Mendoza in the hope of becoming allied with one of the oldest families.

"Such, at least, is the gossip down here. I cannot presume to keep you posted at such a distance, but thought I had better write what is in every one's mouth. As for the inscribed dagger which Norton has taken with him, I rely on you to inform me. There seems to be a great deal of mystery connected with it, and I am unable even to hazard a guess as to its nature. Fortunately, you are on the spot

"Very sincerely yours,

"HAGGERTY."

"So," remarked Kennedy, as he read over the translation of the skiagraph which he had jotted down as we picked out the letters and words, "that's how the land lies. Everybody seems to have appreciated the importance of the dagger."

"Except Norton," I could not help putting in in disgust.

"And now it's gone," he continued, "just as though some one had dropped it overboard. I believe I will keep that appointment you made for me with Whitney, after all."

Thus it happened that I found myself a third time entering Whitney's building. I was about to step into the elevator, when Kennedy tugged at my arm and pulled me back.

"Hello, Norton," I heard him say, as I turned and caught sight of the archaeologist just leaving an elevator that had come down.

Norton's face plainly showed that he was worried.

"What the matter?" asked Kennedy, putting the circum-stances together. "What has Whitney been doing?"

Norton seemed reluctant to talk, but having no alternative motioned to us to step aside in the corridor.

"It's the first time I've talked with him since the dagger was stolen—that is, about the loss," he said nervously. "He called me up half an hour ago and asked me to come down."

I looked at Kennedy significantly. Evidently it must have been just after his return to the office and receipt of the letter which I had stuck in the letter slot.

"He was very angry over something," continued Norton. "I'm sure it was not my fault if the dagger was stolen, and I'm sure that managing an expedition in that God-forsaken country doesn't give you time to read every inscription, especially when it is almost illegible, right on the spot. There was work enough for months that I brought back, along with that. Sometimes Whitney's unreasonable."

"You don't think he could have known something about the dagger all along?" ventured Craig.

Norton puckered his eyes. "He never said anything," he replied. "If he had asked me to drop other things for that, why, of course, I would have done so. We can't afford to lose him as a contributor to the exploration fund. Confound it— I'm afraid I've put my foot in it this time."

Kennedy said nothing, and Norton continued, growing more excited: "Everybody's been talking to Whitney, telling him all kinds of things—Lockwood, the de Moches, heaven knows who else. Why don't they come out and face me? I've a notion to try to carry on my work independently. Nothing plays hob with scholarship like money. You'd think he owned me body and soul, and the collection, too, if you heard him talk. Why, he accused me of carelessness in running the Museum, and heaven knows I'm not the curator —I'm not even the janitor!"

Norton was excited, but I could not help feeling that he was also relieved. "I've been preparing for the time when I'd have to cut loose," he went on finally. "Now, I suppose it is coming. Ah, well, perhaps it will be better—who can tell? I may not do so much, but it will all be mine, with no strings attached. Perhaps, after all, it is for the best."

Talking over his troubles seemed to do Norton some good, for I am sure that he left us in a better frame of mind than we had found him.

Kennedy wished him good-luck, and we again entered the lift.

We found Whitney in an even greater state of excitement than Norton had been. I am sure that if it had been any one else than Kennedy he would have thrown him out, but he seemed to feel that he must control himself in our presence.

"What do you know about that fellow Norton, up at your place?" he demanded, almost before we had seated ourselves.

"A very hard-working, ambitious man his colleagues tell me," returned Kennedy, purposely I thought, as if it had been a red rag flaunted before a bull.

"Hard-working—yes," bellowed Whitney. "He has worked me hard. I send him down to Peru—yes, I put up most of the money. Then what does he do? Just kids me along, makes me think he's accomplishing a whole lot—when he's actually so careless as to let himself be robbed of what he gets with my money. I tell you, you can't trust anybody. They all double-cross you. I swear, I think Lockwood and I ought to go it alone. I'm glad I found that fellow out. Let himself be robbed—a fine piece of work! Why, that fellow couldn't see through a barn door—after the horse was stolen," he concluded, mixing his metaphors in his anger.

"Evidently some one has been telling you something," remarked Kennedy. "We tried to see you twice this morning, but couldn't find you."

His tone was one calculated to impress Whitney with the fact that he had been watching and had some idea of where he really was. Whitney shot a sharp glance at Craig, whose face betrayed nothing.

"Ambitious—I should say so," repeated Whitney, reverting to Norton to cover up this new change of the subject. "Well—let him be ambitious. We can get along without him. I tell you, Kennedy, no one is indispensable. There is always some way to get along—if you can't get over an obstacle, you can get around it. I'll dispense with Mr. Norton. He's an expensive luxury, anyhow. I'm just as well satisfied."

There was real vexation in Whitney's voice, yet as he talked he, too, seemed to cool down. I could not help thinking that both Norton and Whitney were perhaps just a bit glad at the break. Had both of them got out of each other all that they wanted—Norton his reputation and Whitney—what?

He cooled down so rapidly now that almost I began to wonder whether his anger had been genuine. Did he know more about the dagger than appeared? Was this his cover— to disown Norton?

"It seems to me that Senora de Moche is ambitious for her son, too," remarked Kennedy, tenaciously trying to force the conversation into the channel he chose.

"How's that?" demanded Whitney, narrowing his eyes down

into a squint at Kennedy's face, a proceeding that served by contrast to emphasize the abnormal condition of the pupils which I had already noticed both in his eyes and Lockwood's.

"I don't think she'd object to having him marry into one of the leading families in Peru," ventured Kennedy, para-phrasing what we had already read in the letter.

"Perhaps Senorita Mendoza herself can be trusted to see to that," Whitney replied with a quick laugh.

"To say nothing of Mr. Lockwood," suggested Craig.

Whitney looked at him quizzically, as though in doubt just how much this man knew.

"Senora de Moche puzzles me," went on Kennedy. "I often wonder whether superstition or greed would rule her if it came to the point in this matter of the Gold of the Gods, as they all seem to call the buried treasure at Truxillo. She's a fascinating woman, but I can't help feeling that with her one is always playing with fire."

Whitney eyed us knowingly. I had long ago taken his measure as a man quite susceptible to a pretty face, especially if accompanied by a well-turned ankle.

"I never discuss politics during business hours," he laughed, with a self-satisfied air. "You will excuse me? I have some rather important letters that I must get off."

Kennedy rose, and Whitney walked to the door with us, to call his stenographer.

We had scarcely said good-bye and were about to open the

outer door when it was pushed open from outside, and Lockwood bustled in.

"No more anonymous letters, I hope?" he queried, in a tone which I could not determine whether serious or sarcastic.

Kennedy answered in the negative. "Not unless you have one."

"I? I rather think the ready letter-writers know better than to waste time on me. That little billet doux seems to have quite upset the Senorita, though. I don't know how many times she has called me up to see if I was all right. I begin to think that whoever wrote it has done me a good turn, after all."

Lockwood did not say it in a boastful way, but one could see that he was greatly pleased at the solicitude of Inez.

"She thinks it referred to you, then?" asked Kennedy.

"Evidently," he replied; then added, "I won't say but that I have taken it seriously, too."

He slapped his hip pocket. Under the tail of his coat bulged a blue-steel automatic.

"You still have no idea who could have sent it, or why?"

Lockwood shook his head. "Whoever he is, I'm ready," he replied grimly, bowing us out.

XI

THE SHOE-PRINTS

"I'm afraid we've neglected the Senorita a bit, in our efforts to follow up what clues we have in the case," remarked Kennedy, as we rode uptown again. "She needs all the protection we can give her. I think we'd better drop around there, now that she is pretty likely to be left alone."

Accordingly, instead of going back to the laboratory, we dropped off near the apartment of the Mendozas and walked over from the subway.

As we turned the corner, far down the long block I could see the entrance to the apartment.

"There she is now," I said to Kennedy, catching sight of her familiar figure, clad in sombre black, as she came down the steps. "I wonder where she can be going."

She turned at the foot of the steps and, as chance would have it, started in the opposite direction from us.

"Let us see," answered Kennedy, quickening his pace.

She had not gone very far before a man seemed to spring up

Arthur B. Reeve

from nowhere and meet her. He bowed, and walked along beside her.

"De Moche," recognized Kennedy.

Alfonso had evidently been waiting in the shadow of an entrance down the street, perhaps hoping to see her, perhaps as our newspaper friend had seen before, to watch whether Lockwood was among her callers. As we walked along, we could see the little drama with practically no fear of being seen, so earnestly were they talking.

Even during the few minutes that the Senorita was talking with him no one would have needed to be told that she really had a great deal of regard for him, whatever might be her feelings toward Lockwood.

"I should say that she wants to see him, yet does not want to see him," observed Kennedy, as we came closer.

She seemed now to have become restive and impatient, eager to cut the conversation short.

It was quite evident at the same time that Alfonso was deeply in love with her, that though she tried to put him off he was persistent. I wondered whether, after all, some of the trouble had not been that during his lifetime the proud old Castilian Don Luis could never have consented to the marriage of his daughter to one of Indian blood. Had he left a legacy of fear of a love forbidden by race prejudice?

In any event, the manner of Alfonso's actions about the Mendoza apartment was such that one could easily imagine his feelings toward Lockwood, whom he saw carrying off the prize under his very eyes.

As for his mother, the Senora, we had already seen that Peruvians of her caste were also a proud old race. Her son was the apple of her eye. Might not some of her feelings be readily accounted for? Who were these to scorn her race, her family?

We had walked along at a pace that finally brought us up with them. As Kennedy and I bowed, Alfonso seemed at first to resent our intrusion, while Inez seemed rather to welcome it as a diversion.

"Can we not expect you?" the young man repeated. "It will be only for a few minutes this afternoon, and my mother has something of very great importance to tell."

He was half pleading, half apologizing. Inez glanced hastily around at Kennedy, uncertain what to say, and hoping that he might indicate some course. Surreptitiously, Kennedy nodded an affirmative.

"Very well, then," she replied reluctantly, not to seem to change what had been her past refusal too suddenly. "I may ask Professor Kennedy, too?"

He could scarcely refuse before us. "Of course," he agreed, quickly turning to us. "We were speaking about meeting this afternoon at four in the tea room of the Prince Edward. You can come?"

Though the invitation was not over-gracious, Kennedy replied, "We should be delighted to accompany Miss Inez, I am sure. We happened to be passing this way and thought we would stop in to see if anything new had happened. Just as we turned the corner we saw you disappearing down the street, and followed. I trust everything is all right?"

"Nothing more has happened since this morning," she returned, with a look that indicated she understood that Kennedy referred to the anonymous letter. "I had a little shopping to do. If you will excuse me, I think I will take a car. This afternoon—at four."

She nodded brightly as we assisted her into a taxicab and left us three standing there on the curb. For a moment it was rather awkward. To Alfonso her leaving was somewhat as though the sun had passed under a cloud.

"Are you going up toward the University?" inquired Kennedy.

"Yes," responded the young man reluctantly.

"Then suppose we walk. It would take only a few more minutes," suggested Kennedy.

Alfonso could not very well refuse, but started off at a brisk pace.

"I suppose these troubles interfere seriously with your work," pursued Craig, as we fell into his stride.

"Yes," he admitted, "although much of my work just now is only polishing off what I have already learned—getting your American point of view and methods. You see, I have had an idea that the canal will bring both countries into much closer relations than before. And if you will not learn of us, we must learn of you."

"It is too bad we Americans don't take more interest in the countries south of us," admitted Craig. "I think you have the right idea, though. Such men as Mr. Whitney are doing their best to bring the two nations closer together."

I watched the effect of the mention of Whitney's name. It seemed distasteful, only in a lesser degree than Lockwood's.

"We do not need to be exploited," he ventured. "My belief is that we should not attract capital in order to take things out of the country. If we might keep our own earnings and transform them into capital, it would be better. That is why I am doing what I am at the University."

I could not believe that it explained the whole reason for his presence in New York. Without a doubt the girl who had just left us weighed largely in his mind, as well as his and his mother's ambitions, both personal and for Peru.

"Quite reasonable," accepted Kennedy. "Peru for the Peruvians. Yet there seems to be such untold wealth in the country that taking out even quite large sums would not begin to exhaust the natural resources."

"But they are ours, they belong to us," hastened de Moche, then caught the drift of Kennedy's remarks, and was on his guard.

"Buried treasure, like that which you call the Gold of the Gods, is always fascinating," continued Kennedy. "The trouble with such easy money, however, is that it tends to corrupt. In the early days history records its taint. And I doubt whether human nature has changed much under the veneer of modern civilization. The treasure seems to leave its trail even as far away as New York. It has at least one murder to its credit already."

"There has been nothing but murder and robbery from the time that the peje chica was discovered," asserted the young man sadly. "You are quite right."

"Truly it would seem to have been cursed," added Craig. "The spirit of Mansiche must, indeed, watch over it. I suppose you know of the loss of the old Inca dagger from the University Museum and that it was that with which Don Luis was murdered?"

It was the first time Kennedy had broached the subject to de Moche, and I watched closely to see what was its effect.

"Perhaps it was a warning," commented Alfonso, in a solemn tone, that left me in doubt whether it was purely superstitious dread or in the nature of a prophecy of what might be expected from some quarter of which we were ignorant.

"You have known of the existence of the dagger always, I presume," continued Kennedy. "Have you or any one you know ever sought to discover its secret and search it out?"

"I think my mother told you we never dig for treasure," he answered. "It would be sacrilegious. Besides, there is more treasure buried by nature than that dedicated to the gods. There is only one trouble that may hurt our natural resources—the get-rich-quick promoter. I would advise looking out for him. He flourishes in a newly opened country like Peru. That curse, I suppose, is much better understood by Americans than the curse of Mansiche. But as for me, you must remember that the curse is part of my religion, as it were."

We had reached the campus by this time, and parted at the gate, each to go his way.

"You will drop in on me if you hear anything?" invited Craig.

"Yes," promised Alfonso. "We shall see you at four."

With this parting reminder he turned toward the School of Mines while we debouched off toward the Chemistry Building.

"The de Moches are nobody's tools," I remarked. "That young man seems to have a pretty definite idea of what he wants to do."

"At least he puts it so before us," was all that Kennedy would grant. "He seems to be as well informed of what passed at that visit to the Senora as though he had been there too."

We had scarcely opened the laboratory door when the ringing of the telephone told us that some one had been trying to get in touch for some time.

"It was Norton," said Kennedy, hanging up the receiver. "I imagine he wants to know what happened after we left him and went up to see Whitney."

That was, in fact, just what Norton wanted, as well as to make clear to us how he felt on the subject.

"Really, Kennedy," he remarked, "it must be fine to feel that your chair in the University is endowed rather than subsidized. You saw how Whitney acted, you say. Why, he makes me feel as if I were his hired man, instead of head of the University's expedition. I'm glad it's over. Still, if you could find that dagger and have it returned it might look better for me. You have no clue, I suppose?"

"I'm getting closer to one," replied Craig confidently, though on what he could base any optimism I could not see.

The same idea seemed to be in Norton's mind. "You think you will have something tangible soon?" he asked eagerly.

"I've had more slender threads than these to work on," reassured Kennedy. "Besides, I'm getting very little help from any of you. You yourself, Norton, at the start left me a good deal in the dark over the history of the dagger."

"I couldn't do otherwise," he defended. "You understand now, I guess, how I have always been tied, hand and foot, by the Whitney influence. You'll find that I can be of more service, now."

"Just how did you get possession of the dagger?" asked Kennedy, and there flashed over me the recollection of the story told by the Senora, as well as the letter which we had purloined.

"Just picked it up from an Indian who had an abnormal dislike to work. They said he was crazy, and I guess perhaps he was. At any rate, he later drowned himself in the lake, I have heard."

"Could he have been made insane, do you think?" ruminated Craig. "It's possible that he was the victim of somebody, I understand. The insanity might have been real enough without the cause being natural."

"That's an interesting story," returned Norton. "Offhand, I can't seem to recall much about the fellow, although some one else might have known him very well."

Evidently he either did not know the tale as well as the Senora, or was not prepared to take us entirely into his confidence.

"Who is Haggerty?" asked Craig, thinking of the name signed to the letter we had read.

"An agent of Whitney and his associates, who manages things in Lima," explained Norton. "Why?"

"Nothing—only I have heard the name and wondered what his connection might be. I understand better now."

Kennedy seemed to be anxious to get to work on something, and, after a few minutes, Norton left us.

No sooner had the door closed than he took the glass-bell jar off his microscope and drew from a table drawer several scraps of paper on which I recognized the marks left by the carbon sheets. He set to work on another of those painstaking tasks of examination, and I retired to my typewriter, which I had moved into the next room, in order to leave Kennedy without anything that might distract attention from his work.

One after another he examined the sheets which he had marked, starting with a hand-lens and then using one more powerful. At the top of the table lay the specially prepared paper on which he had caught and preserved the marks in the dust of the Egyptian sarcophagus in the Museum.

Besides these things, I noticed that he had innumerable photographs, many of which were labelled with the stamp of the bureau in the Paris Palais de Justice, over which Bertillon had presided.

One after another he looked at the carbon prints, comparing them point by point with the specially prepared copy of the shoe-prints in the sarcophagus. It was, after all, a comparatively simple job. We had the prints of de Moche and Lockwood, as well as Whitney, all of them crossed by steps from Norton.

"Well, what do you think of that?" I heard him mutter.

Arthur B. Reeve

I quit my typewriter, with a piece of paper still in it, and hurried into the main room.

"Have you found anything?"

"I should say I had," he replied, in a tone that betrayed his own astonishment at the find. "Look at that," he indicated to me, handing over one of the sheets. "Compare it with this Museum foot-print."

With his pencil Kennedy rapidly indicated the tell-tale points of similarity on the two shoe-prints.

I looked up at him, convinced now of some one's identity.

"Who was it?" I asked, unable to restrain myself longer.

Kennedy paused a minute, to let the importance of the surprise be understood.

"The man who entered the Museum and concealed himself in the sarcophagus in the Egyptian section adjoining Norton's treasures," replied Kennedy slowly, "was Lockwood himself!"

XII

THE EVIL EYE

Completely at sea as a result of the unexpected revelation of the shoe-prints we had found in the Museum, and with suspicions now thoroughly aroused against Lockwood, I accompanied Kennedy to keep our appointment with the Senorita at the Prince Edward Albert.

We were purposely a bit early, in order to meet Inez, so that she would not have to be alone with the Senora, and we sat down in the lobby in a little angle from which we could look into the tea room.

We had not been sitting there very long when Kennedy called my attention to Whitney, who had just come in. Almost at the same time he caught sight of us, and walked over.

"I've been thinking a good deal of your visit to me just now," he began, seating himself beside us. "Perhaps I should not have said what I did about your friend Norton. But I couldn't help it. I guess you know something about that dagger he lost, don't you?"

"I have heard of the 'great fish' and the 'little fish' and the 'curse of Mansiche,'" replied Kennedy, "if that is what you mean. Somehow the Inca dagger seems to have been mixed up with them."

"Yes—with the peje grande, I believe," went on Whitney.

Beneath his exterior of studied calm I could see that he was very much excited. If I had not already noted a peculiar physical condition in him, I might have thought he had stopped in the cafe with some friends too long. But his eyes were not those of a man who has had too much to drink.

Just then Senorita Mendoza entered, and Kennedy rose and went forward to greet her. She saw Whitney, and flashed an inquiring glance at us.

"We were waiting for Senorita Mendoza," explained Kennedy to both Whitney and her, "when Mr. Whitney happened along. I don't see Senora de Moche in the tea room. Perhaps we may as well sit out here in the corridor until she comes."

It was evidently his desire to see how Whitney and Inez would act, for this was the first time we had ever seen them together.

"We were talking of the treasure," resumed Whitney, omitting to mention the dagger. "Kennedy, we are not the only ones who have sought the peje grande, or rather are seeking it. But we are, I believe, the only ones who are seeking it in the right place, and," he added, leaning over confidentially, "your father, Senorita, was the only one who could have got the concession, the monopoly, from the government to seek in what I am convinced will be the right place. Others have found the 'little fish.' We shall find the 'big fish.'"

He had raised his voice from the whisper, and I caught Inez looking anxiously at Kennedy, as much as to say, "You see? He is like the rest. His mind is full of only one subject."

"We shall find it, too," he continued, still speaking in a high-pitched key, "no matter what obstacles man or devil put in our way. It shall be ours—for a simple piece of engineering —ours! The curse of Mansiche—pouf!"

He snapped his fingers defiantly as he said it. There was an air of bravado about his manner. I could not help feeling that perhaps in his heart he was not so sure of himself as he would have others think.

I watched him closely, and could see that he had suddenly become even more excited than before. It was as though some diabolical force had taken possession of his brain, and he fought it off, but was unable to conquer.

Kennedy followed the staring glance of Whitney's eyes, which seemed almost to pop out of his head, as though he were suffering from the disease exophthalmic goitre. I looked also. Senora de Moche had come from the elevator, accompanied by Alfonso, and was walking slowly down the corridor. As she looked to the right and left, she had caught sight of our little group, all except Whitney, with our backs toward her. She was now looking fixedly in our direction, paying no attention to anything else.

Whitney was a study. I wondered what could be the relations between these two, the frankly voluptuous woman and the calculating full-blooded man. Whitney, for his part, seemed almost fascinated by her gaze. He rose as she bowed, and, for a moment, I thought that he was going over to speak to her, as if drawn by that intangible attraction which Poe has so cleverly expressed in his "Imp of the Perverse." For, clearly, one who talked as Whitney had just been talking would have to be on his guard with that woman. Instead, however, he returned her nod and stood still, while Kennedy bowed at a distance and signalled to her that we would be in the tea room directly.

I glanced up in time to see the anxious look on the face of Inez change momentarily into a flash of hatred toward the Senora.

At the same moment Alfonso, who was on the other side of his mother, turned from looking at a newsstand which had attracted his attention and caught sight of us. There was no mistaking the ardent glance which he directed at the fair Peruvian at my side. I fancied, too, that her face softened a bit. It was only for a moment, and then Inez resumed her normal composure.

"I won't detain you any longer," remarked Whitney. "Somehow, when I start to talk about my—our plans down there at Truxillo I could go on all night. It is marvellous, marvellous. We haven't any idea of what the future holds in store. No one else in all this big city has anything like the prospect which is before us. Gradually we are getting everything into shape. When we are ready to go ahead, it will be the sensation of Wall Street—and, believe me, it takes much to arouse the Street."

He may have been talking wildly, but it was worth while to listen to him. For, whatever else he was, Whitney was one of the most persuasive promoters of the day. More than that, I could well imagine how any one possessed of an imagination susceptible to the influence of mystery and tradition would succumb to the glittering charm of the magic words, peje chica, and feel all the gold-hunter's enthusiasm when Whitney brought him into the atmosphere of the peje grande.

As he talked, visions of hidden treasure seemed to throw a glamour over everything. One saw golden.

"You will excuse us?" apologized Kennedy, taking Inez by the arm. "If you are about, Mr. Whitney, I shall stop to chat with you again on the way out."

"Remember—she is a very remarkable woman," said Whitney, as we left him and started for the tea room.

His tone was not exactly one of warning, yet it seemed to have cost him an effort to say it. I could not reconcile it with any other idea than that he was trying to use her in his own plans, but was still in doubt of the outcome.

We parted from him and entered the darkened tea room, with its wicker tables and chairs, and soft lights, glowing pinkly, to simulate night in the broad light of afternoon outside. A fountain splashed soothingly in the centre. Everything was done to lend to the place an exotic air of romance.

Alfonso and his mother had chosen a far corner, deeper than the rest in the shadows, where two wicker settees were drawn up about a table, effectually cutting off inquisitive eyes and ears.

Alfonso rose as we approached and bowed deeply. I could not help watching the two women as they greeted each other. "Won't you be seated?" he asked, pulling around one of the wicker chairs.

It was then that I saw how he had contrived to sit next to Inez, while Kennedy manoeuvred to sit on the end, where he could observe them all best.

It was a rather delicate situation, and I wondered how

Kennedy would handle it, for, although Alfonso had done the inviting, it was really Craig who was responsible for allowing Inez to accept. The Senora seemed to recognize it, also, for, although she talked to Inez, it was plain she had him in mind.

"I have heard from Alfonso about the cruel death of your father," she began, in a softened tone, "and I haven't had a chance to tell you how deeply I sympathize with you. Of course, I am a much older woman than you, have seen much more trouble. But I know that never in life do troubles seem keener than when life is young. And yours has been so harsh. I could not let it pass without an opportunity to tell you how deeply I feel."

She said it with an air of sincerity that was very convincing, so convincing, in fact, that it shook for the moment the long chain of suspicion that I had been forging both of her and her son. Could she be such a heartless woman as to play on the very heartstrings of one whom she had wronged? I was shaken, moreover, by the late discovery by Kennedy of the foot-prints.

The Senorita murmured her thanks for the condolences in a broken voice. It was evident that whatever enmity she bore against the Senora it was not that of suspicion that she was the cause of her father's death.

"I can sympathize with you the more deeply," she went on, "because only lately I have lost a very dear brother myself. Already I have told Professor Kennedy something about it. It was a matter of which I felt I must speak to you, for it may concern you, in the venture in which Mr. Lockwood and your father were associated, and into which now Mr. Whitney has entered."

Inez said nothing, and Craig bowed, as though he, too, wished her to go on.

"It is about the 'big fish' and the concession which your father has obtained from the government to search for it."

The Senorita started and grew a bit pale at the reference, but she seemed to realize that it was something she ought to hear, and steeled herself to it.

"Yes," she murmured, "I understand."

"As you no doubt know," resumed the Senora, "no one has had the secret of the hiding-place. It has been by mere tradition that they were going to dig. That secret, you may know or may not know now, was in reality contained in the inscriptions on an old Inca dagger."

Inez shuddered at the mention of the weapon, a shudder that was not lost on the Senora.

"I have already told Professor Kennedy that both the tradition and the dagger were handed down in my own family, coming at last to my brother. As I said, I don't know how it happened, but somehow he seemed to be getting crazy, until he talked, and the dagger was stolen from him. It came finally into Professor Norton's hands, from whom it was in turn stolen."

She looked at Inez searchingly, as if to discover just what she knew. I wondered whether the Senora suspected the presence of Lockwood's footprints in the sarcophagus in the Museum—what she would do if she did.

"After he lost it," she continued reminiscently, "my brother threw himself one day into Lake Titicaca. Everywhere the trail of that dagger, of the secret of the Gold of the Gods has been stained by blood. To-day the world scoffs at curses. But surely that gold must be cursed. It has been cursed for us and ours."

She spoke bitterly; yet might she not mean that the loss of the dagger, the secret, was a curse, too?

"There is one other thing I wish to say, and then I will be through. Far back, when your ancestors came into the country of mine, an ancestor of your father lost his life over the treasure. It seems as if there were a strange fatality over it, as if the events of to-day were but living over the events of yesterday. It is something that we cannot escape—fate."

She paused a moment, then added, "Yet it might be possible that the curse could be removed if somehow we, who were against each other then, might forget and be for each other now."

"But Senorita Mendoza has not the dagger," put in Kennedy, watching her face keenly, to read the effect of his remark. "She has no idea where it may be."

"Then it is pure tradition on which Mr. Lockwood and Mr. Whitney depend in their search for the treasure?" flashed back the Senora quickly.

Kennedy did not know, but he did not confess it. "Until we know differently, we must take their word for it," he evaded.

"It was not that that I meant, however," replied Senora de Moche. "I meant that we might stop the curse by ceasing to hunt for the treasure. It has never done any one good; it never will. Why tempt fate, then? Why not pause before it is too late?"

I could not quite catch the secondary implication of her plan. Did it mean that the treasure would then be left for her family? Or was she hinting at Inez accepting Alfonso's suit? Somehow I could not take the Senora at her face value. I constantly felt that there was an ulterior motive back of her actions and words.

I saw Craig watching the young man's face, and followed his eyes. There was no doubt of how he took the remark. He was gazing ardently at Inez. If there had ever been any doubt of his feelings, which, of course, there had not, this would have settled it.

"One thing more," added the Senora, as though she had had an afterthought, "and that is about Mr. Lockwood and Mr. Whitney. Let me ask you to think it over. Suppose they have not the dagger. Then are their chances better than others? And if they have"—she paused to emphasize it—"what does that mean?"

Kennedy had turned his attention to the Senorita. It was evident that the dilemma proposed by de Moche was not without weight. She had now coloured a flaming red. The woman had struck her in a vital spot.

"Mr. Lockwood is not here to defend himself," Inez said quietly. "I will not have him attacked by innuendo."

She had risen. Neither the ardour of Alfonso nor the seeds of doubt of the Senora had shaken her faith. It was a test that Kennedy evidently was glad to have witnessed. For some day she might learn the truth about the foot-prints. He understood her character better. The Senora, too, had learned that if she were to bring pressure on the girl she might break her, but she would not bend.

Arthur B. Reeve

Without another word Inez, scarcely bowing stiffly, moved out of the tea room, and we followed, leaving the mother and son there, baffled.

"I hope you will pardon me for allowing you to come here," said Kennedy, in a low voice. "I did it because there are certain things that you ought to hear. It was in fairness to you. I would not have you delude yourself about Mr. Whitney, about—Mr. Lockwood, even. I want you to feel that, no matter what you hear or see, you can come to me and know that I will tell you the truth. It may hurt, but it will be best."

I thought he was preparing the way for a revelation about the foot-prints, but he said nothing more.

"Oh, that woman!" she exclaimed, as if to change the subject. "I do not know, I cannot say, why she affects me so. I saw a change in my father, when he knew her. I have told you how he was, how sometimes I thought he was mad. Did you notice a change in Mr. Whitney, or haven't you known him long enough? And lately I have fancied that I see the same sort of change beginning in Mr. Lockwood. At times they become so excited, their eyes seem staring, as if some fever were wasting them away. Father seemed to see strange visions, and hear voices, was worse when he was alone than when he was in a crowd. Oh, what is it? I could think of nothing else, not even what she was saying, all the time I was with her."

"Then you fear that in some way she may be connected with these strange changes?" asked Kennedy.

"I don't know," she temporized; but the tone of her answer was sufficient to convey the impression that in her heart she did suspect something, she knew not what.

"Oh, Professor Kennedy," she cried finally, "can't you see it? Sometimes—when she looks out of those eyes of hers—she almost makes people do as she pleases."

We had come to the taxicab stand before the hotel, and Kennedy had already beckoned to a cab to take her home.

As he handed her in she turned with a little shiver.

"Don't please, think me foolish," she added, with bated breath, "but often I fear that it is, as we call it, the mal de ojo—the evil eye!"

XIII

THE POISONED CIGARETTE

There was not a grain of superstition in Kennedy, yet I could see that he was pondering deeply what Inez Mendoza had just said. Was it possible that there might be something in it—not objectively, but subjectively? Might that very fear which the Senorita had of the Senora engender a feeling that would produce the very result that she feared? I knew that there were strange things that modern psychology was discovering. Could there be some scientific explanation of the evil eye?

Kennedy turned and went back into the hotel, to keep his appointment with Whitney, and as he did so I reflected that, whatever credence might be given the evil-eye theory, there was something now before us that was a fact—the physical condition which Inez had observed in her father before his death, saw now in Whitney, and foresaw in Lockwood. Surely that in itself constituted enough of a problem.

We found Whitney in the cafe, sitting alone in a leather-cushioned booth, and smoking furiously. I observed him narrowly. His eyes had even more than before that peculiar, staring look. By the manner in which his veins stood out I could see that his heart action must be very rapid.

"Well," he remarked, as we seated ourselves, "how did you come out in your tete-a-tete?"

"About as I expected," answered Kennedy nonchalantly. "I let it go on merely because I wanted Senorita Mendoza to hear certain things, and I thought that the Senora could tell them best. One of them related to the history of that dagger."

I thought Whitney's eyes would pop out of his head. "What about it?" he asked.

"Well," replied Kennedy briefly, "there was the story of how her brother had it and was driven crazy until he gave it up to somebody, then committed suicide by throwing himself into Titicaca. The other was the tradition that in the days after Pizarro a Mendoza was murdered by it, just as her father has now been murdered."

Whitney was listening intently, and seemed to be thinking deeply of something.

"Do you know," he said finally, with a nod to indicate that he knew what it was that Kennedy referred to, "I've been thinking of that de Moche woman a good deal since I left you with her. I've had some dealings with her."

He looked at Kennedy shrewdly, as though he would have liked to ask whether she had said anything about him, but did not because he knew Kennedy would not tell. He was trying to figure out some other way of finding out.

"Sometimes I think she is trying to double-cross me," he said, at length. "I know that when she talks to others about me she says many things that aren't so. Yet when she is with me everything is fine, and she is ready soon to join us, use her influence with influential Peruvians; in fact, there isn't anything she won't do - manana, to-morrow."

All that Whitney said we now knew to be true.

"She has one interesting dilemma, however, which I do not mind telling you," remarked Kennedy at length. "She cannot expect me to keep secret what she said before all of us. Inez Mendoza would mention it, anyhow."

"What was that?" queried Whitney, dissembling his interest.

"Why," replied Kennedy slowly, "it was that, with the plans for digging for the treasure which you say you have, suppose you and Lockwood and your associates have not the dagger—how are you better off than previous hunters? And supposing you have it—what does that imply?"

Whitney thought a moment over the last proposition of the dilemma. "Imply?" he repeated slowly. Then the significance of it seemed to dawn on him, the possession of the dagger and its implication in regard to the murder of Mendoza. "Well," he answered, "we haven't the dagger. You know that. But, on the other hand, we think our plans for getting at the treasure are better than any one else has ever had, more certain of success."

"Yet the possession of the dagger, with its inscription, is the only thing that absolutely insures success," observed Kennedy.

"That's true enough," agreed Whitney. "Confound that man Norton. How could he be such a boob as to let the chance slip through his fingers?"

"He never told you of it?" asked Kennedy.

"Yes, he told me of the dagger, but hadn't read the inscription, he said," answered Whitney. "I was so busy at the time with Lockwood and Mendoza, who had the concession to dig for the treasure, that I didn't pay much attention to what Norton brought back. I thought that could wait until Lockwood had been persuaded to join the interests I represent."

"Did Lockwood or Mendoza know about the dagger and its importance?" suggested Craig.

"If they did, they never said anything about it," returned Whitney promptly. "Mendoza is dead. Lockwood tells me he knew nothing about it until very lately—since the murder, I suppose."

"You suppose?" persisted Kennedy. "Are you sure that he knew nothing about it before?"

"No," confessed Whitney, "I'm not sure. Only I say that he told me nothing of it."

"Then he might have known?"

"Might have. But I don't think it very probable."

Whitney seemed to be turning something over in his mind. Suddenly he brought his fist down on the little round table before us, rattling the glasses.

"Do you know," he exclaimed, "the more I think about it, the more convinced I am that Norton ought to be held to account for that loss! He ought to have known. Then the presumption is that he did know. By heaven, I'm going to have that fellow watched. I'm going to do it to-day, too. I don't trust him. He shall not double-cross me—even if that woman does!"

I wondered whether Whitney was bluffing. If he was, he was making a lot of fuss over it. He talked more and more wildly, as he grew more excited over his latest idea.

"I'll have detectives put on his trail," he blustered. "I'll talk it over with Lockwood. He never liked the man."

"What did Lockwood say about Norton?" asked Kennedy casually.

Whitney eyed us a moment.

"Say," he ejaculated, "it was Norton brought you into this case, wasn't it?"

"I cannot deny that," returned Kennedy quietly, meeting his eyes. "But it is Inez Mendoza now that keeps me in it."

"So—you're another rival, are you?" purred Whitney sarcastically. "Lockwood and de Moche aren't enough. I have a sneaking suspicion that Norton himself is one of them. Now it's you, too. I suppose Mr. Jameson is another. Well, if I was ten years younger, I'd cut you all out, or know the reason why. Oh, YES, I think I will NOT tell you what Mr. Lockwood suspects."

With every sentence the veins of Whitney's forehead stood out further, until now they were like whipcords. His eyes and face were fairly apoplectic. Slowly the conviction was forced on me. The man acted for all the world like one affected by a drug.

"Well," he went on, "you may tell Norton for me that I am going to have him watched. That will throw a scare into him."

At least it showed that the breach between Whitney and Norton was deep. Kennedy listened without saying much, but I knew that he was gratified. He was playing Lockwood against de Moche, the Senora against Inez. Now if Whitney would play himself against Norton, out of the tangle might emerge just the clues he needed. For when people get fighting among themselves the truth comes out.

"Very well," remarked Craig, rising, with a hurried glance at Whitney's apoplectic face, "go as far as you like. I think we understand each other better, now."

Whitney said nothing, but, rising also, turned on his heel and walked deliberately out of the cafe into the corridor of the Prince Edward Albert, leaving us standing there.

Kennedy leaned over and swept up the ashes of Whitney's cigarettes which lay in the ash-tray, placing them, stubs and all, in an envelope, as he had done before.

"We have one sample, already," he said. "Another won't hurt. You can never have too much material to work with. Let us see where he is going."

Slowly we followed in the direction which Whitney had taken from the cafe. There was Whitney standing by the cigar-stand, gazing intently down the corridor.

Kennedy and I moved over so that we could see what he was gazing at. Just then he started to walk hurriedly in the direction in which he was looking.

"Senora de Moche!" exclaimed Craig, drawing me toward a palm.

It was indeed she. She had left the tea room and gone to her own room. Now she was alighting from the elevator, and had started toward the main dining-room, when her eyes had rested on Whitney. In spite of all that he had said to us about her, he had received the glance as a signal and was fluttering over to her like a moth to a flame.

What was the reason back of it all, I asked, as I thought of those wonderful eyes of hers? Was it a sort of auto-hypnotism? There was, I knew, a form of illusion known as ophthalmophobia—fear of the eye. It ranged from mere aversion at being gazed at all the way to the subjective development of real physical action from an otherwise trivial objective cause. Perhaps Inez was right about the eyes. One might fear them, and that fear might cause the precise thing to happen which the owner of the eyes intended. Still, as I reflected before, there was a much more important problem regarding eyes before us, that of the drug that was evidently being used in the cigarettes. What was it?

There was no chance of our gleaning anything now from these two who made such a strange pair. Kennedy turned and went out of the nearest entrance of the hotel.

"Central Park, West," he directed a cab driver, as we climbed in his machine; then to me, after giving the number, "I must see Inez Mendoza again before I can go ahead."

Inez was not expecting us so soon after leaving her at the hotel, yet I think was just a little glad that we had come.

"Did anything happen after I left?" she asked eagerly.

"We went back and saw Mr. Whitney," returned Craig. "I believe you are right. He is acting queerly,"

"Alfonso called me up," she volunteered.

"Was it about anything I should know?" queried Craig.

"Well," she hesitated, "he said he hoped that nothing that had taken place would change our own relations. That was about all. He was the dutiful son, and made no attempt to explain anything that was said."

Kennedy smiled. "You have not seen Mr. Lock, wood since, I suppose?" he asked.

"You always make me tell what I hadn't intended," she confessed, smiling back. "Yes, I couldn't help it. At least, I didn't see him. I called him up. I wanted to tell him what she had said and that it hadn't made any difference to me."

"What did he say?"

"I can't remember just how he put it, but I think he meant that it was something very much like that anonymous letter I received. We both feel that there is some one who wants to make trouble between us, and we are not going to let it happen."

If she had known of Kennedy's discovery of the shoe-prints, I feel sure that, as far as we were concerned, the case would have ended there. She was in no mood to be convinced by such a thing, would probably have insisted that some one was wearing a second-hand pair of his shoes.

Kennedy's eye had been travelling around the room as though searching for something.

"May I have a cigarette out of that case over there?" he asked, indicating a box of them on a table.

"Why—that is Mr. Lockwood's," she replied. "He left it here

Arthur B. Reeve

the last time he was here and I forgot to send it to him. Wait a minute. Let me get you some of father's."

She left the room. The moment the door closed Kennedy reached over and took one from the case. "I have some of Lockwood's already, but another won't matter, as long as I can get it," he said. "I thought it was her father's. When she brings them, smoke one with me, and be careful to save the stub. I want it."

A moment later she entered with a metal box that must have held several hundred. Kennedy and I each took one and lighted it, then for several minutes chatted as an excuse for staying. As for myself, I was glad enough to leave a pretty large stub, for I did not like it. These cigarettes, like those Whitney had offered us, had a peculiar flavour which I had not acquired a liking for.

"You must let me know whether anything else develops from the meeting in the tea room," said Kennedy finally, rising. "I shall be at the laboratory some time, I think."

XIV

THE INTERFEROMETER

Norton was waiting for us at the laboratory when we returned, evidently having been there some time.

"I was on my way to my apartment," he began, "when I thought I'd drop in to see how things are progressing."

"Slowly," returned Kennedy, throwing off his street clothes and getting into his laboratory togs.

"Have you seen Whitney since I had the break with him?" asked Norton, a trifle anxiously.

I wondered whether Kennedy would tell Norton what to expect from Whitney. He did not, however.

"Yes," he replied, "just now we had an appointment with Senora de Moche and some others and ran into him at the hotel for a few moments."

"What did he say about me?" queried Norton.

"He hadn't changed his mind," evaded Kennedy. "Have you heard anything from him?"

Arthur B. Reeve

"Not a syllable. The break is final. Only I was wondering what he was telling people about me. He'll tell them something—his side of the case."

"Well," considered Kennedy, as though racking his brain for some remark which he remembered, while Norton watched him eagerly, "I do recall that he was terribly sore about the loss of the dagger, and seemed to think that it was your fault."

"I thought so, I knew it," replied Norton bitterly. "I can see it coming. All the trustees will hear of my gross negligence in letting the Museum be robbed. I suppose I ought to sit up there all night. Oh, by the way, there's another thing I wanted to ask you. Have you ever done anything with those shoe-prints you found in the dust of the mummy case?"

I glanced at Kennedy, wondering whether he felt that the time had come to reveal what he had discovered. He said nothing for a moment, but reached into a drawer and pulled out the papers, which I recognized.

"Here they are," he said, picking out the original impression which he had taken.

"Yes," repeated Norton, "but have you been able to do anything toward identifying them?"

"I found it rather hard to collect prints of the shoes of all of those I wished to compare. But I have them at last."

"And?" demanded Norton, leaning forward tensely.

"I find that there is one person whose shoe-prints are precisely the same as those we found in the Museum," went on Kennedy, tossing over the impression he had taken.

Norton scanned the two carefully. "I'm not a criminologist," he said excitedly, "but to my untrained eye it does seem as though you had here a replica of the first prints, all right." He laid them down and looked squarely at Kennedy. "Do you mind telling me whose feet made these prints?"

"Turn the second over. You will see the name written on it."

"Lockwood!" exclaimed Norton in a gasp as he read the name. "No—you don't mean it."

"I mean nothing less," repeated Kennedy firmly. "I do not say what happened afterwards, but Lockwood was in the Museum, hiding in the mummy case, that night."

Norton's mind was evidently working rapidly. "I wish I had your power of deduction, Kennedy," he said, at length. "I suppose you realize what this means?"

"What does it mean to you?" asked Kennedy, changing front.

Norton hesitated. "Well," he replied, "it means to me, I suppose, what it means to any one who stops to think. If Lockwood was there, he got the dagger. If he had the dagger—it was he who used it!"

The inference was so strong that Craig could not deny it. Whether it was his opinion or not was another matter.

"It fits in with other facts, too," continued Norton. "For instance, it was Lockwood who discovered the body of Mendoza."

"But the elevator boy took Lockwood up himself," objected Craig, more for the sake of promoting the discussion than to combat Norton.

"Yes—when he 'discovered' the thing. But it must have been done long before. Who knows? He may have entered. The deed might have been done. He may have left. No one saw him come or go. What then more likely to cover himself up than to return when he knew that his entrance would be known, and find the thing himself?"

Norton's reasoning was clever and plausible. Yet Kennedy scarcely nodded his head, one way or the other.

"You were acquainted with Lockwood?" he asked finally. "I mean to say, of course, before this affair."

"Yes, I met him in Lima just as I was starting out on my expedition. He was preparing to come to New York."

"What did you think of him then?"

"Oh, he was all right, I suppose. He wasn't the sort who would care much for an archaeologist. He cared more for a prospector going off into the hills than he did for me. And I—I admit that I am impossible. Archaeology is my life."

Norton continued to study the prints. "I can hardly believe my eyes," he murmured; then he looked up suddenly. "Does Whitney know about this—or Lockwood?"

Kennedy shook his head negatively.

"Because," pursued Norton, "an added inference to that I spoke of would be that the reason why they are so sure that they will find the treasure is that they are not going on tradition, as they say, but on the fact itself."

"A fair conclusion," agreed Craig.

"I wish the break could have been postponed," continued Norton. "Then I might have been of some service in my relation to Whitney. It's too late for me to be able to help you in that direction now, however."

"There is something you can do, though," said Craig.

"I shall be delighted," hastened Norton. "What is it?"

"You know Senora de Moche and Alfonso?"

"Yes."

"I wish that you would cultivate their acquaintance. I feel that they are very suspicious of me. Perhaps they may not be so with you."

"Is there any special thing you want to find out?"

"Yes—only I have slight hopes of doing so. You know that she is on most intimate terms with Whitney."

"I'm afraid I can't do much for you, then. She'll fight shy of me. He'll tell her his story."

"That will make no difference. She has already warned me against him. He has warned against her. It's a most remarkable situation. He is trying to get her into some kind of deal, yet all the time he is afraid she is double-crossing him. And at the same time he obeys her—well, like Alfonso would Inez if she'd only let him."

Norton frowned. "I don't like the way they hover about Inez Mendoza," he remarked. "Perhaps the Senora is after Whitney, while her son is after Inez. Lockwood seems to be impervious to her. Yes, I'll undertake that commission for you, only I can't promise what success I'll have."

Kennedy restored the shoe-prints to the drawer.

"I think that's gratifying progress," went on Norton. "First we know who stole the dagger. We know that the dagger killed Mendoza. You have even determined what the poison on the blade was. It seems to me that it remains only to determine who struck the actual blow. I tell you, Kennedy, Whitney will regret the day that he ever threw me over on so trivial a pretext."

Norton was pacing up and down excitedly now.

"My only fear is," he went on, "what the shock of such a thing will be on that poor little girl. First her father, then Lockwood. Why—the blow will be terrible. You must be careful, Kennedy."

"Never fear about that," reassured Craig. "Not a word of this has been breathed to her yet. We are a long way from fixing the guilt of the murder; inference is one thing, fact another. We must have facts. And the facts I want, which you may be able to get, relate to the strange actions of the de Moches."

Norton scanned Kennedy's face for some hint of what was back of the remark. But there was nothing there.

"They will bear watching, all right," he said, as he rose to go. "Old Mendoza was never quite the same after he became so intimate with her. And I think I can see a change in Whitney."

"What do you attribute it to?" asked Kennedy, without admitting that it had attracted his attention, too.

"I haven't the slightest idea," confessed Norton.

"Inez is as afraid of her as any of the rest," remarked Kennedy thoughtfully. "She says it is the evil eye."

"Not an uncommon belief among Latin-Americans," commented Norton. "In fact, I suppose there are people among us who believe in the evil eye yet. Still, you can hardly blame that little girl for believing it is almost anything. Well, I won't keep you any longer. I shall let you know of anything I find out from the de Moches. I think you are getting on remarkably."

Norton left us, his face much brighter than it had been when we met him at the door.

Kennedy, alone at last in the laboratory, went over to a cabinet and took out a peculiar-looking apparatus, which seemed, as nearly as I can describe it, to consist of a sort of triangular prism, set with its edge vertically on a rigid platform attached to a massive stand of brass.

"Norton seems to have suddenly become quite solicitous of the welfare of Senorita Mendoza," I hazarded, as he worked over the adjustment of the thing.

Kennedy smiled. "Every one seems to be—even Whitney," he returned, twisting a set-screw until he had the alignment of the various parts as he wanted it.

The telephone bell rang.

"Do you want to answer it?" I asked Craig.

"No," he replied, not even looking up from his work. "Find out who it is. Unless it is something very important say I am out on an investigation and that you have heard from me; that I shall not be either at the laboratory or the apartment until tomorrow morning. I must get this done to-night."

I took down the receiver.

"Hello, is this Professor Kennedy?" I recognized a voice.

"No," I replied. "Is there any message I can take?"

"This is Mr. Lockwood," came back the information I had already guessed. "When do you expect him?"

"It's Lockwood," I whispered to Craig, my hand over the transmitter.

"See what he wants," returned Craig. "Tell him what I told you."

I repeated Kennedy's message.

"Well, that's too bad," replied Lockwood. "I've just seen Mr. Whitney, and he tells me that Kennedy and you are pretty friendly with Norton, Of course, I knew that. I saw you at the Mendozas' together the first time. I'd like to have a talk with him about that man. I suppose he has told you all his side of the story of his relations with Whitney."

I am, if anything, a good listener, and so I said nothing, not even that he had better tell it to Kennedy in the morning, for it was such a novelty to have any of these people talk voluntarily that I really didn't much care whether I believed what they said or not.

"I used to know him down in Lima, you know," went on Lockwood. "What I want to say has to do with that dagger he says was stolen. I want to tell what I know of how he got it. There was an Indian mixed up in it who committed suicide—well, you tell Kennedy I'll see him in the morning."

Lockwood rang off, and I repeated what he had told me, as Kennedy continued to adjust the apparatus.

"Say," I exclaimed, as I finished. "That was a harry's of a commission you gave Norton just now, watching the de Moches. Why, they'd eat him alive if they got a chance, and I don't know that all's like a Sunday school on his part. Lockwood doesn't seem to think so."

Kennedy smiled quietly. "That was why I asked him to do it," he returned. "I thought that he wouldn't let much escape him. They all seem so down on him, he'll have to watch out. It will keep him busy, too, and that means a chance for us to work."

He had finished setting up the machine, and now went over to another drawer, from which he took the envelope of stubs which we had taken down at Whitney's office first. Then from the pocket of his street coat he drew both the second envelope of ashes and stubs, the whole cigarette from Lockwood's case, and the stubs which both of us had saved from the cigarettes that had once belonged to Mendoza.

Carefully he separated and labelled them all, so that there would be no chance for them to get mixed up. Then he picked up one of the stubs and lighted it. The smoke curled up in wreaths between a powerful light and the peculiar instrument, while Craig peered through a lens, manipulating the thing with exhaustless patience and skill. I watched him curiously, but said nothing, for he was studying something carefully, and I did not want to interrupt his train of thought.

Finally he beckoned me over. "Can you make anything out of that?" he asked.

I looked through the eye-piece, also. On a sort of fine grating all I could see was a number of strange lines.

"If you want an opinion from me," I said, with a laugh, "you'll have to tell me first what I am looking at."

"That," he explained, as I continued to gaze, "is one of the latest forms of the spectroscope, known as the interfero-meter, with delicately ruled gratings in which power to resolve the straight, close lines in the spectrum is carried to the limit of possibility. A small watch is delicate. But it bears no comparison to the delicacy of these defraction spectroscopes.

"Every substance, you know, is, when radiating light, characterized by what at first appears to be almost haphazard sets of spectral bands without relation to one another. But they are related by mathematical laws, and the apparent haphazard character is only the result of our lack of knowledge of how to interpret the results."

He resumed his place at the eye-piece to check over his results.

"Walter," he said finally, looking up at me with a twinkle in his eye, "I wish that you'd go out and find me a cat."

"A cat?" I repeated.

"Yes, a cat—felis domesticus, if it sounds better that way—a plain, ordinary cat."

I jammed on my hat and, late as it was, sallied forth on this apparently ridiculous mission.

Several belated passers-by and a policeman watched me as though I were a house-breaker, and I felt like a fool, but at last, by perseverance and tact, I managed to capture a fairly good specimen of the species, and carried it in my arms to the laboratory with some profanity and many scratches.

XV

THE WEED OF MADNESS

In my absence Craig had set to work on a peculiar apparatus, as though he were distilling something from several of the cigarette stubs which he had been studying by means of the interferometer.

"Here's your confounded cat," I ejaculated, as I placed the unhappy feline in a basket and waited patiently until finally he seemed to be rewarded for his patient labours. It was well along toward morning when he obtained in a test-tube a few drops of a colourless, odourless liquid.

"My interferometer gave me a clue," he remarked, as he held the tube up with satisfaction. "Without the tell-tale line in the spectrum which I was able to discover by its use I might have been hunting yet for it. It is so rare that no one would ever have thought, offhand, I suppose, to look for it. But here it is, I'm sure, only I wanted to be able to test it."

"So you are not going to try it on yourself," I said sarcastically, referring to his last experiment with a poison. "This time you are going to make the cat the dog."

"The cat will be better to test it on than a human being," he replied, with a glance that made me wince, for, after his performance with the curare, I felt that once the scientific furore was on him I might be called upon to become an unwilling martyr to science.

It was with an air of relief, both for himself and my own peace and safety, that I saw him take the cat out of the basket and hold her in his arms, smoothing her fur gently, to quiet the feelings that I had severely ruffled.

Then with a dropper he sucked up a bit of the liquid from the test-tube. I watched him intently as he let a small drop fall into the eye of the cat.

The cat blinked a moment, and I bent over to observe it more closely.

"It won't hurt the cat," he explained, "and it may help us."

As I looked at the cat's eye it seemed to enlarge, even under the glare of a light, shining forth, as it were, like the proverbial cat's eye under a bed.

What did it mean?

Was there such a thing, I wondered hastily, as the drug of the evil eye?

"What have you found?" I queried.

"Something very much like the so-called 'weed of madness,' I think," he replied slowly.

"The weed of madness?" I repeated.

"Yes. It is similar to the Mexican toloache and the Hindu

datura, which you must have heard about."

I had heard of these weird drugs, but they had always seemed to be so far away and to belong rather to the atmosphere of civilizations different from New York. Yet, I reflected, what was to prevent the appearance of anything in such a cosmopolitan city, especially in a case so unusual as that which had so far baffled even Kennedy's skill?

"You know the jimson weed—the Jamestown weed, as it is so often called?" he continued, explaining. "It grows almost everywhere in the world, but most thrivingly in the tropics. All the poisons that I have mentioned are related to it in some way, I believe."

"I've seen the thing in lots and fields," I replied, "but I never thought it was of much importance."

"Well," he resumed, "the jimson weed on the Pacific coast, in some parts of the Andes, has large white flowers which exhale a faint, repulsive odour. It is a harmless-looking plant, with its thick tangle of leaves, a coarse green growth, with trumpet-shaped flowers. But to one who knows its properties it is quite too dangerously convenient for safety."

"But what has that to do with the evil eye?" I asked.

"Nothing; but it has much to do with the cigarettes that Whitney is smoking," he went on positively. "Those cigarettes have been doped!"

"Doped?" I interrogated, in surprise. "With this weed of madness, as you call it?"

"No, it isn't toloache that was used," he corrected. "I think it must be some particularly virulent variety of the jimson weed that was used, though that same weed in Mexico is, I am sure, what there they call toloache. Perhaps its virulence in this case lies in the method of concentration in preparing it. For instance, the seeds of the stramonium, which is the same thing, contain a much higher percentage of poison than the leaves and flowers. Perhaps the seeds were used. I can't say. But, then, that isn't at all necessary. It is the fact of its use that concerns us most now."

He took a drop of the liquid which he had isolated and added a drop of nitric acid. Then he evaporated it by gentle heat and it left a residue slightly yellow.

Next he took from the shelf over his table a bottle marked "Alcoholic Solution—Potassium Hydrate." He opened it and let a drop fall on the place where the liquid had evaporated.

Instantly the residue became a beautiful purple, turning rapidly to violet, then to dark red, and, finally, it disappeared altogether.

"Stramonium, all right," he nodded, with satisfaction at the achievement of his night's labours. "That was known as Vitali's test. Yes, there was stramonium in those cigarettes— datura stramonium—perhaps a trace of hyoscyamine."

I tried to look wise, but all I could think of was that, whatever his science showed me now, my instinct had been enough to prompt me not to smoke those cigarettes, though, of course, only Kennedy's science could tell what it was that caused that instinctive aversion.

"They are all like atropine, mydriatic alkaloids," he proceeded, "so called from the effect they have on the eye. Why, one-one hundred thousandth of a grain will affect the eye of a cat. You saw how it acted on our subject. It is more active in that way than atropine. Better yet, you remember how Whitney's eyes looked, how Inez said her father stared, and how she feared for Lockwood?"

"I remember," I said, still not able to detach the evil-eye idea quite from my mind. "How about the Senora's eyes? What makes them so—well, effective?"

"Oh," Craig answered quickly, "her pupils were normal enough. Didn't you notice that? It was the difference in Whitney's and the others' that first suggested making some tests."

"What is the effect?" I asked, wondering whether it might have contributed to the cause of Mendoza's death.

"The concentrated poison which has been used in these cigarettes does not kill—at least not outright. It is worse than that. Slowly it accumulates in the system. It acts on the brain."

I was listening, spellbound, as he made his disclosure. No wonder, I thought, even a scientific criminal stood in awe of Craig.

"Of all the dangers to be met with in superstitious countries, these mydratic alkaloids are among the worst. They offer a chance for crimes of the most fiendish nature—worse than with the gun or the stiletto. They are worse because there is so little fear of detection. That crime is the production of insanity!"

Horrible though the idea, and repulsive, I could not doubt it in the face of Craig's investigations and what I had already seen with my own eyes. In fact, it was necessary for me only to recall the mild sensations I myself had experienced, in order to be convinced of the possible effect intended by the insidious poison contained in the many cigarettes which Whitney, for instance, had smoked.

"But don't you suppose they know it?" I wondered. "Can't they tell it?"

"I suppose they have gradually become accustomed to it," Craig ventured. "If you have ever smoked one particular brand of cigarette you must have noticed how the manufacturer can gradually substitute a cheaper grade of tobacco without any large number of his patrons knowing anything about it. I imagine it might have been done in some way like that."

"But you would think they'd feel the effect and attribute it to smoking."

"Perhaps they do feel the effect. But when it comes to tracing causes, some people are loath to admit that tobacco and liquor can be the root of the evil. No, some one is slipping these cigarettes in on them, perhaps substituting the doped brand for those that are ordered. If you will notice, both Whitney and Lockwood have cigarettes that are made especially for them. So had Mendoza. It is a circumstance which some one has turned to account, though how and by whom the substitution has been made I cannot say yet. I wish I had time to follow out this one line, to the exclusion of everything else. But I've got to keep my fingers on every rope at once, else the thing will pull away from me. It is enough for the present that we know what the poison is. I shall take up the tracing of the person who is administering it the moment I get a hint."

It was almost daylight before Craig and I left the laboratory after his discovery of the manner of the cigarette poisoning by stramonium. But that was the only way in which he was able to make progress—taking time for each separate point by main force.

I was thoroughly tired, though not so much so that my dreams were not haunted by a succession of baleful eyes peering at me from the darkness.

I slept late, but was awakened by a knocking on the door. As I rose to answer it I saw through the open door of Kennedy's room that he had been about early and must already be at the laboratory. How he did it I don't know. My own newspaper experience had made me considerable of a nighthawk. But I always paid for it by sleeping the next day. With Kennedy, when he was on a case, even five hours of sleep was more than he seemed able to stand.

"Hello, Jameson," greeted a voice, as I opened the door. "Is Kennedy in—oh, he hasn't come back yet?"

It was Lockwood, at first eager to see Craig, then naturally crestfallen because he saw that he was not there.

"Yes," I replied, rubbing my eyes. "He must be at the laboratory. If you'll wait a minute while I slip on my clothes, I'll walk over there with you."

While I completed my hasty toilet, Lockwood sat in our living room, gazing about with fascination at the collection of trophies of the chase of criminals.

"This is positively a terrifying array of material, Jameson," he declared, as at last I emerged. "Between what Kennedy has here and what he has stowed away in that laboratory of his, I wonder that any one dares be a crook."

I could not help eying him keenly. Could he have spoken so heartily if he had known what it was, damning to himself, that Kennedy had tucked away in the laboratory? If he knew, he must have been a splendid actor, one of those whom only the minute blood-pressure test of the sphygmograph could induce to give up a secret, and then only in spite of himself.

"It is wonderful," I agreed. "Are you ready?"

We left the apartment and walked along in the bracing morning air toward the campus and the Chemistry Building. Sure enough, as I had expected, Kennedy was in his laboratory.

As we entered he was verifying his experiments and checking over his results, carefully endeavouring to isolate any of the other closely related mydriatic alkaloids that might be contained in the noxious fumes of the poisoned tobacco.

Though Craig was already convinced of what was going on, I knew that he always considered it a matter of considerable medico-legal importance to be exact, for if the affair ever came to the stage of securing an indictment the charge could be sustained only by specific proof.

As we appeared in the door, however, he laid aside his work, and greeted us.

"I suppose Jameson has already told you that I called you up last night—and what I said?" began Lockwood.

Kennedy nodded. "It was something about Norton, wasn't it?"

Lockwood leaned over impressively and almost whispered: "Of course, you are in no position to know, but there are ugly rumours current down in Lima among the natives regarding that dagger."

Kennedy did not appear to be particularly impressed. "Is that so?" he said merely. "What are they?"

"Well," resumed Lockwood, "I wasn't in Lima at the time. I was up here. But they tell me that there was something crooked about the way that that dagger was got away from an Indian—a brother of Senora de Moche." "Yes," replied Kennedy, "I know something about it. He committed suicide. But what has that to do with Norton?"

Lockwood hesitated, then shrugged his shoulders. "I should think the inference was plain," he insinuated. Then, looking at Craig fixedly, as though to take his measure, he added, "We are not out of touch with what is going on down there, even if we are several thousand miles away."

I wondered whether he had any information more than we had already obtained by X-raying the letter to Whitney signed "Haggerty." If he had, it was not his purpose, evidently, yet to disclose it. I felt from his manner that he was not playing a trump-card, but was just feeling us out by this lead.

"There was some crooked business about that dagger down there as well as here," he pursued. "There are many interests connected with it. Don't you think that it would be worth while watching Norton?" he paused, then added: "We do— and we're going to do it."

"Thank you very much," returned Kennedy quietly. "Mr. Whitney has already told me he intended to do so."

Lockwood eyed us critically, as though not quite sure what to make of the cool manner in which Craig took it.

"I think if I were you," he said at length, "I'd keep a close watch on the de Moches, both of them, too."

"Exactly," agreed Craig, without showing undue interest.

Lockwood had risen. "Well," he snapped, "you may not think much of what I am telling you now. But just wait until OUR detectives begin to dig up facts." No sooner had he left than I turned to Craig. "What was that?" I asked. "A plant?"

"Perhaps," he returned, clearing up the materials which he had been using.

The telephone rang.

"Hello, Norton," I heard Craig answer. "What's that? You are shadowed by some one—you think it is by Whitney?"

I had been expecting something of the sort, and listened attentively, but it was impossible to gather the drift of the one-sided conversation.

As Kennedy hung up the receiver I remarked, "So it was not a bluff, after all."

"I think my plan is working," he remarked thoughtfully. "You heard what he said? He guesses right the first time, that it is Whitney. The last thing he said was, 'I'll get even! I'll take some action!' and then he rang off. I think we'll hear something soon."

Instead of going out, Kennedy pulled out the several unsigned letters we had collected, and began the laborious process of studying the printing, analyzing it, in the hope that he might discover some new clue.

XVI

THE EAR IN THE WALL

Perhaps an hour later our laboratory door was flung open suddenly, and both Kennedy and I leaped to our feet.

There was Inez Mendoza, alone, pale and agitated.

"Tell me, Professor Kennedy," she cried, her hands clasped before her in frantic appeal, "tell me—it isn't true—is it? He wasn't there—no—no—no!"

She would have fainted if Craig had not sprung forward and caught her in time to place her in our only easy-chair.

"Walter," he said, "quick—that bottle of aromatic spirits of ammonia over there—the second from the left."

I handed it to him, and threw open the window to allow the fresh air to blow in. As I did so one of the papers Kennedy had been studying blew off the table, and, as luck would have it, fell almost before her. She saw it, and in her hypersensitive condition recognized it instantly.

"Oh—that anonymous letter!" she cried. "Tell me—you do not think that—the friend of my father's that it warned me to beware of—was—"

She did not finish the sentence. She did not need to do so.

"Please, Senorita," pleaded and soothed Kennedy, "try to be calm. What has happened? Tell me. What is it?"

The ammonia and the fresh air seemed to have done their work, for she managed to brace herself, gripping the arms of the chair tightly and looking up searchingly into Craig's face.

"It's about Chester," she managed to gasp; then seemed unable to go on.

It was the first time I had ever heard her use Lockwood's first name, and I knew that something had stirred her emotions more deeply than at any time since the death of her father.

"Yes," prompted Kennedy. "Go on."

"I have heard that you found foot-prints, shoe-prints, in the dust in the Museum after the dagger was stolen," she said, speaking rapidly, suppressing her feelings heroically. "Since then you have been collecting prints of shoes—and I've heard that the shoe-prints that were found are those of—of Mr. Lockwood. Oh, Professor Kennedy, it cannot be—there must be some mistake."

For a moment Kennedy did not say anything. He was evidently seeking some way in which to lead up to the revelation of the truth without too much shock.

"You remember that time in the tea room when we were sitting with Senora de Moche?" he asked finally.

"Yes," she said shortly, as though the very recollection were disagreeable to her.

Kennedy, however, had a disagreeable task, and he felt that it must be performed in the kindest manner.

"You remember then that she said she had one thing more to say, that it was about Mr. Whitney and Mr. Lockwood."

She was about to interrupt, but he hurried on, giving her no chance to do so. "She asked you to think it over. Suppose they did not have the dagger, she said. Then were their chances of finding the treasure any better than any one else had? And if they did have it, she asked what that meant. It is a dilemma, my dear Senorita, which you must meet some time. Why not meet it now?"

Her face was set. "You will remember, also, Professor Kennedy," she said, with a great effort controlling her voice, "that I said that Mr. Lockwood was not there to defend himself and I would not have him attacked by innuendo. I meant it to the Senora—I mean it to you!"

She had also meant it to defy him; but as she proceeded her voice broke, and before she knew it her nature had triumphed, and she was alternately sobbing and pleading.

For a minute or two Kennedy let her give vent to her emotions.

"It cannot be. It cannot be," she sobbed over and over. "He could not have been there. He could not have done it."

It was a terrible thing to have to disillusion her, but it was something now that had to be done. Kennedy had not sought to do so. He had postponed it in the hope of finding some other way. But now the thing was forced upon him.

"Who told you?" he asked finally.

"I was trying to read, to keep my mind occupied, as you asked me, when Juanita told me that there was some one in the living room who wanted to see me—a man. I thought it was either you or Mr. Jameson. But it was—Professor Norton—"

Kennedy and I exchanged glances. That was the action in revenge to Lockwood and Whitney which he had contemplated over the telephone. It was so cruel and harsh that I could have hated him for it, the more so as I recollected that it was he himself who had cautioned us against doing the very thing which now he had done in the heat of passion.

"Oh," she wailed, "he was very kind and considerate about it. He said he felt that it was his duty to tell me, that he would be anything, like an older brother, to me; that he could not see me blinded any longer to what was going on, and everybody knew, but had not love enough for me to tell. It was such a shock. I could not even speak. I simply ran from the room without another word to him, and Juanita found me lying on the bed. Then—I decided—I would come to you."

She paused, and her great, deep eyes looked up pathetically. "And you," she added bitterly, "you are going to tell me that he was right, that it is true. You can't prove it. Show me what it is that you have. I defy you!"

Somehow, as she rested and relieved her feelings, a new strength seemed to come to her. It was what Kennedy had been waiting for, the reaction that would leave her able for him to go on and plan for the future.

He reached into a drawer of a cabinet and pulled out the various shoe-prints which he had already shown Norton, and which he had studied and restudied so carefully.

"That is the print of the shoe in the dust of the Egyptian sarcophagus of the Museum," he said quietly. "Some one got in during the daytime and hid there until the place was locked. That is the print of Alfonso de Moche's shoe, that of Mr. Whitney's, and that of Mr. Lockwood's."

He said it quickly, as though trying to gloss it over. But she would not have it that way. She felt stronger, and she was going to see just what there was there. She took the prints and studied them, though her hand trembled. Hers was a remarkable mind. It took only seconds to see what others would have seen only in minutes. But it was not the reasoning faculty that was aroused by what she saw. It sank deep into her heart.

She flung the papers down.

"I don't believe it!" she defied. "There is some mistake. No— it cannot be true!"

It was a noble exhibition of faith. I think I have never seen any instant more tense than that in Kennedy's laboratory. There stood the beautiful girl declaring her faith in her lover, rejecting even the implication that it might have been he who had taken the dagger, perhaps murdered her father to insure the possession of her father's share of the treasure as well as the possession of herself.

Kennedy did not try to combat it. Instead he treated her very intuitions with respect. In him there was room for both fact and feeling.

"Senorita," he said finally, in a voice that was deep and thrilling with feeling, "have I ever been other than a friend to you? Have I ever given you cause to suspect even one little motive of mine?"

She faced him, and they looked into each other's eyes an instant. But it was long enough for the man to understand the woman and she to understand him.

"No," she murmured, glancing down again.

"Then trust me just this once. Do as I ask you."

For an instant she struggled with herself. What would he ask?

"What is it?" she questioned, raising her eyes to him again.

"Have you seen Mr. Lockwood?"

"No."

"Then, I want you to see him. Surely you wish to have no secrets from him any more than you would wish him to have anything secret from you. See him. Ask him frankly about it all. It is the only fair thing to him—it is only fair to yourself."

Senorita Mendoza was no coward. "I—I will," she almost whispered.

"Splendid!" exclaimed Kennedy in admiration. "I knew that you would. You are not the woman who could do otherwise. May I see that you get home safely? Walter, call a taxicab."

Senorita Mendoza was calmer, though pale and still nervous, when I returned. Kennedy handed her into the car and then returned to the laboratory for two rather large packages, which he handed to me.

"You must come along with us, Walter," he said. "We shall need you."

Scarcely a word was spoken as we jolted over the city pavements and at last reached the apartment. Inez and Craig entered and I followed, carrying just one of the packages as Craig had indicated by dumb show, leaving the other in the car, which was to wait.

"I think you had better write him a note," suggested Craig, as we entered the living room. "I don't want you to see him until you feel better—and, by the way, see him here."

She nodded with a wan smile, as though thinking how unusual it was for a meeting of lovers to be an ordeal, then excused herself to write the note.

She had no sooner disappeared than Kennedy unwrapped the package which I had brought. From it he took a cedar box, oblong, with a sort of black disc fixed to an arm on the top. In the face of the box were two little square holes, with sides of cedar which converged inward into the box, making a pair of little quadrangular pyramidal holes which ended in a small black circle in the interior.

He looked about the room quickly. Beside a window that opened out over a house several stories below stood a sectional bookcase. Into this bookcase, back of the books, in the shadow, he shoved the little box, to which he had already attached a spool of twisted wires. Then he opened the window and dropped the spool out, letting it unwind of its own weight until it fell on the roof far below. He shut the window and rejoined me without a word.

A moment later she returned with the dainty note which she had written. "Shall I send it by a messenger?" she asked.

"Yes, please," answered Kennedy, rising. As he moved a step to the door he held out his hand to her. "Senorita Mendoza," he said simply, in a tone that meant more than words, "you are a wonderful woman."

She took his hand without a word, and a moment later we were whisked down in the elevator.

"I must get on that roof on some pretext," remarked Kennedy, as we reached the street and he got his bearings. "Let me see, that house which backs up to the apartment is around the corner. Have the man drive us around there."

We located the house and mounted the steps. On the wall beside the brownstone door was pasted a little slip of paper, "Furnished Rooms."

"Splendid!" exclaimed Kennedy, as he read it. "Dismiss the taxi and meet me inside with the other package."

By the time I had paid the man and come up the steps again Kennedy had made a dicker with the landlady for a double room on the third floor for both of us, and, by payment of a week's rent, we were to have immediate possession.

"Our baggage will follow to-day," he explained, as we mounted the stairs to the room.

I thought the landlady would never get through expatiating upon what a select place she ran, and thus leave us alone in our room, but at last even her flood of words was stilled by demands from a servant downstairs who must be instructed if the selectness of the establishment were to be maintained.

No sooner were we alone than Kennedy tiptoed into the hall and made sure that we were not watched. It was then the work of only a few seconds to mount a ladder to a scuttle, unhook it, and gain the roof.

There, dangling down from the dizzy height above, swayed the twisted wire. He seized it, unrolled it some more, and sent me downstairs to catch it, as he swung it over the edge of the roof to one of our own windows. Then he rejoined me.

The other package, which had been heavier, consisted of another of those mysterious boxes, as well as several dry cells. Quickly he attached the wires to the box, placing the dry cells in the circuit. Then he began adjusting the mechanism of the box. So far I had only a vague idea of just what he had in mind, but gradually it began to dawn on me.

It was perhaps half an hour, perhaps longer, after we had left the Senorita, before, sure that everything was all right with his line and the batteries which he had brought, Kennedy turned a little lever that moved in a semicircle, touching one after another of a series of buttons on the face of the cedar box, meanwhile holding a little black disc from the back of the box to his ear as he adjusted the thing.

Nothing seemed to happen, but I could tell by the look of intentness on his face that he was getting along all right and was not worrying.

Suddenly the look on his face changed to one of extreme satisfaction. He dropped the disc he was holding to his ear back into its compartment and turned to me.

All at once it seemed as if the room in which we were was peopled by spirits. There was the sound of voices, loud, clear, distinct. It was uncanny.

"He has just come in," remarked Craig.

"Who?" I asked.

"Lockwood—can't you recognize his voice? Listen."

I did listen intently, and the more my ears became adjusted, the more plainly I could distinguish two voices, that of a man and that of a woman. It was indeed Lockwood and the Senorita, far above us.

I would have uttered an exclamation of amazement, but I could not miss what they were saying.

"Then you—you believe what he says?" asked Lockwood earnestly.

"Professor Kennedy has the prints," replied Inez tremulously.

"You saw them?"

"Yes."

"And you believe what HE says, too?"

There was a silence.

"What is it?" I asked, tapping the box lightly.

"A vocaphone," replied Kennedy. "The little box that hears and talks."

"Can they hear us?" I asked, in an awestruck whisper.

"Not unless I want them to hear," he replied, indicating a switch. "You remember, of course, the various mechanical and electrical ears, such as the detectaphone, which we have used for eavesdropping in other cases?"

I nodded.

"Well, this is a new application which has been made of the detectaphone. When I was using that disc from the compartment there, I had really a detectaphone. But this is even better. You see how neat it all is? This is the detective service, and more. We can 'listen in' and we don't have to use ear-pieces, either, for this is a regular loud-speaking telephone—it talks right out in meeting. Those square holes with the converging sides act as a sort of megaphone to the receivers, those little circles back there inside magnifying the sound and throwing it out here in the room, so that we can hear just as well as if we were up there in the room where they are talking. Listen—I think they are talking again."

"I suppose you know that Whitney and I have placed detectives on the trail of Norton," we could hear Lockwood say.

"You have?" came back the answer in a voice which for the first time sounded cold.

Lockwood must have recognized it. He had made a mistake. It was no sufficient answer to anything that he had done to assert that some one else had also done something.

"Inez," he said, and we could almost hear his feet as he moved over the floor in her direction in a last desperate appeal, "can't you trust me, when I tell you that everything is all right, that they are trying to ruin me—with you?"

There was a silence, during which we could almost hear her quick breath come and go.

"Women—not even Peruvian women are like the women of the past, Chester," she said at length. "We are not playthings. Perhaps we have hearts—but we also have heads. We are not to be taken up and put down as you please. We may love—but we also think. Chester, I have been to see Professor Kennedy, and—"

She stopped. It hurt too much to repeat what she had seen.

"Inez," he implored.

There was evidently a great struggle of love and suspicion going on in her, her love of him, her memory of her father, the recollection of what she had heard and seen. No one could have been as we were without wishing to help her. Yet no one could help her. She must work out her own life herself.

"Yes," she said finally, the struggle ended. "What is it?"

"Do you want me to tell you the truth?"

"Yes," she murmured.

His voice was low and tense.

"I was there—yes—but the dagger was gone!"

XVII

THE VOICE FROM THE AIR

"Do you believe it?" I asked Kennedy, as the voices died away, leaving us with a feeling that some one had gone out of the very room in which we were.

He shrugged his shoulders and said nothing. But I cannot say that he seemed ill pleased at the result of the interview.

"We'll just keep this vocaphone in," he remarked. "It may come in handy some time. Now, I think we had better go back to the laboratory! Things have begun to move."

On the way back he stopped to telephone Norton to meet us and a few minutes after we arrived, the archaeologist entered.

Kennedy lost no time in coming directly to the point, and Norton could see, in fact seemed to expect and be prepared for what was coming.

"Well," exclaimed Kennedy, "you've done it, this time!"

"I know what you are going to ask," returned Norton. "You are going to ask me why I did it. And I'm going to tell you.

After I left you, the other day, I thought about it a long time. The more I thought, the more of a shame it seemed to me that a girl like that should be made a victim of her feelings. It wasn't so much what they have done to me that made me do it. I would have acted the same if it had been de Moche instead of Lockwood who was playing on her heart. I was afraid, to tell the truth, that you wouldn't tell her until it was too late. And she's too good to throw herself away and allow her fortune to be wasted by a couple of speculators."

"Very well," said Craig. "For the sake of argument, let us admit all that. What did you expect to accomplish by it?"

"Why—put an end to it, of course."

"But do you think she was going to accept as truth what you told her? Would that be natural for one so high-strung?"

"Perhaps not—right away. But I supposed she would come to you—as I see she has, for you know about it. After that, it was only a question of time. It may have been a heroic remedy, but the disease was critical."

"Suppose," suggested Craig, "that, after all, he told her that he was there in the Museum, but that he did not get the dagger. And suppose that she believed it. What then?"

Norton looked up quickly. "Did he tell her that?"

"I am supposing that he did," repeated Craig, declining to place himself in a position which might lead to disclosing how he found out.

"Then I should say that he was a great deal cleverer than I gave him credit for being," returned Norton.

"Well, it's done now, and can't be undone. Have you found out anything about the de Moches?"

"Not very much, I must admit. Of course, you know I'm not on the best of terms with them, for some reason or other. But I've been around the Prince Edward Albert a good deal, and I don't think they've been able to do much that I haven't some kind of line on. Alfonso seems to be moping. His professors here tell me that he has been neglecting his work sadly for the past few days. The Senora and Whitney seem to be as friendly as ever. I should say that they were going the pace fast, and it shows on him."

I glanced significantly at Kennedy, but he betrayed nothing that might lead one to suppose he had discovered the cause. Evidently he was not ready yet to come out into the open and expected further developments on the poisoned cigarette clue.

The telephone rang and Craig took down the receiver.

"Yes, this is Kennedy," he answered. "Oh, hello, Lockwood. What's that? You've been trying to get me all day? I just came in. Why, yes, I can see you in about half an hour."

"I guess I'd better clear out," said Norton with a bitter laugh, as Kennedy hung up the receiver. "There have been enough crimes committed without adding another murder to the list."

"Keep on watching the de Moches," requested Kennedy as Norton made his way to the door.

"Yes," agreed Norton. "They will bear it—particularly Alfonso. They are hot-blooded. You never know what they are going to do, and they keep their own counsel. I might hope that Lockwood would forget; but a de Moche—never."

I cannot say that I envied him very much, for doubtless what he said was true, though his danger might be mitigated by the fact that the dagger was no longer in his Museum. Still, it would never have left Peru, I reflected, if it had not been for him, and there is, even in the best of us, a smouldering desire for revenge.

Lockwood was more than prompt. I had expected that he would burst into the laboratory prepared to clean things out. Instead he came in as though nothing at all had happened.

"There's no use mincing words, Kennedy," he began. "You know that I know what has happened. That scoundrel, Norton, has told Inez that you had shoe-prints of some one who was in the Museum the night of the robbery and that those shoe-prints correspond with mine. As a matter of fact, Kennedy, I was there. I was there to get the dagger. But before I could get it, some one else must have done so. It was gone."

I wanted to believe Lockwood. As for Craig he said nothing.

"Then, when I did have a chance to get away that night," he continued, "I went over to Mendoza's. The rest you know."

"You have told Inez that?" asked Kennedy in order to seem properly surprised.

"Yes—and I think she believes me. I can't say. Things are strained with her. It will take time. I'm not one of those who can take a girl by main force and make her do what she won't do. I wish I could smooth things over. Let me see the prints."

Kennedy handed them over to him. He looked at them, long and closely, then handed back the damning evidence against himself.

Arthur B. Reeve

"I know it would be no use to destroy these," he remarked. "In the first place that would really incriminate me. And in the second I suppose you have copies."

Craig smiled blandly.

"But I can tell you," he exclaimed, bringing his fist down on the laboratory table with a bang, "that before I lose that girl, somebody will pay for it—and there won't be any mistakes made, either."

The scowl on his face and the menacing look in his eye showed that now, with his back up against the wall, he was not bluffing.

He seemed to get little satisfaction out of his visit to us, and in fact I think he made it more in a spirit of bravado than anything else.

Lockwood had scarcely gone before Kennedy pulled out the University schedule, and ran his finger down it.

"Alfonso ought to be at a lecture in the School of Mines," he said finally, folding up the paper. "I wish you'd go over and see if he is there, and, if he is, ask him to step into the laboratory."

The lecture was in progress all right, but when I peered into the room it was evident that de Moche was not there. Norton was right. The young man was neglecting his work. Evidently the repeated rebuffs of Inez had worked havoc with him.

Nor was he at the hotel, as we found out by calling up.

There was only one other place that I could think of where

he would be likely to be and that was at the apartment of Inez. Apparently the same idea occurred to Kennedy, for he suggested going back to our observation point in the boarding-house and finding out.

All the rest of the day we listened through the vocaphone, but without finding out a thing of interest. Now and then we would try the detective instrument, the little black disc in the back, but with no better success. Then we determined to listen in relays, one listening, while the other went out for dinner.

It must have been just a bit after dark that we could hear Inez talking in a low tone with Juanita.

A buzzing noise indicated that there was some one at the hall door.

"If it's any one for me," we heard Inez say, "tell them that I will be out directly. I'm not fit to be seen now."

The door was opened and a voice which we could not place asked for the senorita. A moment later Juanita returned and asked the visitor to be seated a few moments.

It was not long before we were suddenly aware that there was another person in the room. We could hear whispers. The faithful little vocaphone even picked them up and shot them down to us.

"Is everything all right?" whispered one, a new voice which was somewhat familiar I thought, but disguised beyond recognition.

"Yes. She'll be out in a minute."

"Now, remember what I told you. If this thing works you get fifty dollars more. I'd better put this mask on—damn it!—the slit's torn. It'll do. I'll hide here as soon as we hear her. That's a pretty nice private ambulance you have down there. Did you tell the elevator boy that she had suddenly been taken ill? That's all fixed, then. I've got the stuff—amyl nitrite—she'll go off like a shot. But we'll have to work quick. It only keeps her under a few minutes. I can't wear this mask down and I'm afraid some one will recognize me. Oh, you brought a beard. Good. I'll give you the signal. There must be no noise. Yes, I saw the stretcher where you left it in the hall."

"All right, Doc," returned the first and unfamiliar voice.

It all happened so quickly that we were completely bowled over for the moment. Who was the man addressed as "Doc"? There was no time to find out, no time to do anything, apparently, so quickly had the plot been sprung.

I looked at Kennedy, aghast, not knowing what to do in this unexpected crisis.

A moment later we heard a voice, "I'm sorry to have had to keep you waiting, but what is it that I can do for you?"

"Good God!" exclaimed Kennedy. "It is Inez herself!"

It was altogether too late to get over there to warn her, perhaps even to rescue her. What could we do? If we could only shout for help. But what good would that do, around a corner and so far away?

The vocaphone itself!

Quickly Kennedy turned another switch, of a rheostat, which accentuated a whisper to almost a shout.

"Don't be alarmed, Senorita," he cried. "This is Kennedy talking. Look under the bookcase by the window. You will find a cedar box. It is a detective vocaphone through which I can hear you and which is talking out to you. I have heard something just there just now - "

"Yes, yes. Go on!"

"You are threatened. Shout! Shout!"

Just then there came a sound of a scuffle and a muffled cry which was not much above a whisper, as though a strong hand was clapped over her mouth.

What could we do?

"Juanita—Juanita—help!—police!" shouted Craig himself through the vocaphone.

An instant later we could hear other screams as Juanita heard and spread the alarm, not a second too soon.

"Come on, Walter," shouted Kennedy dashing out of the room, now that he was assured the alarm had been given.

We hurried around the corner, and into the apartment. One of the elevators was up, and no one was running the other, but we opened the gates and Kennedy ran it up by himself.

In the Mendoza apartment all was a babel of voices, every one talking at once.

"Did you get them?" Craig asked, looking about.

"No, sir, replied the elevator boy. "One of them came in from the ambulance and told me Miss Mendoza was suddenly taken sick. He rode up with the stretcher. The other one must have walked up."

"Do you know him? Has he ever been here before?"

"I can't say, sir. I didn't see him. At least, sir, when I heard the screams I ran in from the elevator, which the other one told me to wait with—left the door open. Just as I ran in, they dodged out past me, jumped into the car and rode down. I guess they must have had the engine of the ambulance motor running, sir, if they got away without you seeing them."

We were too late to head them from speeding off. But, at least, we had saved the Senorita. She was terribly upset by the attack, much shaken, but really all right.

"Have you any idea who it could be?" asked Craig as the faithful Juanita cared for her.

"I don't know the man who was waiting and 'Nita never saw him, either," she replied. "The one who jumped out from behind the portieres had on a mask and a false beard. But I didn't recognize anything about him."

Sudden as the attack had been and serious as might have been the outcome, we could not but feel happy that it had been frustrated.

Yet it seemed that some one ought to be delegated to see that such a thing could not occur again.

"We must think up some means of protecting you," soothed Kennedy. "Let me see, Mr. Lockwood and Mr. Whitney seem to be the closest to you. If you don't mind I'll call them up. I wonder if you'd object if we had a little luncheon up here, to-morrow? I have a special reason for asking it. I want to insure your safety and we may as well meet on common ground."

"There isn't the slightest objection in the world," she replied, as Kennedy reached for the telephone.

We had some little difficulty in locating both Lockwood and Whitney, but finally after a time managed to find them and arrange for the conference on the Senorita's safety for the next day.

Outside Kennedy gave instructions to the officer on the beat to watch the apartment particularly, and there was no reason now to fear a repetition of the attempt, at least that night.

XVIII

THE ANTIDOTE

Early the following morning Kennedy left me alone in the laboratory and made a trip downtown, where he visited a South American tobacco dealer and placed a rush order for a couple of hundred cigarettes exactly similar in shape and quality to those which Mendoza had smoked and which the others seemed also to prefer, except, however, that the deadly drug was left out.

While he was gone, it occurred to me to take up again the hunt for Alfonso. Norton was not in his little office, nor could I find Alfonso anywhere about the campus. In fact he seemed to have almost dropped out of his University work for the time. Accordingly, I turned my steps toward the Prince Edward Albert Hotel, in the hope that he might be there.

Inquiries of the clerk at the desk told me that he had been there, but was out just at that moment. I did not see Whitney around, nor the Senora, so I sat down to wait, having nothing better to do until Kennedy's return.

I was about to give it up and go, when I heard a cab drive up to the door and, looking up, I saw Alfonso get out. He saw me about the same time and we bowed. I do not think he even tried to avoid me.

"I haven't seen you for some time," I remarked, searching his face, which seemed to me to be paler than it had been.

"No," he replied. "I haven't been feeling very well lately and I've been running up into the country now and then to a quiet hotel—a sort of rest cure, I suppose you would call it. How are you? How is Senorita Inez?"

"Very well," I replied, wondering whether he had said what he did in the hope of establishing a complete alibi for the events of the night before.

Briefly I told him what had happened, omitting reference to the vocaphone and our real part in it.

"That is terrible," he exclaimed. "Oh, if she would only allow me to take care of her—I would take her back to our own country, where she would be safe, far away from these people who seek to prey on all of us."

He paced up and down nervously, and I could see that my information had added nothing to his peace of mind, though, at the same time, he had betrayed nothing on his part.

"I was just passing through," I said finally, looking at my watch, "and happened to see you. I hope your mother is well?"

"As well as is to be expected, surrounded by people who watch every act," he replied, I thought with a rap at us for having Norton about and so active, though I could not be sure.

Arthur B. Reeve

We separated, and I hastened back to the laboratory to report to Craig that Alfonso was rusticating for his health.

Kennedy, on his part, had had an experience, though it was no more conclusive than my own. After he had left the tobacco district, he had walked up Wall Street to the subway. In the crowd he had seen Senora de Moche, although she had not seen him. He had turned and followed her until she entered the building in which Whitney and his associates had their offices. Whether it indicated that she was still leading them a chase, or they her, was impossible to determine, but it at least showed that they were still on friendly terms with each other.

In the laboratory he could always find something to do on the case, either in perfecting his chemical tests of the various drugs we had discovered, or in trying to decipher some similarities in the rough printing of the four warnings and the anonymous letter with the known handwriting of those connected with the case, many specimens of which he bad been quietly collecting. That in itself was a tremendously minute job, entailing not only a vast amount of expert knowledge such as he had collected in his years of studying crime scientifically, but the most exact measurements and careful weighing and balancing of trifles, which to the unscientific conveyed no meanings at all. Still, he seemed to be forging ahead, though he never betrayed what direction the evidence seemed to be taking.

The package of cigarettes which he had ordered downtown was delivered about an hour after his return and seemed to be the signal for him to drop work, for the meeting with Lockwood and Whitney had been set early. He stowed the package in his pockets and then went over to a cabinet in which he kept a number of rather uncommon drugs. From it he took a little vial which he shoved into his waistcoat pocket.

"Are you ready, Walter?" he asked.

"Whenever you are," I said, laying aside my writing.

Together we made our way down to the Mendoza apartment which had been the scene of the near-tragedy the night before. Outside, he paused for several moments to make inquiries about any suspicious persons that might have been seen lurking about the neighbourhood. None of the attendants in the apartment remembered having seen any, and they were now very alert after the two events, the murder and the attempted abduction. Not a clue seemed to have been left by the villain who had been called "Doc."

"How do you feel after your thrilling experience?" greeted Craig pleasantly, as Juanita admitted us and Inez came forward.

"Oh, Mr. Kennedy," she answered, with a note of sadness in her tone. "It makes me feel so alone in the world. If it were not for 'Nita—and you, I don't know what I should do."

"Doesn't Mr. Lockwood count?" asked Kennedy observantly.

"Of course—everything," she answered hastily. "But he has to be away so much on business, and—"

She paused and sighed. I could not help wondering whether, after all, his explanation of the dagger episode had been enough to satisfy her. Had she really accepted it?

Neither Lockwood nor Whitney had arrived, and Kennedy improved the opportunity to have a quiet talk aside with her, at which, I imagine, he was arranging a programme of what was to happen at this meeting and her part in it to co-operate with him.

She had left the room for a moment and we were alone. It was evidently a part of his plan, for no sooner was she gone than he opened the package of cigarettes which he had ordered and took out from the box in which Mendoza had kept his cigarettes those that were there, substituting those he had brought.

We had not long to wait, now. Lockwood and Whitney came together. I was interested to see the greeting of Inez and her lover. Was it pure fancy, or did I detect a trace of coldness as though there had sprung up something between them? As far as Lockwood was concerned, I felt sure that he was eager to break down any barrier that kept them from being as they had been.

Whitney took her hand and held it, in a playful sort of way. "I wish I were a young buck," he smiled. "No one would dare look at you—much less try to carry you off. Yes, we must be more careful of our little beauty, or we shall lose her."

They turned to greet us. I felt, as we shook hands, that it was much the same sort of handshake that one sees in the prize ring—to be followed by the clang of a bell, then all going to it, in battle royal, with the devil after the hindmost.

There was scarcely a chance for a preliminary bout before luncheon was announced, and we entered the cozy little dining-room to seat ourselves at the daintiest of tables. One could feel the hostess radiating hospitality, even on such a cross-current set of guests as we were, and for the time, I almost felt that it had been Kennedy's purpose to promote a love-feast instead of an armed truce.

Nothing was said about the main cause of our being together for some time, and the small talk almost lifted for a time the incubus that had settled down on all our lives since the tragedy in the den at the other end of the suite. But the fact could not be blinked.

Tacitly every one seemed to wait on Kennedy to sound the gong. Finally he did so.

"Of course," he began, clearing his throat, "there is no use making believe about anything. I think we all understand each other better now than we have ever done before. As for me, I am in this case under a promise to stick to it and fight it to the end. I suppose the rest of you are, also. But that need not prevent us agreeing on one thing. We can work together to protect Senorita Mendoza, at least, from such danger as threatened her last night."

"It's a dastardly shame," Lockwood exclaimed angrily, "that a man who would attempt a thing like that should go unpunished." "Show me how to trace him and I'll guarantee the punishment," rejoined Craig drily.

"I am not a detective," replied Lockwood.

Kennedy forebore to reply in kind, though I knew there was a ready answer on his tongue for the lover.

Ever since they had arrived, the Senorita had seen that they were well supplied with cigarettes from the case in which she and they supposed were the genuine South American brand of her father. Kennedy and I smoked them, too, although neither of us liked them very much. The others were smoking furiously.

"However," resumed Kennedy, "I do not feel that I want to intrude myself in this matter without being perfectly frank and having the approval of Senorita Mendoza. She has

Arthur B. Reeve

known both of you longer and more intimately than she has known me, although she has seen fit to place certain of her affairs in my hands, for which I trust I shall render a good account of my stewardship. It seems to me, though, that if there is, as we now know there is, some one whom we do not know"—he paused—"who has sunk so low as to wish to carry her off, apparently where she shall be out of the influence of her friends, it is only right that precautions should be taken to prevent it."

"What is your suggestion?" demanded Whitney, rather contentiously.

"Would there be any objection," asked Kennedy, "if I should ask my old friend,—or any of you may do it,—Deputy Commissioner O'Connor to detail a plainclothesman to watch this house and neighbourhood, especially at night?"

We watched the faces of the others. But it was really of no use.

"I think that is an excellent plan," decided Inez herself. "I shall feel much safer and surely none of you can be jealous of the city detectives."

Kennedy smiled. She had cut the Gordian knot with a blow. Neither Lockwood nor Whitney could object. The purpose of the luncheon was accomplished.

In fact he did not wait for further consideration, but excused himself from the table for a moment to call up our old friend O'Connor and tell him how gravely his man was needed. It was a matter of only a few minutes when he returned from the other room.

"He will detail Burke for this special service as long as we want him," reported Craig, sitting down again.

Inez was delighted, naturally, for the affair had been a terrific shock to her. I could see how relieved she felt, for I was sitting directly next to her.

The maid had, meanwhile brought in the coffee and Inez had been waiting to pour until Kennedy returned. She did not do so, now, either, however. It seemed as if she were waiting for some kind of signal from Kennedy.

"What a splendid view of the park you get here," remarked Kennedy turning toward the long, low windows that opened on a balustraded balcony. "Just look at that stream of automobiles passing on the west drive."

Common politeness dictated that all should turn and look, although there was no novelty in the sight for any of us.

As I have said, I was sitting next to Inez. To me she was a far more attractive sight than any view of the park. I barely looked out of the window. Imagine my surprise, then, at seeing her take advantage of the diversion to draw from the folds of her dress a little vial and pour a bit of yellowish, syrupy liquid into the cup of coffee which she was preparing for Whitney.

I could not help looking at her quickly. She saw that I had seen her and raised her other hand with a finger to her lips and an explanatory glance at Kennedy who was keeping the others interested. Instantly, I recognized the little vial which Craig had shoved into his waistcoat pocket. That had been the purpose of his whispered conference with her when we arrived. I said nothing, but determined to observe more closely.

Arthur B. Reeve

More coffee and more cigarettes followed, always from the same box which was now on the table. The luncheon developed almost a real conversation. For the time, under the spell of our hostess, we nearly forgot that we were in reality bitter enemies.

My real interest, as time passed, centred in Whitney and I could not help watching him closely. Was it a fact, or was it merely my imagination? He seemed quite different. The pupils of his eyes did not seem to be quite so dilated as they had been at other times, or even when he arrived. Even his heart action appeared to be more normal. I think Inez noticed it, too. There was none of the wildness in his conversation, such as there often had been at other times.

Our party was prolonged beyond the time we had expected, but, although he had much on his mind, Kennedy made no move to break it up. In fact he did everything to encourage it.

At last, however, the others did notice the time, and I think it was with sincere regret that the truce was broken. Even then, no parting shots were indulged in.

As we left, Inez thanked Kennedy for his consideration, and I am sure that that in itself was reward enough. We parted from Lockwood, who wished to remain a little while, and rode down in the elevator with Whitney, a changed man.

"I'll walk over to the elevated with you," he said. "I was going to my hotel, but I think I'll go down to the office instead."

Evidently he had got Senora de Moche out of his mind, at least temporarily, I thought. Then for the first time I recalled that during the whole luncheon there had been no reference to either the Senora or Alfonso, though both must have been in our minds often.

"What was it you had Inez drop into Whitney's coffee?" I asked Craig as we parted from him and rode uptown.

"You saw that?" he smiled. "It was pilocarpine, jaborandi, a plant found largely in Brazil, one of the antidotes for stramonium poisoning. It doesn't work with every one. But it seems to have done so with him. Besides, the caffeine in the coffee probably aided the pilocarpine. Then, too, I made them smoke cigarettes without the dope that is being fed them. Lockwood's case, for some reason, hasn't gone far. But did you notice how the treatment contracted the pupils of Whitney's eyes almost back to normal again?"

I had and said so, adding, "But what was your idea?"

"I think I've got at the case from a brand-new angle," he replied. "Unless I am greatly mistaken, when the person who is doing the doping sees that Whitney is getting better—why, I think you all noticed it, Inez and Lockwood as well as you—it will mean another attempt to substitute more cigarettes doped with that drug. I think it's by substitution that it's being done. We'll see."

At the laboratory, Kennedy called Norton and described briefly what had happened, especially to Whitney.

"Now is your chance, Norton," he added, "to do some real good work. I want some one to watch the Senora, see if she, too, notes the difference in him. Understand?"

"Perfectly," returned Norton. "That is something I think I can do."

Arthur B. Reeve

XIX

THE BURGLAR POWDER

It was not until after dinner that we heard again from Norton. He had evidently spent the time faithfully hanging about the Prince Edward Albert, but Whitney had not come in, although the Senora and Alfonso were about.

"I saw them leaving the dining-room," he reported to us in the laboratory directly afterward, "just as Whitney came in. They could not see me. I took good care of that. But, say, there is a change in Whitney, isn't there? I wonder what caused it?"

"It's as noticeable as that?" asked Kennedy. "And did she notice it?"

"I'm sure of it," replied Norton confidently. "She couldn't help it. Besides, after he left her and went into the dining-room himself she and Alfonso seemed to be discussing something. I'm sure it was that."

Kennedy said nothing, except to thank Norton and compliment him on his powers of observation. Norton took the praise with evident satisfaction, and after a moment excused himself, saying that he had some work to do over in the Museum.

He had no sooner gone than Kennedy took from a drawer a little packet of powder and an atomizer full of liquid, which he dropped into his pocket.

"I think the Prince Edward Albert will be the scene of our operations, to-night, Walter," he announced, reaching for his hat.

He seemed to be in a hurry and it was not many minutes before we entered. As he passed the dining-room he glanced in. There was Whitney, not half through a leisurely dinner. Neither of the de Moches seemed to be downstairs.

Kennedy sauntered over to the desk and looked over the register. We already knew that Whitney and the Senora had suites on the eighth floor, on opposite sides and at opposite ends of the hall. The de Moche suite was under the number 810. That of Whitney was 825.

"Is either 823 or 827 vacant?" asked Kennedy as the clerk came over to us.

He turned to look over his list. "Yes, 827 is vacant," he found.

"I'd like to have it," said Kennedy, making some excuse about our luggage being delayed, as he paid for it for the night.

"Front!" called the clerk, and a moment later we found ourselves in the elevator riding up.

The halls were deserted at that time in the evening except for a belated theatre-goer, and in a few minutes there would ensue a period in which there was likely to be no one about.

Arthur B. Reeve

We entered the room next to Whitney's without being observed by any one of whom we cared. The boy left us, and it was a simple matter after that to open a rather heavy door that communicated between the two suites and was not protected by a Yale lock.

Instead of switching on the lights, Kennedy first looked about carefully until he was assured that there was no one there. It seemed to me to be an unnecessary caution, for we knew Whitney was down-stairs and would probably be there a long time. But he seemed to think it necessary. Positive that we were alone, he made a hasty survey of the rooms. Then he seemed to select as a starting-point a table in one corner of the sitting-room on which lay a humidor and a heavy metal box for cigarettes.

Quickly he sprinkled on the floor, from the hall door to the table on which the case of cigarettes lay, some of the powder which I had seen him wrap up in the laboratory before we left. Then, with the atomizer, he sprayed over it something that had a pungent, familiar odour—walking backwards from the hall door to the table, as he sprayed.

"Don't you want more light?" I asked, starting to cross to a window to let the moonlight stream in.

"Don't walk on it, Walter," he whispered, pushing me back. "No, I don't need any more light."

"What are you doing?" I asked, mystified at his actions.

"First I sprinkled some powdered iodine on the floor," he replied, "and then sprayed over just enough ammonia to moisten it. It will evaporate quickly, leaving what I call my anti-burglar powder."

"I'm sure I wouldn't be thought one of the fraternity for the world," I observed, stepping aside to give him all the room he wanted in which to operate.

He had finished his work by this time and now the evening wind was blowing away the slight fumes that had arisen. For a few moments he left our door into Whitney's room open, in order to insure clearing away the odour. Then he quietly closed it, but did not lock it again.

We waited a few minutes, then Craig leaned over to me. "I wish you'd go down and see how near Whitney is through dinner," he said. "If he is through, do something, anything to keep him down there. Only be as careful as you can not to be seen by any one who knows us."

I rode down in an empty elevator and cautiously made my way to the dining-room. Whitney had finished much sooner than I had expected and was not there. Much as I wanted not to be seen, I found that it was necessary to make a tour of the hotel to find him and I did so, wondering what expedient I would adopt to keep him down there if I found him. I did not have to adopt any, however. Whitney was almost alone in the writing-room, and a big pile of letters beside him showed me that he would be busy for some time. I rode back to the room to tell Craig, flattering myself that I had not been seen.

"Good," he exclaimed. "I don't think we'll have to wait much longer, if anything at all is going to happen."

In the darkness we settled ourselves for another vigil that was to last we knew not how long. Neither of us spoke as we half crouched in the shadow of our room, listening.

Slowly the time passed. Would any one take advantage of the opportunity to tamper with the box of cigarettes on the table?

I fell to speculating. Who could it possibly have been that had conceived this devilish plot? What was back of it all? I wondered whether it were possible that Lockwood, now that Mendoza was out of the way, could desire to remove Whitney, the sole remaining impediment to possessing the whole of the treasure as well as Inez? Then there were the Senora and Alfonso, the one with a deep race and family grievance, the other a rejected suitor. What might not they do with some weird South American poison?

Once or twice we heard the elevator door clang and waited expectantly, but nothing happened. I began to wonder whether, even if some one had a pass-key to the suite, we could hear him enter if he was quiet. The outside hall was thickly carpeted, and deadened every footfall if one exercised only reasonable care. The rooms themselves were much the same.

"Don't you think we might have the door ajar a little?" I suggested anxiously.

"Sh!" was Kennedy's only comment in the negative.

I glanced now and then at my watch and by straining my eyes was surprised to see how early it was yet. The minutes were surely leaden-footed.

In the darkness, I fell again to reviewing the weird succession of events. I am not by nature superstitious, but in the black silence I could well imagine a staring succession of eyes, beginning with the dilated pupils of Whitney and passing on to the corpse-like expression of Mendoza, but always ending with the remarkable, piercing, black eyes of the Indian woman with the melancholy-visaged son, as they had impressed me the first time I saw them and, in fact, ever since. Was it a freak of my mind, or was there some reason for it?

Suddenly I heard in the next room what sounded like a series of little explosions, as though some one were treading on match heads.

"My burglar powder works," muttered Craig to me in a hoarse whisper. "Every step, even those of a mouse running across, sets it off!"

He rose quickly and threw open the door into Whitney's suite. I sprang after him.

There, in the shadows, I saw a dark form, starting back in quick retreat. But we were too late. He was cat-like, too quick for us.

In the dim light of the little explosions we could catch a glimpse of the person who had been craftily working with the dread drug to drive Whitney and others insane. But the face was masked!

He banged shut the door after him and fled down the hall, making a turn to a flight of steps.

We followed, and at the steps paused a moment. "You go up, Walter," shouted Kennedy. "I'll go down."

It was fifteen minutes later before we met downstairs, neither of us with a trace of the intruder. He seemed to have vanished like smoke.

"Must have had a room, like ourselves," remarked Craig somewhat chagrined at the outcome of his scheme. "And if he was clever enough to have a room, he is clever enough to have a disguise that would fool the elevator boys for a minute. No, he has gone. But I'll wager he won't try any more substitutions of stramonium-poisoned cigarettes for a while. It was too close to be comfortable."

We were baffled again, and this time by a mysterious masked man. Could it be the same whom we heard over the vocaphone addressed as "Doc"? Perhaps it was, but that gave us no hint as to his identity. He seemed just as far away as ever.

We waited around the elevators for some time, but nothing happened. Kennedy even sought out the manager of the hotel, and after telling who he was, had a search made of the guests who might be suspected. The best we could do was to leave word that the employees might be put on the lookout for anything of a suspicious nature.

Whitney, the innocent cause of all this commotion, was still in the writing-room with his letters.

"I think I ought to tell him," decided Kennedy as we passed down the lobby.

He seemed surprised to see us, as we strolled up to his writing desk, but pushed aside the few letters which he had not finished and asked us to sit down.

"I don't know whether you have noticed it," began Craig, "but I wonder how you feel?"

Whitney had expected something else rather than his health as the subject of a quiz. "Pretty good now," he answered before he knew it, "although I must admit that for the past few days I have wondered whether I wasn't slowing up a bit—or rather going too fast."

"Would you like to know why you feel that way?" asked Craig.

Whitney was now genuinely puzzled. It was perfectly evident, as it had been all the time, that he had not the slightest inkling of what was going on.

As Craig briefly unfolded what we had discovered and the reason for it, Whitney watched him aghast.

"Poisoned cigarettes," he repeated slowly. "Well, who would ever have thought it. You can bet your last jitney I'll be careful what I smoke in the future, if I have to smoke only original packages. And it was that, partly, that ailed Mendoza?"

Kennedy nodded. "Don't take any pilocarpine, just because I told you that was what I used. You have given yourself the best prescription, just now. Be careful what you smoke. And, don't get excited if you seem to be stepping on matches up there in your room for a little while, either. It's nothing."

Whitney's only known way of thanking anybody was to invite them to adjourn to the cafe, and accordingly we started across the hall, after he had gathered up his correspondence. The information had made more work that night impossible for him.

As we crossed from the writing-room, we saw Alfonso de Moche coming in from the street. He saw us and came over to speak. Was it a coincidence, or was it merely a blind? Was he the one who had got away and now calculated to come back and throw us off guard?

Whitney asked him where he had been, but he replied quickly that his mother had not been feeling very well after dinner and had gone to bed, while he strolled out and had dropped into a picture show. That, I felt, was at least clever. The intruder had been a man.

Arthur B. Reeve

De Moche excused himself, and we continued our walk to the cafe, where Whitney restored his shattered peace of mind somewhat.

"What's the result of your detective work on Norton?" ventured Kennedy at last, seeing that Whitney was in a more expansive frame of mind, and taking a chance.

"Oh," returned Whitney, "he's scared, all right. Why, he has been hanging around this hotel—watching me. He thinks I don't know it, I suppose, but I do."

Kennedy and I exchanged glances.

"But he's slippery," went on Whitney. "He knows that he is being shadowed and the men tell me that they lose him, now and then. To tell the truth I don't trust most of these private detectives. I think their little tissue paper reports are half-faked, anyhow."

He seemed to want to say no more on the subject, from which I took it that he had discovered nothing of importance.

"One thing, though," he recollected, after a moment. "He has been going to see Inez Mendoza, they tell me."

"Yes?" queried Kennedy.

"Confound him. He pretty nearly got Lockwood in bad with her, too," said Whitney, then leaning over confidentially added, "Say, Kennedy, honestly, now, you don't believe that shoe-print stuff, do you?"

"I see no reason to doubt it," returned Kennedy with diplomatic firmness. "Why?"

"Well," continued Whitney, still confidential, "we haven't got the dagger—that's all. There—I never actually asserted that before, though I've given every one to understand that our plans are based on something more than hot-air. We haven't got it, and we never had it."

"Then who has it?" asked Kennedy colourlessly.

Whitney shook his head. "I don't know," he said merely.

"And these attacks on you—this cigarette business—how do you explain that," asked Craig, "if you haven't the dagger?"

"Jealousy, pure jealousy," replied Whitney quickly. "They are so afraid that we will find the treasure. That's my dope."

"Who is afraid?"

"That's a serious matter," he evaded. "I wouldn't say anything that I couldn't back up in a case of that kind. I'd get into trouble."

There was nothing to be gained by prolonging the conversation and Kennedy made a move as though to go.

"Just give us a square deal," said Whitney as we left. "That's all we want—a square deal."

Kennedy and I walked out of the Prince Edward Albert and turned down the block.

"Well, have you found out anything more?" asked a voice in the shadow beside us.

We turned. It was Norton.

"I saw you talking to Whitney in the writing-room," he said, with a laugh, "then in the cafe, and I saw Alfonso come in. He still has those shadows on me. I wouldn't be surprised if there was one of them around in a doorway, now."

"No," returned Kennedy, "he didn't say anything that was important. They still say they haven't the dagger."

"Of course," said Norton.

"You'll wait around a little longer?" asked Kennedy as we came to a corner and stopped.

"I think so," returned Norton. "I'll keep you posted."

Kennedy and I walked on a bit.

"I'm going around to see how Burke, O'Connor's man, is getting on watching the Mendoza apartment, Walter," he said at length. "Then I have two or three other little outside matters to attend to. You look tired. Why don't you go home and take a rest? I shan't be working in the laboratory to-night, either."

"I think I will," I agreed, for the strain of the case was beginning to tell on me.

XX

THE PULMOTOR

I went directly to our apartment after Craig left me and for a little while sat up, speculating on the probabilities of the case.

Senora de Moche had told us of her ancestor who had been intrusted with the engraved dagger, of how it had been handed down, of the death of her brother; she had told us of the murder of the ancestor of Inez Mendoza, of the curse of Mansiche. Was this, after all, but a reincarnation of the bloody history of the Gold of the Gods?

There were the shoe-prints in the mummy case. They were Lockwood's. How about them? Was he telling the truth? Now had come the poisoned cigarettes. All had followed the threats:

BEWARE THE CURSE OF MANSICHE ON THE GOLD OF THE GODS.

Several times I had been forced already to revise my theories of the case. At first I had felt that it pointed straight toward Lockwood. But did it seem to do so now?

Arthur B. Reeve

Suppose Lockwood had stolen the dagger from the Museum, although he denied even that. Did that mean, necessarily that he committed the murder with it, that he now had it? Might he not have lost it? Might not some one else—the Senora, or Alfonso, or both—have obtained it? Might not Mendoza have been murdered with it by some other hand to obtain or to hide the secret on its bloody blade?

I went to bed, still thinking, no nearer a conclusion than before, prepared to dream over it.

That is the last I remember.

When I regained consciousness, I was lying on the bed still, but Craig was bending over me. He had just taken a rubber cap off my face, to which was attached a rubber tube that ran to a box perhaps as large as a suitcase, containing a pump of some kind.

I was too weak to notice these things right away, too weak to care much about them, or about anything else.

"Are you all right now, old man?" he asked, bending over me.

"Y-Yes," I gasped, clutching at the choking sensation in my throat. "What has happened?"

Perhaps I had best tell it as though I were not the chief actor; for it came to me in such disjointed fragmentary form, that it was some time before I could piece it together.

Craig had seen Burke, and had found that everything was all right. Then he had made the few little investigations that he intended. But he had not been to the laboratory. There had been no light there that night.

At last when he arrived home, he had found a peculiar odour in the hall, but had thought nothing of it, until he opened our door. Then there rushed out such a burst of it that he had to retreat, almost fainting, choking and gasping for breath.

His first thought was for me; and protecting himself as best he could he struggled through to my room, to find me lying on the bed, motionless, almost cold.

He was by this time too weak to carry me. But he managed to reach the window and throw it wide open. As the draught cleared the air, he thought of the telephone and with barely strength enough left called up one of the gas companies and had a pulmotor sent over.

Now that the danger was past for me, and he felt all right, his active mind began at once on the reconstruction of what had happened.

What was it—man or devil? Could a human fly have scaled the walls, or an aeroplane have dropped an intruder at the window ledge? The lock on the door did not seem to have been tampered with. Nor was there any way by which entrance could have been gained from a fire escape. It was not illuminating gas. Every one agreed on that. No, it was not an accident. It was an attempt at murder. Some one was getting close to us. Every other weapon failing, this was desperation.

I had been made comfortable, and he was engaged in one of his characteristic searches, with more than ordinary eagerness, because this was his own apartment, and it was I who had been the victim.

I followed him languidly as he went over everything, the furniture, the walls, the windows, the carpets—there looking for finger-prints, there for some trace of the poisonous gas that had filled the room. But he did not have the air of one who was finding anything. I was too tired to reason. This was but another of the baffling mysteries that confronted us.

A low exclamation caused me to open my eyes and try to discover what was the cause. He was bending over the lock of the door looking at it intently.

"Broken?" I managed to say.

"No—corroded," he replied. "You keep still. Save your energy. I've got strength enough for two, for a while."

He came over to the bed and bent over me. "I won't hurt you," he encouraged, "but just let me get a drop of your blood."

He took a needle and ran it gently into my thumb beside the nail. A drop or two of blood oozed out and he soaked it up with a piece of sterile gauze.

"Try to sleep," he said finally.

"And you?" I asked.

"It's no use. I'm going over to the laboratory. I can't sleep. There's a cop down in front of the house. You're safe enough. By George, if this case goes much further we'll have half the force standing guard. Here—drink that."

I had made up my mind not to go to sleep, if he wouldn't, but I slipped up when I obeyed him that time. I thought it was a stimulant but it turned out to be a sedative.

I did not wake up until well along in the morning, but when I did I was surprised to find myself so well. Before any one could stop me, I was dressed and had reached the door.

A friend of ours who had volunteered to stay with me was dozing on a couch as I came out.

"Too late, Johnson," I called, trying hard to be gay, though I felt anything but like it. "Thank you, old man, for staying with me. But I'm afraid to stop. You're stronger than I am this morning—and besides you can run faster. I'm afraid you'll drag me back."

He did try to do it, but with a great effort of will-power I persuaded him to let me go. Out in the open air, too, it seemed to do me good. The policeman who had been stationed before the house gazed at me as though he saw a ghost, then grinned encouragingly.

Still, I was glad that the laboratory was only a few blocks away, for I was all in by the time I got there, and hadn't even energy enough to reply to Kennedy's scolding.

He was working over a microscope, while by his side stood in racks, innumerable test-tubes of various liquids. On the table before him lay the lock of our door which he had cut out after he gave me the sleeping draught.

"What was it?" I asked. "I feel as if I had been on a bust, without the recollection of a thing."

He shook his head as if to discourage conversation, without taking his eyes off the microscope through which he was squinting. His lips were moving as if he were counting. I waited in impatient silence until he seemed to have finished.

Then, still without a word, he took up a test-tube and

dropped into it a little liquid from a bottle on a shelf above the table. His face lighted up, and he regarded the reaction attentively for some time. Then he turned to me, still holding the tube.

"You have been on a bust," he said with a smile as if the remark of a few minutes before were still fresh. "Only it was a laughing gas jag—nitrous oxide."

"Nitrous oxide?" I repeated. "How—what do you mean?"

"I mean simply that a test of your blood shows that you were poisoned by nitrous oxide gas. You remember the sample of blood which I squeezed from your thumb? I took it because I knew that a gas—and it has proved to be nitrous oxide—is absorbed through the lungs into the circulation and its presence can be told for a considerable period after administration."

He paused a moment, then went on: "To be specific in this case I found by microscopic examination that the number of corpuscles in your blood was vastly above the normal, something like between seven and eight million to a drop that should have had somewhat more than only half that number. You were poisoned by gas that—"

"Yes," I interrupted, "but how, with all the doors locked?"

"I was coming to that," he said quietly, picking up the lock and looking at it thoughtfully.

He had already placed it in a porcelain basin, and in this basin he had poured some liquids. Then he passed the liquids through a fine screen and at last took up a tube containing some of the resulting liquid.

"I have already satisfied myself," he explained, "but for your benefit, seeing that you're the chief sufferer, I'll run over a part of the test. You saw the reaction which showed the gas a moment ago. I have proved chemically as well as microscopically that it is present in your blood. Now if I take this test-tube of liquid derived from my treatment of the lock and then test it as you saw me do with the other, isn't that enough for you? See—it gives the same reaction."

It did, indeed, but my mind did not react with it.

"Nitrous oxide," he continued, "in contact with iron, leaves distinct traces of corrosion, discernible by chemical and microscopic tests quite as well as the marks it leaves in the human blood. Manifestly, if no one could have come in by the windows or doors, the gas must have been administered in some way without any one coming into the room. I found no traces of an intruder."

It was a tough one. Never much good at answering his conundrums when I was well, I could not even make a guess now.

"The key-hole, of course!" he explained. "I cut away the entire lock, and have submitted it to these tests which you see."

"I don't see it all yet," I said.

"Some one came to our door in the night, after gaining entrance to the hall—not a difficult thing to do, we know. That person found our door locked, knew it would be locked, knew that I always locked it. Knowing that such was the case, this person came prepared, bringing perhaps, a tank of compressed nitrous oxide, certainly the materials for making the gas expeditiously."

I began to understand how it had been done.

"Through the keyhole," he resumed, "a stream of the gas was injected. It soon rendered you unconscious, and that would have been all, if the person had been satisfied. A little bit would have been harmless enough. But the person was not satisfied. The intention was not to overcome, but to kill. The stream of gas was kept up until the room was full of it.

"Only my return saved you, for the gas was escaping very slowly. Even then, you had been under it so long that we had to resort to the wonderful little pulmotor after trying both the Sylvester and Schaefer methods and all other manual means to induce respiration. At any rate we managed to undo the work of this fiend."

I looked at him in surprise, I, who didn't think I had an enemy in the world.

"But who could it have been?" I asked.

"We are pretty close to that criminal," was the only reply he would give, "providing we do not spread the net in sight of the quarry."

"Why should he have wanted to get me?" I repeated.

"Don't flatter yourself," replied Craig. "He wanted me, too. There wasn't any light in the laboratory last night. There was a light in our apartment. What more natural than to think that we were both there? You were caught in the trap intended for both of us."

I looked at him, startled. Surely this was a most desperate criminal. To cover up one murder—perhaps two—he did not hesitate to attempt a third, a double murder. The attack had been really aimed at Kennedy. It had struck me alone. But it had miscarried and Craig had saved my life.

As I reflected bitterly, I had but one satisfaction. Wretched as I felt, I knew that it had spared Craig from slowing up on the case at just the time when he was needed.

The news of the attempt spread quickly, for it was a police case and got into the papers.

It was not half an hour after I reached the laboratory that the door was pushed open by Inez Mendoza, followed by a boy spilling with fruit and flowers like a cornucopia.

"I drove to the apartment," she cried, greatly excited and sympathetic, "but they told me you had gone out. Oh, I was glad to hear it. Then I knew it wasn't so serious. For, some-how, I feel guilty about it. It never would have happened if you hadn't met me."

"I'm sure it's worth more than it cost," I replied gallantly.

She turned toward Kennedy. "I'm positively frightened," she exclaimed. "First they direct their attacks against my father—then against me—now against you. What will it be next? Oh—it is that curse—it is that curse!"

"Never fear," encouraged Kennedy, "we'll get you out—we'll get all of us out, now, I should say. It's just because they are so desperate that we have these things. As long as there is nothing to fear a criminal will lie low. When he gets scared he does things. And it's when he does things that he begins to betray himself."

She shuddered. "I feel as though I was surrounded by enemies," she murmured. "It is as if an unseen evil power was watching over me all the time—and mocking me—striking down those I love and trust. Where will it end?"

Kennedy tried his best to soothe her, but it was evident that the attack on us could not have had more effect, if it had been levelled direct at her.

"Please, Senorita," he pleaded, "stand firm. We are going to win. Don't give in. The Mendozas are not the kind to stop defeated."

She looked at him, her eyes filled with tears.

"It was my father's way," she choked back her emotion. "How could you, a stranger, know?"

"I didn't know," returned Kennedy. "I gathered it from his face. It is also his daughter's way."

"Yes," she said, straightening up and the fire flashing from her eyes, "we are a proud, old, unbending race. Good-bye. I must not interrupt your work any longer. We are also a race that never forgets a friend."

A moment later she was gone.

"A wonderful woman," repeated Kennedy absently.

Then he turned again to his table of chemicals.

The telephone had begun to tinkle almost continuously by this time, as one after another of our friends called us up to know how we were getting on and be assured of our safety. In fact I didn't know that it was possible to resuscitate so many of them with a pulmotor.

"By George, I'm glad it wasn't any more serious," came Norton's voice from the doorway a moment later. "I didn't see a paper this morning. The curator of the Museum just told me. How did it happen?"

Kennedy tried to pass it off lightly, and I did the same, for as I was up longer I really did feel better.

Norton shook his head gravely, however.

"No," he said, "there were four of us got warnings. They are a desperate, revengeful people."

I looked at him quickly. Did he mean the de Moches?

XXI

THE TELESCRIBE

I decided that discretion was the better part of valour and that I had better go slow that day and regain my strength, a fortunate decision, as it turned out.

Kennedy, also, spent most of the time in the laboratory, so that, after all, I did not feel that I was missing very much.

It was along in the afternoon that the telephone began acting strangely, as it will do sometimes when a long distance connection is being made. Twice Kennedy answered, without getting any response.

"Confound that central," he muttered. "What do you suppose is the matter?"

Again the bell rang.

"Hello," shouted Kennedy, exasperated. "Who's this?"

There was a pause. "Just a minute," he replied.

Quickly he jammed the receiver down on a little metal base which he had placed near the instrument. Three prongs reaching upward from the base engaged the receiver tightly, fitting closely about it.

Then he took up a watch-case receiver to listen through in place of the regular receiver.

"Who is it?" he answered.

Apparently the voice at the other end of the wire replied rather peevishly, for Kennedy endeavoured to smooth over the delay. I wondered what was going on, why he was so careful. His face showed that, whatever it was, it was most important.

As he restored the telephone to its normal condition, he looked at me puzzled.

"I wonder whether that was a frame-up!" he exclaimed, pulling a little cylinder off the instrument into which he had inserted the telephone receiver. "I thought it might be and I have preserved the voice. This is what is known as the telescribe—a recent invention of Edison which records on a specially prepared phonograph cylinder all that is said—both ways—over a telephone wire."

"What was it about?" I asked eagerly.

He shoved the cylinder on a phonograph and started the instrument.

"Professor Kennedy?" called an unfamiliar voice.

"Yes," answered a voice that I recognized as Craig's.

"This is the detective agency employed by Mr. Whitney. He has instructed us to inform you that he has obtained the

Arthur B. Reeve

Peruvian dagger for which you have been searching. That's all. Good-bye."

I looked at Kennedy in blank surprise.

"They rang off before I could ask them a question," said Craig. "Central tells me it was a pay station call. There doesn't seem to be any way of tracing it. But, at least I have a record of the voice."

"What are you going to do?" I queried. "It may be a fake."

"Yes, but I'm going to investigate it. Do you feel strong enough to go down to Whitney's with me?"

The startling news had been like a tonic. "Of course," I replied, seizing my hat.

Kennedy paused only long enough to call Norton. The archaeologist was out, and we hurried on downtown to Whitney's.

Whitney was not there and his clerk was just about to close the office. All the books were put away in the safe and the desks were closed. Now and then there echoed up the hall the clang of an elevator door.

"Where is Mr. Whitney?" demanded Craig of the clerk.

"I can't say. He went out a couple of hours ago."

"Did he have a visit from one of his detectives?" shot out Craig suddenly.

The clerk looked up suspiciously at us.

"No," he replied defiantly.

"Walter—stand by that door," shouted Craig. "Let no one in until they break it down."

His blue-steel automatic gleamed a cold menace at the clerk. A downtown office after office hours is not exactly the place to which one can get assistance quickly. The clerk started back.

"Did he have a visit from one of his detectives?"

"Yes."

"What was it about?"

The clerk winced. "I don't know," he replied, "honest—I don't."

Craig waved the gun for emphasis. "Open the safe," he said.

Reluctantly the clerk obeyed. Under the point of the gun he searched every compartment and drawer of the big chrome steel strong-box which Whitney had pointed out as the safest place for the dagger on our first visit to him. But there was absolutely no trace of it. Had we been hoaxed and was all this risk in vain?

"Where did Mr. Whitney go?" demanded Craig, as he directed the clerk to shut the door and lock the safe again, baffled.

"If I should try to tell you," returned the man, very much frightened, "I would be lying. You would soon find out. Mr. Whitney doesn't make a confidant of me, you know."

It was useless. If he had the dagger, at least we knew that it was not at the office. We had learned only one thing. He had had a visit from one of his detectives.

As fast as the uptown trend of automobiles and surface cars during the rush hour would permit, Kennedy and I hurried in a taxicab to the Prince Edward Albert in the hope of surprising him there.

"It's no use to inquire for him," decided Craig as we entered the hotel. "I still have the key to that room, 827, next to his. We'll ride right up in the elevator boldly and get in."

No one said anything to us, as we let ourselves into the room next to Whitney's. A new lock had been placed on the door between the suites, but, aside from the additional time it took to force it, it presented no great difficulty.

"He wouldn't leave the dagger here, of course," remarked Kennedy, as at last we stepped into Whitney's suite. "But we may as well satisfy ourselves. Hello—what's this?"

The room was all upset, as though some one had already gone through it. For a moment I thought we had been forestalled.

"Packed a grip hastily," Craig remarked, pointing to the marks on the bedspread where it had rested while he must literally have thrown things into it.

We made a hasty search ourselves, but we knew it was hopeless. Two things we had learned. Whitney had had a visit from his detectives, and he had gone away hurriedly. An anonymous telephone message had been sent to Kennedy. Had it been for the purpose of throwing us off the track?

The room telephone rang. Quickly Craig jumped to it and took down the receiver.

"Hello," he called. "Yes, this is Mr. Whitney."

A silence ensued during which, of course, I could not gather any idea of what was going on over the wire.

"The deuce!" exclaimed Kennedy, working the hook up and down but receiving no response. "The fellow caught on. Something must have happened to Norton, too."

"How's that?" I asked.

"Why," he replied, "some one just called up Whitney and said that Norton had got away from him."

"Perhaps they're trying to keep him out of the way just as they are with us," I suggested. "I think the thing is a plant."

Down the hall, Kennedy stopped and tapped lightly at the door of 810, the de Moche suite. I think he was surprised when the Senora's maid opened it.

"Tell Senora de Moche it is Professor Kennedy," he said quickly, "and that I must see her."

The maid admitted us into the sitting-room where we had had our first interview with her and a moment later she appeared. She was evidently not dressed for dinner, although it was almost time, and I saw Kennedy's eye travel from her to a chair in the corner over which was draped a linen automobile coat and a heavy veil. Had she been preparing to go somewhere, too? The door to Alfonso's room was open and he clearly was not there. What did it all mean?

"Have you heard anything of a report that the dagger has been found?" demanded Kennedy abruptly.

"Why—no," she replied, greatly surprised, apparently.

"You were going out?" asked Kennedy with a significant glance at the coat and veil.

"Only for a little ride with Alfonso, who has gone to hire a car," she answered quickly.

I felt sure that she had heard something about the dagger.

We had no further excuse for staying and on the way out, now that he had satisfied himself that Whitney was not there, Craig inquired at the office for him. They could tell us nothing of his whereabouts, except that he had left in his car late in the afternoon in a great hurry.

Kennedy stepped into a telephone booth and called up Lockwood, but no one answered. Inquiry in the garages in the neighbourhood finally located that at which Lockwood kept his car. There, all that they could tell us was that the car had been filled with gas and oil as if for a trip. Lockwood was gone, too.

Kennedy hastily ordered a touring car himself and placed it at a corner of the Prince Edward Albert where he could watch two of the entrances, while I waited on the next corner where I could see the entrance on the other street.

For some time we waited and still she did not come out. Had she telephoned to Alfonso and had he gone alone? Perhaps she had already been out and had taken this method of detaining us, knowing that we would wait to watch her.

It must have been a mixture of both motives, for at length I was rewarded by seeing her come cautiously out of the rear entrance of the hotel alone and start to walk hurriedly up the street. I signalled to Craig who shot down and picked me up.

By this time the Senora had reached a public cab stand and had engaged a hack.

Sinking back in the shadows of the top, which was up, Craig directed our driver to follow the hack cautiously, keeping a couple of blocks behind. There was some satisfaction, though slight, in it, at least. We felt the possibility of the trail leading somewhere, now.

On uptown the hack went, while we kept discreetly in the rear. We had reached a part of the city where it was sparsely populated, when the hack suddenly turned and doubled back on us.

There was not time for us to turn and we trusted that by shrinking back in the shadow we might not be observed.

As the hack passed us, however, the Senora leaned out until it was perfectly evident that she must recognize us. She said nothing but I fancied I saw a smile of satisfaction as she settled back into the cushions. She was deliberately going back along the very road by which she had led us out. It had been an elaborate means of wasting our time.

She did not have the satisfaction, however, of shaking us off, for we followed all the way back to the hotel and saw her go in. Then Kennedy placed the car where we had it before and left the driver with instructions to follow her regardless of time if she should come out again.

Surely, I reasoned, there must be something very queer going on, if they were all it to eliminate us and Norton. What had happened to him?

Kennedy hastened back to the campus, late as it was, there to start anew. Norton was not in his quarters and, on the chance that he might have sought to elude Whitney's detectives by doing the unexpected and going to the Museum, Kennedy walked over that way.

There was nothing to indicate that anybody had been at the Museum, but, as we passed our laboratory, we could hear the telephone ringing inside, as though some one had been trying to get us for a long time.

Kennedy opened the door and switched on the lights. Waiting only long enough to jam the receiver down into place on the telescribe, he answered the call.

"The deuce you will!" I heard him exclaim, then apparently whoever was talking rang off and he could not get them back.

"Another of those confounded telephone messages," he said, turning to me and taking the cylinder off. "I looks as though the ready-letter writer who used to send warnings had learned his lesson and taken to the telephone as leaving fewer clues than handwriting."

He placed the record on the phonograph so that I could hear it. It was brief and to the point, as had been the first.

"Hello, is that you, Kennedy? We've got Norton. Next we'll get you. Good-bye."

Kennedy repeated the first message. It was evident that both had been spoken by the same voice.

"Whose is it?" I asked blankly. "What does it mean?"

Before Craig could answer there was a knock at our door and he sprang to open it.

Arthur B. Reeve

XXII

THE VANISHER

It was Juanita, Inez Mendoza's maid, frantic and almost speechless.

"Why, Juanita," encouraged Kennedy, "what's the matter?"

"The Senorita!" she gasped, breaking down now and sobbing over and over again. "The Senorita!"

"Yes, yes," repeated Kennedy, "but what about her? Is there anything wrong?"

"Oh, Mr. Kennedy," sobbed the poor girl, "I don't know. She is gone. I have had no word from her since this afternoon."

"Gone!" we exclaimed together. "Where was Burke—that man that the police sent up to protect her?"

"He is gone, too—now," replied Juanita in her best English, sadly broken by the excitement.

Kennedy and I looked at each other aghast. This was the hardest blow of all. We had thought that, at least, Inez would be safe with a man like Burke, whom we could trust, detailed to watch her.

"Tell me," urged Kennedy, "how did it happen? Did they carry her off—as they tried to do the other time?"

"No, no," sobbed Juanita. "I do not know. I do not know even whether she is gone. She went out this afternoon for a little walk. But she did not come back. After it grew dark, I was frightened. I remembered that you were here and called up, but you were out. Then I saw that policeman. I told him. He has others working with him now. But I could not find you—until now I saw a light here. Oh, my poor, little girl, what has become of her? Where have they taken her? Oh, MADRE DE DIOS, it is terrible!"

Had that been the purpose for which we had been sent on wild-goose chases? Was Inez really kidnapped this time? I knew not what to think. It seemed hardly possible that all of them could have joined in it.

If she were kidnapped, it must have been on the street in broad daylight. Such things had happened. It would not be the first disappearance of the kind.

Quickly Kennedy called up Deputy O'Connor. It was only too true. Burke had reported that she had disappeared and the police, especially those at the stations and ferries and in the suburbs had been notified to look for her. All this seemed to have taken place in those hours when the mysterious telephone calls had sent us on the wrong trail.

Kennedy said nothing, but I could see that he was doing some keen thinking.

Just then the telephone rang again. It was from the man whom we had left at the Prince Edward Albert. Senora de

Moche had gone out and driven rapidly to the Grand Central. He had not been able to find out what ticket she bought, but the train was just leaving.

Kennedy paced up and down, muttering to himself. "Whitney first—then Lockwood—and Alfonso. The Senora takes a train. Suppose the first message were true? Gas and oil for a trip."

He seized the telephone book and hastily turned the pages over. At last his finger rested on a name in the suburban section. I read: "Whitney, Stuart. Res. 174-J Rockledge."

Quickly he gave central the number, then shoved the receiver again into the telescribe.

"Hello, is Mr. Whitney there?" I heard later as he placed the record again in the phonograph for repetition.

"No—who is this?"

"His head clerk. Tell him I must see him. Kennedy has been to the office and—"

"Say—get off the line. We had that story once."

"That's it!" exclaimed Craig. "Don't you see—they've all gone up to Whitney's country place. That clerk was faking. He has already telephoned. And listen. Do you see anything peculiar?"

He was running all three records which we had on the telescribe. As he did so, I saw unmistakably that it was the same voice on all three. Whitney must have had a servant do the telephoning for him.

"Don't fret, Juanita," reassured Kennedy. "We shall find your mistress for you. She will be all right. You had better go back to the apartment and wait. Walter look up the next train to Rockledge while I telephone O'Connor."

We had an hour to wait before the next train left and in the meantime we drove Juanita back to the Mendoza apartment.

It was a short run to Rockledge by railroad, but it seemed to me that it took hours. Kennedy sat in silence most of the time, his eyes closed, as if he were trying to place himself in the position of the others and figure out what they would do.

At last we arrived, the only passengers to get off at the little old station. Which way to turn we had not the slightest idea. We looked about. Even the ticket office was closed. It looked as though we might almost as well have stayed in New York.

Down the railroad we could see that a great piece of engineering was in progress, raising the level of the tracks and building a steel viaduct, as well as a new station, and at the same time not interrupting the through traffic, which was heavy.

"Surely there must be some one down there," observed Kennedy, as we picked our way across the steel girders, piles of rails, and around huge machines for mixing concrete.

We came at last to a little construction house, a sort of general machine-and work-shop, in which seemed to be everything from a file to a pneumatic riveter.

"Hello!" shouted Craig.

There came a sound from a far corner of a pile of ties and a

Arthur B. Reeve

moment later a night-watchman advanced suspiciously swinging his lantern.

"Hello yourself," he growled.

"Which way to Stuart Whitney's estate?" asked Craig.

My heart sank as he gave the directions. It seemed miles away.

Just then the blinding lights of a car flashed on us as it came down the road parallel to the tracks. He waved his light and the car stopped. It was empty, except for a chauffeur evidently returning from a joy ride.

"Take these gentlemen as far as Smith's corner, will you?" asked the watchman. "Then show 'em the turn up to Whitney's."

The chauffeur was an obliging chap, especially as it cost him nothing to earn a substantial tip with his master's car. However, we were glad enough to ride in anything on wheels, and not over-particular at that hour about the ownership.

"Mr. Whitney hasn't been out here much lately," he volunteered as he sped along the beautiful oiled road, and the lights cast shadows on the trees that made driving as easy as in daylight.

"No, he has been very busy," returned Craig glad to turn to account the opportunity to talk with a chauffeur, for it is the chauffeur in the country who is the purveyor of all knowledge and gossip.

"His car passed us when I was driving up from the city. My

boss won't let me speed or I wouldn't have taken his dust. Gee, but he does wear out the engines in his cars, Whitney."

"Was he alone?" asked Craig.

"Yes—and then I saw him driving back again when I went down, to the station for some new shoes we had expressed up. Just a flying trip, I guess—or does he expect you?"

"I don't think he does," returned Craig truthfully.

"I saw a couple of other cars go up there. House party?"

"Maybe you'd call it that," returned Craig with a twinkle of the eye. "Did you see any ladies?"

"No," returned the chauffeur. "Just a man driving his own car and another with a driver."

"There wasn't a lady with Mr. Whitney?" asked Craig, now rather anxious.

"Neither time."

I saw what he was driving at. The Senora might have got up there in any fashion without being noticed. But for Inez not to be with Whitney, nor with the two who must evidently have been Lockwood and Alfonso, was indeed strange. Could it be that we were only half right—that they had gathered here but that Inez had really disappeared?

The young man set us down at Smith's Corner and it proved to be only about an eighth of a mile up the road and up-hill when Whitney's house burst in sight, silhouetted against the sky.

Arthur B. Reeve

There were lights there and it was evident that several people had gathered for some purpose.

We made our way up the path and paused a moment to look through the window before springing the little surprise. There we could see Lockwood, Alfonso, and Senora de Moche, who had arrived, after all and probably been met at the station by her son. They seemed like anything but a happy party. Never on the best of terms, they could not be expected to be happy. But now, if ever, one would have thought they might do more than tolerate each other, assuming that some common purpose had brought them here.

Kennedy rang the bell and we could see that all looked surprised, for they had heard no car approach. A servant opened the door and before he knew it, Kennedy had pushed past him, taking no chances at a rebuff after the experience over the wire.

"Kennedy!" exclaimed Lockwood and Alfonso together.

"Where is Inez Mendoza?" demanded Craig, without returning the greeting.

"Inez?" they repeated blankly.

Kennedy faced them squarely.

"Come, now. Where is she? This is a show-down. You may as well lay your cards on the table. Where is she—what have you done with her?"

The de Moches looked at Lockwood and he looked at them, but neither spoke for a moment.

"Walter," ordered Kennedy, "there's the telephone. Get the

managing editor of the Star and tell him where we are. Every newspaper in the United States, every police officer in every city will have the story, in twelve hours, if you precious rascals don't come across. There—I give you until central gets die Star."

"Why—what has happened?" asked Lockwood, who was the first to recover his tongue.

"Don't stand there asking me what has happened," cried Kennedy impatiently. "Tickle that hook again, Walter. You know as well as I do that you have planned to get Inez Mendoza away from my influence—to kidnap her, in other words—"

"We kidnap her?" gasped Lockwood. "What do you mean, man? I know nothing of this. Is she gone?" He wheeled on the de Moches. "This is some of your work. If anything happens to that girl—there isn't an Indian feud can equal the vengeance I will take!"

Alfonso was absolutely speechless. Senora de Moche started to speak, but Kennedy interrupted her. "That will do from you," he cut short. "You have passed beyond the bounds of politeness when you deliberately went out of your way to throw me on a wrong trail while some one was making off with a young and innocent girl. You are a woman of the world. You will take your medicine like a man, too."

I don't think I have ever seen Kennedy in a more towering rage than he was at that moment.

"When it was only a matter of a paltry poisoned dagger at stake and a fortune that may be mythical or may be like that of Croesus, for all I care, we could play the game according to rules," he exclaimed. "But when you begin to tamper with a life like that of Inez de Mendoza—you have passed the bounds of all consideration. You have the Star? Telephone the story anyhow. We'll arbitrate afterward."

I think, as I related the facts to my editor, it sobered us all a great deal.

"Kennedy," appealed Lockwood at last, as I hung up the receiver, "will you listen to my story?"

"It is what I am here for," replied Craig grimly.

"Believe it or not, as far as I am concerned," asserted Lockwood, "this is all news to me. My God—where is she?"

"Then how came you here?" demanded Craig.

"I can speak only for myself," hastened Lockwood. "If you had asked where Whitney was, I could have understood, but—"

"Well, where is he?"

"We don't know. Early this afternoon I received a hurried message from him—at least I suppose it was from him—that he had the dagger and was up here. He said—I'll be perfectly frank—he said that he was arranging a conference at which all of us were to be present to decide what to do."

"Meanwhile I was to be kept away at any cost," supplied Kennedy sarcastically. "Where did he get it?"

"He didn't say."

"And you didn't care, as long as he had it," added Craig, then, turning to the de Moches, "And what is your tale?"

Senora de Moche did not lose her self-possession for an instant. "We received the same message. When you called, I thought it would be best for Alfonso to go alone, so I telephoned and caught him at the garage and when my train arrived here, he was waiting."

"None of you have seen Whitney here?" asked Kennedy, to which all nodded in the negative. "Well, you seem to agree pretty well in your stories, anyhow. Let me take a chance with the servants."

It is no easy matter to go into another's household and without any official position quiz and expect to get the truth out of the servants. But Kennedy's very wrath seemed to awe them. They answered in spite of themselves.

It seemed clear that as far as they went both guests and servants were telling the truth. Whitney had made the run up from the city earlier in the afternoon, had stayed only a short time, then had gone back, leaving word that he would be there again before his guests arrived.

They all professed to be as mystified as ourselves now over the outcome of the whole affair. He had not come back and there had been no word from him.

"One thing is certain," remarked Craig, watching the faces before him as he spoke. "Inez is gone. She has been spirited away without even leaving a trace. Her maid Juanita told me that. Now if Whitney is gone, too, it looks as if he had planned to double-cross the whole crowd of you and leave you safely marooned up here with nothing left but your common hatred of me. Much good may it do you."

Lockwood clenched his fists savagely, not at Kennedy but at the thought that Craig had suggested. His face set itself in

Arthur B. Reeve

tense lines as he swore vengeance on all jointly and severally if any harm came to Inez. I almost forgot my suspicions of him in admiration.

"Nothing like this would ever have happened if she had stayed in Peru," exclaimed Alfonso bitterly. "Oh, why did her father ever bring her here to this land of danger?"

The idea seemed novel to me to look on America as a lawless, uncultured country, until I reflected on the usual Latin-American opinion of us as barbarians.

Lockwood frowned but said nothing, for a time. Then he turned suddenly to the Senora, "You were intimate enough with him," he said. "Did he tell you any more than he told us?"

It was clear that Lockwood felt now that every man's hand was against him.

I thought I could discover a suppressed gleam of satisfaction in her wonderful eyes as she answered, "Nothing more. It was only that I carried out what he asked me."

Could it be that she was taking a subtle delight in the turn of events—the working out of a curse on the treasure-secret which the fatal dagger bore? I could not say. But it would not have needed much superstition to convince any one that the curse on the Gold of the Gods was as genuine as any that had ever been uttered, as it heaped up crime on crime.

We waited in silence, the more hopeless as the singing of the night insects italicized our isolation from the organized instruments of man for the righting of wrong. Here we were, each suspecting the other, in the home of a man whom all mistrusted.

"There's no use sitting here doing nothing," exclaimed Lockwood in whose mind was evidently the same thought, "not so long as we have the telephone and the automobiles."

These, at least, were our last bonds with the great world that had wrapped a dark night about a darker mystery.

"There are many miles of wire—many miles of road. Which way shall we turn?"

Senora de Moche seemed to take a fiendish delight in the words as she said them. It was as though she challenged our helplessness in the face of a power that was greater than us all.

Lockwood flashed a look of suspicion in her direction. As for myself, I had never been able to make the woman out. To-night she seemed like a sort of dea ex machina, who sat apart, playing on the passions of a group of puppet men whom she set against each other until all should be involved in a common ruin.

It was impossible, in the silence of this far-off lonely place in the country, not to feel the weirdness of it all.

Once I closed my eyes and was startled by the uncanny vividness of a mind-picture that came unbidden. It was of a scrap of paper on which, in rough capitals was printed:

BEWARE THE CURSE OF MANSICHE ON THE GOLD OF THE GODS.

XXIII

THE ACETYLENE TORCH

Do you suppose he really had the dagger, or was that a lie?" I asked, with an effort shaking off the fateful feeling that had come over me as if some one were casting a spell.

"There is one way to find out," returned Craig, as though glad of the suggestion.

Though they hated him, they seemed forced to admit, for the time, his leadership. He rose and the rest followed as he went into Whitney's library.

He switched on the lights. There in a corner back of the desk stood a safe. Somehow or other it seemed to defy us, even though its master was gone. I looked at it a moment. It was a most powerful affair, companion to that in the office of which Whitney was so proud, built of layer on layer of chrome steel, with a door that was air tight and soup-proof, bidding defiance to all yeggmen and petermen.

Lockwood fingered the combination hopelessly. There were some millions of combinations and permutations that only a mathematician could calculate. Only one was any good. That one was locked in the mind of the man who now seemed to baffle us as did his strong-box.

I placed my hand on the cold, defiant surface. It would take hours to drill a safe like that, and even then it might turn the points of the drills. Explosives might sooner wreck the house and bring it down over the head of the man who attacked this monster.

"What can we do?" asked Senora de Moche, seeming to mock us, as though the safe itself were an inhuman thing that blocked our path.

"Do?" repeated Kennedy decisively, "I'll show you what we can do. If Lockwood will drive me down to the railroad station in his car, I'll show you something that looks like action. Will you do it?"

The request was more like a command. Lockwood said nothing, but moved toward the porte-cochere, where he had left his car parked just aside from the broad driveway.

"Walter, you will stay here," ordered Kennedy. "Let no one leave. If any one comes, don't let him get away. We shan't be gone long."

I sat awkwardly enough, scarcely speaking a word, as Kennedy dashed down to the railroad station. Neither Alfonso nor his mother betrayed either by word or action a hint of what was passing in their minds. Somehow, though I did not understand it, I felt that Lockwood might square himself. But I could not help feeling that these two might very possibly be at the bottom of almost anything.

It was with some relief that I heard the car approaching again. I had no idea what Kennedy was after, whether it was dynamite or whether he contemplated a trip to New York. I was surprised to see him, with Lockwood, hurrying up the steps to the porch, each with a huge tank studded with bolts like a boiler.

"There," ordered Craig, "set the oxygen there," as he placed his own tank on the opposite side. "That watchman thought I was bluffing when I said I'd get an order from the company, if I had to wake up the president of the road. It was too good a chance to miss. One doesn't find such a complete outfit ready to hand every day."

Out of the tanks stout tubes led, with stop-cocks and gauges at the top. From a case under his arm Kennedy produced a curious arrangement like a huge hook, with a curved neck and a sharp beak. Really it consisted of two metal tubes which ran into a sort of cylinder, or mixing chamber, above the nozzle, while parallel to them ran a third separate tube with a second nozzle of its own.

Quickly he joined the ends of the tubes from the tanks to the metal hook, the oxygen tank being joined to two of the tubes of the hook, and the second tank being joined to the other. With a match he touched the nozzle gingerly. Instantly a hissing, spitting noise followed, and an intense, blinding needle of flame.

"Now we'll see what an oxyacetylene blow-pipe will do to you, old stick-in-the-mud," cried Kennedy, as he advanced toward the safe, addressing it as though it had been a thing of life that stood in his way. "I think this will make short work of you."

Almost as he said it, the steel beneath the blow-pipe became incandescent. For some time he laboured to get a starting-point for the flame of the high-pressure torch.

It was a brilliant sight. The terrific heat from the first nozzle caused the metal to glow under the torch as if in an open-hearth furnace. From the second nozzle issued a stream of oxygen, under which the hot metal of the door was completely consumed.

The force of the blast, as the compressed oxygen and acetylene were expelled, carried a fine spray of the disintegrated metal visibly before it. And yet it was not a big hole that it made—scarcely an eighth of an inch wide, but clean and sharp as if a buzz-saw were eating its way through a plank of white-pine.

With tense muscles Kennedy held this terrific engine of destruction and moved it as easily as if it had been a mere pencil of light. He was the calmest of all of us as we crowded about him, but at a respectful distance.

"I suppose you know," he remarked hastily, never pausing for a moment in his work, "that acetylene is composed of carbon and hydrogen. As it burns at the end of the nozzle it is broken into carbon and hydrogen—the carbon gives the high temperature and the hydrogen forms a cone that protects the end of the blow-pipe from being itself burnt up."

"But isn't it dangerous?" I asked, amazed at the skill with which he handled the blow-pipe.

"Not particularly—when you know how to do it. In that tank is a porous asbestos packing saturated with acetone, under pressure. Thus they carry acetylene safely, for it is dissolved and the possibility of explosion is minimized.

"This mixing chamber, by which I am holding the torch, where the oxygen and acetylene mix, is also designed in such a way as to prevent a flash-back. The best thing about this style of blow-pipe is the ease with which it can be transported and the curious purposes—like this—to which it can be put."

He paused a moment to test what had been burnt. The rest of the safe seemed as firm as ever.

"Humph!" I heard one of them, I think it was Alfonso, mutter. I resented it, but Kennedy affected not to hear.

"When I shut off the oxygen in this second jet," he resumed, "you see the torch merely heats the steel. I can get a heat of approximately sixty-three hundred degrees Fahrenheit, and the flame will exert a pressure of fifty pounds to the square inch."

"Wonderful!" exclaimed Lockwood, who had not heard the suppressed disapproval of Alfonso, and was watching, in undisguised admiration at the thing itself, regardless of consequences. "Kennedy, how did you ever think of such a thing?"

"Why, it's used for welding, you know," answered Craig, as he continued to work calmly in the growing excitement. "I first saw it in actual use in mending a cracked cylinder in an automobile. The cylinder was repaired without being taken out at all. I've seen it weld new teeth and build up worn teeth on gearing, as good as new."

He paused to let us see the terrifically heated metal under the flame.

"You remember when we were talking to the watchman down there at the station, Walter?" he asked. "I saw this thing in that complete little shop of theirs. It interested me. See. I turn on the oxygen now in the second nozzle. The blow-pipe is no longer an instrument for joining metals together, but for cutting them asunder.

"The steel burns just as you, perhaps, have seen a watch-spring burn in a jar of oxygen. Steel, hard or soft, tempered, annealed, chrome, or Harveyized, it all burns just about as fast, and just about as easily under this torch. And it's cheap, too. This attack—aside from what it costs to the safe—may amount to a couple of dollars as far as the blow-pipe is concerned—quite a difference from the thousands of dollars' loss that would follow an attempt to blow a safe like this one."

We had nothing to say. We stood in awe-struck amazement as the torch slowly, inexorably traced a thin line along the edge of the combination.

Minute after minute sped by, as the line burned by the blow-pipe cut around the lock. It seemed hours, but really it was minutes. I wondered when he would have cut about the whole lock. He was cutting clear through and around it, severing it as if with a superhuman knife.

With something more than half his work done, he paused a moment to rest.

"Walter," he directed, mopping his forehead, for it was real work directing that flaming knife, "get New York on the wire. See if O'Connor is at his office. If he has any report, I want to talk to him."

It was getting late and the service was slackening up. I had some trouble, especially in getting a good connection, but at last I got headquarters and was overjoyed to hear O'Connor's bluff, Irish voice boom back at me.

"Hello, Jameson," he called. "Where on earth are you? I've been trying to get hold of Kennedy for a couple of hours. Rockledge? Well, is Kennedy there? Put him on, will you?"

I called Craig and, as I did so, my curiosity got the better of me and I sought out an extension of the wire in a den across the hall from the library, where I could listen in on what was said.

"Hello, O'Connor," answered Craig. "Anything from Burke yet?"

"Yes," came back the welcome news. "I think he has a clue. We found out from here that she received a long distance message during the afternoon. Where did Jameson say you were—Rockledge?—that's the place. Of course we don't know what the message was, but anyhow she went out to meet some one right after that. The time corresponds with what the maid says."

"Anything else?" asked Craig. "Have you found any one who saw her?"

"Yes. I think she went over to your laboratory. But you were out."

"Confound it!" interrupted Craig.

"Some one saw a woman there."

"It wasn't the maid?"

"No, this was earlier—in the afternoon. She left and walked across the campus to the Museum."

"Oh, by the way, any word of Norton?"

"I'm coming to that. She inquired for Norton. The curator has given a good description. But he was out—hadn't been there for some time. She seemed to be very much upset over something. She went away. After that we've lost her."

"Not another trace?"

"Wait a minute. We had this Rockledge call to work on. So we started backward on that. It was Whitney's place, I found out. We could locate the car at the start and at the finish. He left the Prince Edward Albert and went up there first. Then he must have come back to the city again. No one at the hotel saw him the second time.

"What then?" hastened Craig.

"She may have met him somewhere, though it's not likely she had any intention of going away. All the rest of those people you have up there seem to have gone prepared. We got something on each of them. Also you'll be interested to know I've got a report of your own doings. It was right, Kennedy, I don't blame you. I'd have done the same with Burke on the job. How are you making out? What? You're cracking a crib? With what?"

O'Connor whistled as Kennedy related the story of the blow-pipe. "I think you're on the right track," he commended. "There's nothing to show it, but I believe Whitney told her something that changed her mind about going up there. Probably met her in some tea room, although we can't find anything from the tea rooms. Anyhow, Burke's out trailing along the road from New York to Rockledge and I'm getting reports from him whenever he hits a telephone."

"I wish you'd ask him to call me, here, if he gets anything."

"Sure I will. The last call was from the Chateau Rouge,—that's about halfway. There was a car with a man and a woman who answers her description. Then, there was another car, too."

"Another car?"

"Yes—that's where Norton crosses the trail again. We searched his apartment. It was upset—like Whitney's. I haven't finished with that. But we have a list of all the private hacking places. I've located one that hired a car to a man answering Norton's description. I think he's on the trail. That's what I meant by another car."

"What's he doing?"

"Maybe he has a hunch. I'm getting superstitious about this case. You know Luis de Mendoza has thirteen letters in it. Leslie told me something about a threat he had—a curse. You better look out for those two greasers you have up there. They may have another knife for you."

Kennedy glanced over at the de Moches, not in fear but in amusement at what they would think if they could hear O'Connor's uncultured opinion.

"All right, O'Connor," said Craig, "everything seems to be going as well as we can expect. Don't forget to tell Burke I'm here."

"I won't. Just a minute. He's on another wire for me."

Kennedy waited impatiently. He wanted to finish his job on the safe before some one came walking in and stopped it, yet there was always a chance that Burke might turn up something.

"Hello," called O'Connor a few minutes later. "He's still following the two cars. He thinks the one with the woman in it is Whitney's, all right. But they've got off the main road. They must think they're being followed.

"Or else have changed their destination," returned Craig. "Tell him that. Maybe Whitney had no intention of coming up here. He may have done this thing just to throw these people off up here, too. I can't say. I can tell better whether he intended to come back after I've got this safe open. I'll let you know."

Kennedy rang off.

"Any news of Inez?" asked Lockwood who had been fuming with impatience.

"She's probably on her way up here," returned Craig briefly, taking up the blow-pipe again.

Alfonso remained silent. The Senora could scarcely hide her excitement. If there were anything in telepathy, I am sure that she read everything that was said over the wire.

Quickly Craig resumed his work, biting through the solid steel as if it had been mere pasteboard, the blow-pipe showering on each side a brilliant spray of sparks, a gaudy, pyrotechnic display.

Suddenly, with a quick motion, Kennedy turned off the acetylene and oxygen. The last bolt had been severed, the lock was useless. A gentle push of the hand, and he swung the once impregnable door on its delicately poised hinges as easily as if he had merely said, "Open sesame."

Craig reached in and pulled open a steel drawer directly in

Arthur B. Reeve

front of him.

There in the shadow lay the dagger—with its incalculably valuable secret, a poor, unattractive piece of metal, but with a fascination such as no other object, I had ever seen, possessed.

There was a sudden cry. The Senora had darted ahead, as if to clasp its handle and unloose the murderous blade that nestled in its three-sided sheath.

Before she could reach it, Kennedy had seized her hand in his iron grasp, while with the other he picked up the dagger.

They stood there gazing into each other's eyes.

Then the Senora burst into a hysterical laugh.

"The curse is on all who possess it!"

"Thank you," smiled Kennedy quietly, releasing her wrist as he dropped the dagger into his pocket, "I am only the trustee."

XXIV

THE POLICE DOG

Craig faced us, but there was no air of triumph in his manner. I knew what was in his mind. He had the dagger. But he had lost Inez.

What were we to do? There seemed to be no way to turn. We knew something of the manner of her disappearance. At first she had, apparently, gone willingly. But it was inconceivable that she stayed willingly, now.

I recalled all the remarks that Whitney had ever made about her. Had the truth come out in his jests? Was it Inez, not the dagger, that he really wanted?

Or was he merely the instrument of one or all of these people before us, and was this an elaborate plan to throw Kennedy off and prove an alibi for them? He had been the partner of Lockwood, the intimate of de Moche. Which was he working for, now—or was he working for himself alone?

No answer came to my questions, and I reflected that none would ever come, if we sat here. Yet there seemed to be no way to turn, without risking putting ourselves in a worse position than before. At least, until we had some better plan of campaign, we occupied a strategic advantage in Whitney's own house.

The hours of the night wore on. Midnight came. This inaction was killing. Anything would be better than that

Suddenly the telephone startled us. We had wanted it to ring, yet when it rang we were afraid of it. What was its message? It was with palpitating hearts that we listened, while Craig answered.

"Yes, Burke," we heard him reply, "this is Kennedy."

There came a pause during which we could scarcely wait.

"Where are you now? Cold Stream. That is about twelve miles from Rockledge—not on the New York road—the other road. I see. All right. We'll be there. Yes, wait for us."

As Craig hung up the receiver, we crowded forward. "Have they found her?" asked Lockwood hoarsely.

"It was from Burke," replied Kennedy deliberately. "He is at a place called Cold Stream, twelve miles from here. He tells me that we can find it easily—on a state road, at a sharp curve that has been widened out, just this side of the town. There has been an accident—Whitney's car is wrecked."

Lockwood seized his elbow. "My God," he exclaimed, "tell me—she isn't—hurt, is she? Quick!"

"So far Burke has not been able to discover a trace of a thing, except the wrecked car," replied Kennedy. "I told him I would be over directly. Lockwood, you may take Jameson and Alfonso. I will go with the Senora and their driver."

I saw instantly why he had divided the party. Neither mother nor son was to have a chance to slip away from us. Surely both Lockwood and I should be a match for Alfonso. Senora de Moche he would trust to none but himself.

Eagerly now we prepared for the journey, late though it was. No one now had a thought of rest. There could be no rest with that mystery of Inez challenging us.

We were off at last, Lockwood's car leading, for although he did not know the roads exactly, he had driven much about the country. I should have liked to have sat in front with him, but it seemed safer to stay in the back with Alfonso. In fact, I don't think Lockwood would have consented, otherwise, to have his rival back of him.

Kennedy and the Senora made a strange pair, the ancient order and the ultra-modern. There was a peculiar light in her eyes that gleamed forth at the mere mention of the words, "wreck." Though she said nothing, I knew that through her mind was running the one tenacious thought. It was the working out of the curse! As for Craig, he was always seeking the plausible, natural reason for what to the rest of us was inexplicable, often supernatural. To him she was a fascinating study.

On we sped, for Lockwood was a good driver and now was spurred on by an anxiety that he could not conceal. Yet his hand never faltered at the wheel. He seemed to read the signs at the cross-roads without slackening speed. In spite of all that I knew, I found myself compelled to admire him. Alfonso sat back, for the most part silent. The melancholy in his face seemed to have deepened. He seemed to feel that he was but a toy in the hands of fate. Yet I knew that underneath must smoulder the embers of a bitter resentment.

It seemed an interminable ride even at the speed which we were making. Twelve miles in the blackness of a country night can seem like a hundred.

At last as we turned a curve, and Lockwood's headlights shone on the white fence that skirted the outer edge of the road as it swung around a hill that rose sharply to our left and dropped off in a sort of ravine at the right beyond the fence, I felt the car tremble as he put on the brakes.

A man was waving his arms for us to stop, and as we did, he ran forward. He peered in at us and I recognized Burke.

"Whe-where's Kennedy?" he asked, disappointed, for the moment fearing he had made a mistake and signalled the wrong car.

"Coming," I replied, as we heard the driver of the other car sounding his horn furiously as he approached the curve.

Burke jumped to the safe side of the road and ran on back to signal to stop. It was then for the first time that I paid particular attention to the fence ahead of us on which now both our own and the lights of the other car shone. At one point it was torn and splintered, as though something had gone through it.

"Great heavens, you don't mean to say that they went over that?" muttered Lockwood, jumping down and running forward.

Kennedy had joined us by this time and we all hurried over. Down in the ravine we could see a lantern which Burke had brought and which was now resting on the overturned chassis of the car.

Lockwood was down there ahead of us all, peering under the heavy body fearfully, as if he expected to see two forms of mangled flesh. He straightened up, then took the lantern and flashed it about. There was nothing except cushions and a few parts of the car within the radius of its gleam.

"Where are they?" he demanded, turning to us. "It's Whitney's car, all right."

Burke shook his head. "I've traced the car so far. They were getting ahead of me, when this happened."

Together we managed to right the car which was on a hillock. It sank a little further down the hill, but at least we could look inside it.

"Bring the lantern," ordered Kennedy.

Minutely, part by part, he went over the car. "Something went wrong," he muttered. "It is too much wrecked to tell what it was. Flash the light over here," he directed, stepping over the seat into the back of the tonneau.

A moment later he took the light himself and held it close to the rods that supported the top. I saw him reach down and pull from them a few strands of dark hair that had caught between the rods and had been pulled out or broken.

"No need of Bertillon's palette of human hair to identify that," he exclaimed." There isn't time to study it and if there were it would be unnecessary. She was with him, all right."

"Yes," agreed Lockwood. "But where is she now—where is he? Could they have been hurt, picked up by some one and carried where they could get aid?"

Burke shook his head. "I inquired at the nearest house ahead. I had to do it in order to telephone. They knew nothing."

"But they are gone," persisted Lockwood. "There is the bottom of the bank. You can see that they are not here."

Kennedy had taken the light and climbed the bank again and was now going over the road as minutely as if he were searching for a lost diamond.

"Look!" he exclaimed.

Where the Whitney car had skidded and gone over the bank, the tires had dug deep into the top dressing, making little mounds. Across them now we could see the tracks of other tires that had pressed down the mounds.

"Some one else has been here," reconstructed Kennedy. "He passed, then stopped and backed up. Perhaps they were thrown out, unconscious, and he picked them up."

It seemed to be the only reasonable supposition.

"But they knew nothing at the next house," persisted Burke.

"Is there a road leading off before you get to the house?" asked Kennedy.

"Yes—it crosses the line into Massachusetts."

"It is worth trying—it is the only thing we can do," decided Kennedy. "Drive slowly to the crossroads. Perhaps we can pick out the tire-prints there. They certainly won't show on the road itself. It is too hard."

At the crossing we stopped and Kennedy dropped down on

his hands and knees again with the light.

"There it is," he exclaimed. "The same make of anti-skid tire, at least. There was a cut in the rear tire—just like this. See? It is the finger-print of the motor car. I think we are right. Turn up here and run slowly."

On we went slowly, Kennedy riding on the running-board of the car ahead. Suddenly he raised his hand to stop, and jumped down.

We gathered about him. Had he found a continuation of the tire-tracks? There were tracks but he was not looking at them. He was looking between them. There ran a thin line.

He stuck his finger in it and sniffed. "Not gas," he remarked. "It must have been the radiator, leaking. Perhaps he ran his car into Whitney's—forced it too far to the edge of the road. We can't tell. But he couldn't have gone far with that leak without finding water—or cracked cylinders."

With redoubled interest now we resumed the chase. We had mounted a hill and had run down into the shadows of a valley when, following in the second car, we heard a shout from Kennedy in the first.

Halfway up the hill across the valley, he had come upon an abandoned car. It had evidently reached its limit, the momentum of the previous hill had carried it so far up the other, then the driver had stopped it and let it back slowly off the road into a clump of bushes that hid a little gully.

But that was all. There was not a sign of a person about. Whatever had happened here had happened some hours before. We looked about. All was Cimmerian darkness. Not a house or habitation of man or beast was in sight, though

Arthur B. Reeve

they might not be far away.

We beat about the under-brush, but succeeded in stirring up nothing but mosquitoes.

What were we to do? We were wasting valuable time. Where should we go?

"I doubt whether they would have kept on the road," reasoned Kennedy. "They must have known they would be followed. The hardest place to follow them would be across country."

"With a lantern?" I objected. "We can't do it."

Kennedy glanced at his watch. "It will be three hours before there is light enough to see anything by," he considered. "They have had at least a couple of hours. Five hours is too good a start. Burke - take one of the cars. Go ahead along the road. We mustn't neglect that. I'll take the other. I want to get back to that house and call O' Connor. Walter, you stay here with the rest."

We separated and I felt that, although I was doing nothing, I had my hands full watching these three.

Lockwood was restless and could not help beating around in the under-brush, in the hope of turning up something. Now and then he would mutter to himself some threat if anything happened to Inez. I let him occupy himself, for our own, as much as his, peace of mind. Alfonso had joined his mother in the car and they sat there conversing in low tones in Spanish, while I watched them furtively.

Of a sudden, I became aware that I missed the sound of Lockwood beating about the under-brush. I called, but there was no answer. Then we all called. There came back nothing but a mocking echo. I could not follow him. If I did, I would lose the de Moches.

Had he been laying low, waiting his opportunity to get away? Or was he playing a lone hand? Much as I suspected about him, during the past few hours I had come to admire him.

I sent the de Moche driver out to look for him, but he seemed afraid to venture far, and, of course, returned and said that he could not find him. Even in his getaway, Lockwood had been characteristic. He had been strong enough to bide his time, clever enough to throw every one off guard. It put a new aspect on the case for me. Had Whitney intended the capture of Inez for Lockwood? Had our coming so unexpectedly into the case thrown the plans awry and was it the purpose to leave them marooned at Rockledge while we were shunted off in the city? That, too, was plausible. I wished Kennedy would return before anything else happened.

It was not long by the clock before Kennedy did return. But it seemed ages to me.

He was not alone. With him was a man in a uniform, and a powerful dog, for all the world like a huge wolf.

"Down, Searchlight," he ordered, as the dog began to show an uncanny interest in me. "Let me introduce my new dog detective," he chuckled. "She has a wonderful record as a police dog. I got O'Connor out of bed and he telephoned out to the nearest suburban station. That saved a good deal of time in getting her up here."

I mustered up courage to tell Kennedy of the defection of

266   Arthur B. Reeve

Lockwood. He did not seem to mind it especially.

"He won't get far, with the dog after him, if we want to take the time," he said. "She's a German sheep dog, a Schaeferhund."

Searchlight seemed to have many of the characteristics of the wild, prehistoric animal, among them the full, upright ears of the wild dog, which are such a great help to it. She was a fine, alert, upstanding dog, hardy, fierce, and literally untiring, of a tawny light brown like a lioness, about the same size and somewhat of the type of the smooth-coated collie, broad of chest and with a full brush of tail. Untamed as she seemed, she was perfectly under Kennedy's control and rendered him absolute and unreasoning obedience.

They took her over to the abandoned car. There they let her get a good whiff of the bottom of the car about the driver's feet, and a moment later she started off.

Alfonso and his mother insisted on going with us and that made our progress across country slow.

On we went over the rough country, through a field, then skirting a clump of woods until at last we came to a lane.

We stopped in the shadow of a thicket. There was an empty summer home. Was there some intruder there? Was it really empty?

Now and then we could hear Searchlight scouting about in the under-brush, crouching and hiding, watching and guarding. We paused and waited in the heavily-laden night air, wondering. The soughing of the night wind in the evergreens was mournful. Did it betoken a further tragedy?

There was a slight noise from the other side of the house. Craig reached out and drew us back into the shadow of the thicket, deeper.

"Some one is prowling about, I think. Leave it to the dog."

Searchlight, who had been near us, was sniffing eagerly. From our hiding-place we could just see her. She had heard the sounds, too, even before we had, and for an instant stood with every muscle tense.

Then, like an arrow, she darted into the underbrush. An instant later, the sharp crack of a revolver rang out. Searchlight kept right on, never stopping a second, except, perhaps, in surprise.

"Crack!" almost in her face came a second spit of fire in the darkness, and a bullet crashed through the leaves and buried itself in a tree with a ping. The intruder's marksmanship was poor, but the dog paid no attention to it.

"One of the few animals that show no fear of gun-fire," muttered Kennedy, in undisguised admiration.

"G-r-r-r," we heard from the police dog.

"She has made a leap at the hand that holds the gun," cried Kennedy, now rising and moving rapidly in the same direction. "She has been taught that a man once badly bitten in the hand is nearly out of the fight."

We followed also. As we approached we were just in time to see Searchlight running in and out between the legs of a man who had heard us approach and was hastily making tracks away. As he tripped, the officer who brought her blew shrilly on a police whistle just in time to stop a fierce lunge at his back.

Arthur B. Reeve

Reluctantly, Searchlight let go. One could see that with all her canine instinct she wanted to "get" that man. Her jaws were open, as, with longing eyes, she stood over the prostrate form in the grass. The whistle was a signal, and she had been taught to obey unquestioningly.

"Don't move until we get to you, or you are a dead man," shouted Kennedy, pulling an automatic as he ran. "Are you hurt?"

There was no answer, but, as we approached, the man moved, ever so little, through curiosity to see his pursuers.

Searchlight shot forward. Again the whistle sounded and she dropped back. We bent over to seize him, as Kennedy secured the dog.

"She's a devil," ground out the prone figure on the grass.

"Lockwood!" exclaimed Kennedy.

XXV

THE GOLD OF THE GODS

"What are you doing here?" demanded Craig, astonished.

"I couldn't wait for you to get back. I thought I'd do a little detective work on my own account. I kept getting further and further away, knew you'd find me, anyhow. But I didn't think you'd have a brute like that," he added, binding up his hand ruefully. "Is there any trace of Inez?"

"Not yet. Why did you pick out this house?" asked Kennedy, still suspicious.

"I saw a light here, I thought," answered Lockwood frankly. "But as I approached, it went out. Maybe I imagined it."

"Let us see."

Kennedy spoke a few words to the man with the dog. He slipped the leash, with a word that we did not catch, and the dog bounded off, around the house, as she was accustomed to do when out on duty with an officer in the city suburbs, circling about the backs of houses as the man on the beat walked the street. She made noise enough about it, too, tumbling over a tin pail that had been standing on the back porch steps.

"Bang!"

Some one was in the house and was armed. In the darkness he had not been able to tell whether an attack was being made or not, but had taken no chances. At any rate, now we knew that he was desperate.

I thought of all the methods Kennedy had adopted to get into houses in which the inmates were desperate. But always they had been about the city where he could call upon the seemingly exhaustless store of apparatus in his laboratory. Here we were faced by the proposition with nothing to rely on but our native wit and a couple of guns.

Besides, I did not know whether to count on Lockwood as an ally or not. My estimation of him had been rising and falling like the barometer in a summer shower. I had been convinced that he was against us. But his manner and plausibility now equally convinced me that I had been mistaken. I felt that it would take some supreme action on his part to settle the question. That crisis was coming now.

I think all of us would willingly have pushed Alfonso forward. But the relations of the de Moches with Whitney had been so close that I no more trusted him than I did Lockwood. And if I could not make out Lockwood, a man at least of our own race and education, how could I expect to fathom Alfonso?

It seemed, then, to rest with Kennedy and myself. At least so Craig appraised the situation.

"You have a gun, Walter," he directed, "Lockwood, give yours to Jameson."

Lockwood hesitated. Could he trust being unarmed, while Kennedy and I had all the weapons?

Craig had not stopped to ask Alfonso. As he laid out the attack he merely tapped the young man's pockets to see whether he was armed or not, and finding nothing faced us again, Lockwood still hesitating.

"I want Walter," explained Craig, "to go around back of the house. It is there they must be expecting an attack. He can take up his position behind that oak. It will be safe enough. By firing one gun on each side of the tree he can make enough noise for half a dozen. Then you and I can rush the front of the house."

Lockwood had nothing better to suggest. Reluctantly he handed over his revolver.

I dropped back from them and skirted the house at a safe distance so as not to be seen, then came up back of the tree.

Carefully I aimed at the glass of a window on the first floor, as offering the greatest opportunity for making a racket, which was the object I had in mind.

I fired from the right and the glass was shattered in a thousand bits. Another shot from the left broke the light out of another window on the opposite side.

The house was a sort of bungalow, with most of the rooms on the first floor, and a small second story or attic window. That went next. Altogether I felt that I was giving a splendid account of myself.

From the house came a rapid volley in reply. Whoever was in there was not going to surrender without a fight. One after another I plugged away with my shots, now bent on making the most of them. With the answering shots it made quite a merry little fusillade, and I was glad enough to have the shelter of the staunch oak which two or three times was hit squarely at about the level of my shoulders. I had never before heard the whirr of so many bullets about me, and I cannot say that I enjoyed it.

But my attack was what Craig wanted. I heard a noise in the front of the house, as of feet running, and then I knew that in spite of all he had given me the least dangerous part of the attack.

I plugged away valiantly with what shots I had left, then leaving just one more in the chamber of each gun, I hurried around in the shadow, my blood up, to help them.

With the aid of the officer, they had just forced the light door and Searchlight had been allowed to leap in ahead of them, as I came up.

"Here," I said to Lockwood, handing him back his gun, "take it, there is just one shot left."

I, at least, had expected to find one, perhaps two desperate men waiting for us. Evidently our ruse had worked. The room was dark, but there seemed to be no one in it, though we could hear sounds as though some one were hastily barricading the door that led from the front to the room at which I had been firing.

Lockwood struck a match.

"Confound it, don't!" muttered Craig, knocking it from his hand. "They can see us well enough without helping them."

"Chester!"

We stood transfixed. It was a woman's voice. Where did it come from? Could she be in the room?

"Chester—is that you?"

"Yes, Inez. Where are you?"

"I ran up here—in this attic—when I heard the shots."

"Come down, then. All is right, now."

She came down a half ladder, half flight of steps. At the foot she paused just a moment and hesitated. Then, like a frightened bird, she flew to the safety of Lockwood's arms.

"Mr. Whitney," she sobbed, "called me up and told me that he had something very important to say, a message from you. He said that he had the dagger, in his safe, up in the country. He told me you'd be there and that you expected me to come up with him in his car. I went. We had some trouble with the engine. And then that other car—the one that followed us, came up behind and forced us off the bank. Mr. Whitney and I were both stunned. I don't remember a thing after that, until I woke up here. Where is it?"

I listened, with one eye on that door that had been barricaded. Was Lockwood really innocent, after all? I could not think that Inez Mendoza could make such a mistake, if he were not.

Lockwood clenched his fists. "Some one shall pay for this," he exclaimed.

There was the problem—the inner room. Who would go in?

Arthur B. Reeve

We looked at each other a moment.

The room in which we were was a living room, and perhaps, when there were visitors in the little house, was a guest-room. At any rate, on one side was a huge davenport by day which could be transformed into a folding bed at night.

Lockwood looked about hastily and his eye fell on the door, then on this folding bed.

With a wrench, he opened it and seized the cotton mattress from the inside. With his gun ready he advanced toward the barricaded door, holding the mattress as a shield, for his experience in wild countries had taught him that a cotton mattress is about as good a thing to stop bullets as one could find on the spur of the moment.

Kennedy and the officer followed just behind, and the three threw their weights on the door almost before we knew what they were about.

"Chester—don't!" cried Inez in alarm, too late. "He'll—kill you!"

The excitement had been too much for her. She reeled, fainting, and I caught her.

Before I could restore the davenport to something like its original condition so that we could take care of her, the first onslaught was over.

Three guns were sticking their blue noses into the darkness of the next room.

"Hands up!" shouted Craig, "Drop your gun! Let me hear it fall!"

There followed a thud and Kennedy, followed by Lockwood and the officer entered.

As they fumbled to strike a light, I managed to open a window and let in some fresh air, while the Senora, for once human, loosened the throat of Inez' dress and fanned her.

Through the open door, now, I could hear what was going on in the next room, but could not see.

"It was you, Lockwood," I heard a familiar voice accusing, "who was in the Museum the night the dagger disappeared."

"Yes," replied Lockwood, a bit disdainfully. "I suspected something crooked about that dagger. I thought that if I made a copy of the inscription on the blade, I might decipher it myself, or get some one to do it for me. I went in and, when a chance came, I hid in the sarcophagus. There I waited until the Museum was closed. Then, when finally I got to the place where I thought the dagger was—it was gone!"

"The point is," cut in Craig, interrupting, "who was the mysterious visitor to Mendoza the night of his murder?"

He paused. No one seemed to be disposed to answer and he went on, "Who else than the man who sought to sell the secret on its blade, in return for Inez for whom he had a secret passion? I have reasoned it all out—the offer, the quarrel, the stabbing with the dagger itself, and the escape down the stairs, instead of by the elevator."

"And I," put in Lockwood, "coming to report to Mendoza my failure to find the dagger, found him dead—and at once was suspected of being the murderer!"

Inez had revived and her quick ears had caught her lover's

voice and the last words.

Weak as she was, she sprang up and fairly ran into the next room. "No—Chester—No!" she cried. "I never suspected—not even when I saw the shoe-prints. No—that is the man,—there—I know it—I know it!"

I hurried after her, as she flung herself again between Lockwood and the rest of us, as if to shield him, while Lockwood proudly caressed the stray locks of dark hair that fluttered on his shoulder.

I looked in the direction all were looking.

Before us stood, unmasked at last, the scientific villain who had been plotting and scheming to capture both the secret and Inez—well knowing that suspicion would rest either on Lockwood, the soldier of fortune, or on the jealous Indian woman whose son had been rejected and whose brother he had himself already, secretly, driven to an insane suicide in his unscrupulous search for the treasure of Truxillo.

It was Professor Norton, himself—first thief of the dagger which later he had hidden but which Whitney's detectives had stolen in turn from him; writer of anonymous letters, even to himself to throw others off the trail; maker of stramonium cigarettes with which to confuse the minds of his opponents, Whitney, Mendoza, and the rest; secret lover of Inez whom he demanded as the price of the dagger; and murderer of Don Luis.

Senora de Moche and Alfonso, behind me, could only gasp their astonishment. Much as she would have liked to have the affair end in a general vindication of the curse she could not control a single, triumphant thrust.

"His blood," she cried, transfixing Norton with her stern eyes, "has cried out of Titicaca for vengeance from that day to this!"

"Want any help?"

We all turned toward the door as Burke, dust-covered and tired, stamped in, followed by a man whose face was bandaged and bloody.

"I heard shots. Is it all over?"

But we paid no attention to Burke.

There was Whitney, considerably banged up by the fall, but lucky to be alive.

"I tried to shake him," he explained, catching sight of Norton. "But he stuck to us, even on our detours. Finally he grew desperate—forced my car off the road. What happened after that, I don't know. He must have carried me some miles, insensible, and dumped me in the bushes again. I was several miles up the hill, tramping along, looking for a road-house, when this gentleman found me and said I had gone too far."

Senora de Moche turned from Lockwood and Inez who were standing, oblivious to the rest of us, and stared at Whitney's bruised and battered face.

"It is the curse," she muttered. "It will never—

"Just a moment," interrupted Craig, drawing the dagger from his pocket, and turning toward Inez. "It was to your ancestor that the original possessor of the secret promised to give the 'big fish,' when he was killed."

He paused and handed the dagger to her. She touched it shuddering, but as though it were a duty.

"Take it," he said simply. "The secret is yours. Only love can destroy the curse on the Gold of the Gods."

THE END

Other books by this author

Constance Dunlop

The Master Mystery

Arthur B. Reeve

Choose from Thousands of 1stWorldLibrary Classics By

A. M. Barnard
Ada Leverson
Adolphus William Ward
Aesop
Agatha Christie
Alexander Aaronsohn
Alexander Kielland
Alexandre Dumas
Alfred Gatty
Alfred Ollivant
Alice Duer Miller
Alice Turner Curtis
Alice Dunbar
Allen Chapman
Alleyne Ireland
Ambrose Bierce
Amelia E. Barr
Amory H. Bradford
Andrew Lang
Andrew McFarland Davis
Andy Adams
Angela Brazil
Anna Alice Chapin
Anna Sewell
Annie Besant
Annie Hamilton Donnell
Annie Payson Call
Annie Roe Carr
Annonaymous
Anton Chekhov
Archibald Lee Fletcher
Arnold Bennett
Arthur C. Benson
Arthur Conan Doyle
Arthur M. Winfield
Arthur Ransome
Arthur Schnitzler
Arthur Train
Atticus
B.H. Baden-Powell
B. M. Bower
B. C. Chatterjee
Baroness Emmuska Orczy
Baroness Orczy
Basil King
Bayard Taylor
Ben Macomber
Bertha Muzzy Bower
Bjornstjerne Bjornson

Booth Tarkington
Boyd Cable
Bram Stoker
C. Collodi
C. E. Orr
C. M. Ingleby
Carolyn Wells
Catherine Parr Traill
Charles A. Eastman
Charles Amory Beach
Charles Dickens
Charles Dudley Warner
Charles Farrar Browne
Charles Ives
Charles Kingsley
Charles Klein
Charles Hanson Towne
Charles Lathrop Pack
Charles Romyn Dake
Charles Whibley
Charles Willing Beale
Charlotte M. Braeme
Charlotte M. Yonge
Charlotte Perkins Stetson
Clair W. Hayes
Clarence Day Jr.
Clarence E. Mulford
Clemence Housman
Confucius
Coningsby Dawson
Cornelis DeWitt Wilcox
Cyril Burleigh
D. H. Lawrence
Daniel Defoe
David Garnett
Dinah Craik
Don Carlos Janes
Donald Keyhoe
Dorothy Kilner
Dougan Clark
Douglas Fairbanks
E. Nesbit
E. P. Roe
E. Phillips Oppenheim
E. S. Brooks
Earl Barnes
Edgar Rice Burroughs
Edith Van Dyne
Edith Wharton

Edward Everett Hale
Edward J. O'Biren
Edward S. Ellis
Edwin L. Arnold
Eleanor Atkins
Eleanor Hallowell Abbott
Eliot Gregory
Elizabeth Gaskell
Elizabeth McCracken
Elizabeth Von Arnim
Ellem Key
Emerson Hough
Emilie F. Carlen
Emily Bronte
Emily Dickinson
Enid Bagnold
Enilor Macartney Lane
Erasmus W. Jones
Ernie Howard Pie
Ethel May Dell
Ethel Turner
Ethel Watts Mumford
Eugene Sue
Eugenie Foa
Eugene Wood
Eustace Hale Ball
Evelyn Everett-green
Everard Cotes
F. H. Cheley
F. J. Cross
F. Marion Crawford
Fannie E. Newberry
Federick Austin Ogg
Ferdinand Ossendowski
Fergus Hume
Florence A. Kilpatrick
Fremont B. Deering
Francis Bacon
Francis Darwin
Frances Hodgson Burnett
Frances Parkinson Keyes
Frank Gee Patchin
Frank Harris
Frank Jewett Mather
Frank L. Packard
Frank V. Webster
Frederic Stewart Isham
Frederick Trevor Hill
Frederick Winslow Taylor

Friedrich Kerst
Friedrich Nietzsche
Fyodor Dostoyevsky
G.A. Henty
G.K. Chesterton
Gabrielle E. Jackson
Garrett P. Serviss
Gaston Leroux
George A. Warren
George Ade
Geroge Bernard Shaw
George Cary Eggleston
George Durston
George Ebers
George Eliot
George Gissing
George MacDonald
George Meredith
George Orwell
George Sylvester Viereck
George Tucker
George W. Cable
George Wharton James
Gertrude Atherton
Gordon Casserly
Grace E. King
Grace Gallatin
Grace Greenwood
Grant Allen
Guillermo A. Sherwell
Gulielma Zollinger
Gustav Flaubert
H. A. Cody
H. B. Irving
H. C. Bailey
H. G. Wells
H. H. Munro
H. Irving Hancock
H. R. Naylor
H. Rider Haggard
H. W. C. Davis
Haldeman Julius
Hall Caine
Hamilton Wright Mabie
Hans Christian Andersen
Harold Avery
Harold McGrath
Harriet Beecher Stowe
Harry Castlemon
Harry Coghill
Harry Houidini

Hayden Carruth
Helent Hunt Jackson
Helen Nicolay
Hendrik Conscience
Hendy David Thoreau
Henri Barbusse
Henrik Ibsen
Henry Adams
Henry Ford
Henry Frost
Henry James
Henry Jones Ford
Henry Seton Merriman
Henry W Longfellow
Herbert A. Giles
Herbert Carter
Herbert N. Casson
Herman Hesse
Hildegard G. Frey
Homer
Honore De Balzac
Horace B. Day
Horace Walpole
Horatio Alger Jr.
Howard Pyle
Howard R. Garis
Hugh Lofting
Hugh Walpole
Humphry Ward
Ian Maclaren
Inez Haynes Gillmore
Irving Bacheller
Isabel Cecilia Williams
Isabel Hornibrook
Israel Abrahams
Ivan Turgenev
J. G.Austin
J. Henri Fabre
J. M. Barrie
J. M. Walsh
J. Macdonald Oxley
J. R. Miller
J. S. Fletcher
J. S. Knowles
J. Storer Clouston
J. W. Duffield
Jack London
Jacob Abbott
James Allen
James Andrews
James Baldwin

James Branch Cabell
James DeMille
James Joyce
James Lane Allen
James Lane Allen
James Oliver Curwood
James Oppenheim
James Otis
James R. Driscoll
Jane Abbott
Jane Austen
Jane L. Stewart
Janet Aldridge
Jens Peter Jacobsen
Jerome K. Jerome
Jessie Graham Flower
John Buchan
John Burroughs
John Cournos
John F. Kennedy
John Gay
John Glasworthy
John Habberton
John Joy Bell
John Kendrick Bangs
John Milton
John Philip Sousa
John Taintor Foote
Jonas Lauritz Idemil Lie
Jonathan Swift
Joseph A. Altsheler
Joseph Carey
Joseph Conrad
Joseph E. Badger Jr
Joseph Hergesheimer
Joseph Jacobs
Jules Vernes
Julian Hawthrone
Julie A Lippmann
Justin Huntly McCarthy
Kakuzo Okakura
Karle Wilson Baker
Kate Chopin
Kenneth Grahame
Kenneth McGaffey
Kate Langley Bosher
Kate Langley Bosher
Katherine Cecil Thurston
Katherine Stokes
L. A. Abbot
L. T. Meade

L. Frank Baum
Latta Griswold
Laura Dent Crane
Laura Lee Hope
Laurence Housman
Lawrence Beasley
Leo Tolstoy
Leonid Andreyev
Lewis Carroll
Lewis Sperry Chafer
Lilian Bell
Lloyd Osbourne
Louis Hughes
Louis Joseph Vance
Louis Tracy
Louisa May Alcott
Lucy Fitch Perkins
Lucy Maud Montgomery
Luther Benson
Lydia Miller Middleton
Lyndon Orr
M. Corvus
M. H. Adams
Margaret E. Sangster
Margret Howth
Margaret Vandercook
Margaret W. Hungerford
Margret Penrose
Maria Edgeworth
Maria Thompson Daviess
Mariano Azuela
Marion Polk Angellotti
Mark Overton
Mark Twain
Mary Austin
Mary Catherine Crowley
Mary Cole
Mary Hastings Bradley
Mary Roberts Rinehart
Mary Rowlandson
M. Wollstonecraft Shelley
Maud Lindsay
Max Beerbohm
Myra Kelly
Nathaniel Hawthrone
Nicolo Machiavelli
O. F. Walton
Oscar Wilde

Owen Johnson
P.G. Wodehouse
Paul and Mabel Thorne
Paul G. Tomlinson
Paul Severing
Percy Brebner
Percy Keese Fitzhugh
Peter B. Kyne
Plato
Quincy Allen
R. Derby Holmes
R. L. Stevenson
R. S. Ball
Rabindranath Tagore
Rahul Alvares
Ralph Bonehill
Ralph Henry Barbour
Ralph Victor
Ralph Waldo Emmerson
Rene Descartes
Ray Cummings
Rex Beach
Rex E. Beach
Richard Harding Davis
Richard Jefferies
Richard Le Gallienne
Robert Barr
Robert Frost
Robert Gordon Anderson
Robert L. Drake
Robert Lansing
Robert Lynd
Robert Michael Ballantyne
Robert W. Chambers
Rosa Nouchette Carey
Rudyard Kipling
Saint Augustine
Samuel B. Allison
Samuel Hopkins Adams
Sarah Bernhardt
Sarah C. Hallowell
Selma Lagerlof
Sherwood Anderson
Sigmund Freud
Standish O'Grady
Stanley Weyman
Stella Benson
Stella M. Francis

Stephen Crane
Stewart Edward White
Stijn Streuvels
Swami Abhedananda
Swami Parmananda
T. S. Ackland
T. S. Arthur
The Princess Der Ling
Thomas A. Janvier
Thomas A Kempis
Thomas Anderton
Thomas Bailey Aldrich
Thomas Bulfinch
Thomas De Quincey
Thomas Dixon
Thomas H. Huxley
Thomas Hardy
Thomas More
Thornton W. Burgess
U. S. Grant
Upton Sinclair
Valentine Williams
Various Authors
Vaughan Kester
Victor Appleton
Victor G. Durham
Victoria Cross
Virginia Woolf
Wadsworth Camp
Walter Camp
Walter Scott
Washington Irving
Wilbur Lawton
Wilkie Collins
Willa Cather
Willard F. Baker
William Dean Howells
William le Queux
W. Makepeace Thackeray
William W. Walter
William Shakespeare
Winston Churchill
Yei Theodora Ozaki
Yogi Ramacharaka
Young E. Allison
Zane Grey